# TRICKSHOT
## THE STORY OF A BLACK PIMP
### by
# RANDOLPH HARRIS

An Original Holloway House Edition
**HOLLOWAY HOUSE PUBLISHING CO.**
LOS ANGELES, CALIFORNIA

Published by
HOLLOWAY HOUSE PUBLISHING COMPANY
8060 Melrose Avenue, Los Angeles, CA 90046
All rights reserved. No part of this book may be reproduced or transmitted in any form or by any means, electronic or mechanical, including photocopying, recording or by any information storage and retrieval system, without permission in writing from the Publisher.
Copyright © 1974, 1986 by Randolph Harris.

This novel is a work of fiction. Names, characters, places and incidents are either the product of the author's imagination or are used fictitiously. Any resemblance to actual events or locales or persons, living or dead, is entirely coincidental.

International Standard Book Number 0-87067-724-1
Printed in the United States of America
Cover photograph by Charles Adams; posed by a professional model.
Cover design by Kim Smock

Mark was talking to a girl as they both descended the steps. I shifted my chair and leaned back so that the pistol in my coat pocket would be aimed up without my having to remove it. . . . Mark and his lady companion walked right past me without so much as a nod of recognition. I relaxed, bringing my chair to its upright position and settled back in it, immensely relieved. Then the shots rang out. Five of them. A confused panic blanketed the crowd ... Mark's body, all bloody and punctured, was in the front seat of the late model car. His head was lying back as though he was looking at the car ceiling with his bulging, lifeless eyes. Chunks of flesh had been ripped from his neck, and the windows were blood spattered from the two large holes in his head. Oh, yes. He was thoroughly dead. A police car entered the mouth of the alley, and I split. The next day, the police came looking for me.

*"There is no duty we so much underrate as the duty of being happy."*

**Stevenson**

*"What I have done is due to past thought."*

**Newton**

*"Since when was genius found respectable?"*

**E.B. Browning**

## DEDICATED

to Mary Anne, with thanks to Richard Durham, Lionel Tyler and Beverly Wohner. They helped to make this book possible.

R.H.

## Chapter One

MY LIFE BEGAN IN ST. LOUIS, MISSOURI, in the early 1920's. I was an only child, born of a black woman from the rolling hills of Tennessee. I was brought to Chicago at the early age of one. Never having had my father live with us, I do, however, remember visiting him throughout the years, until his death in 1942.

Dropping out of school at the callow age of fourteen was seemingly a fad amongst blacks of this particular era; I followed the fad.

As to be expected, I eventually wound up in trouble; joy-riding in a stolen car of which netted me thirteen months in Saint Charles, an Illinois institution for boys under sixteen years old.

Ted and Ben, two boys from my neighborhood were also there. Our association and friendship was destined to last the rest of our lives.

But, of course, I had no way of knowing that Ben's youthful life would be surprisingly short.

Ted, six feet two, with a brown complexion, was almost as tall as me; I was six feet, three and a half and complete ebony. Ben was the strange weed in the garden, very light complexioned, straight brown sandy hair, dark brown eyes and his height was about five feet ten. I dare say, there was a mixup somewhere.

Within the following thirteen to twenty months, we were all three on the street again. However, six months later, Ben and I were in the House of Correction, commonly known as the Bridewell: this was concerning a minor charge of theft, for which we served eight months. That did it; I had had enough. I was going to find an easier way to make a fast buck.

I was nineteen years old at the time.


The lounge at Fifty-fifth Street and Michigan Avenue was filled with hilarious weekend drinkers when I arrived. My girl Marion worked there. I had stopped in that night to talk to her and have a drink. The little Jew who owned the joint was at the front counter busily filling the package goods orders of the patrons from the Savoy Hotel across the street. World War II was just declared and the hostilities had brought new jobs and fat paychecks to Chicago's ebony hired crowd of promiscuous funseekers, and the city, especially the southside, was jumping.

Leroy, the bartender, roamed the length of the bar dispensing gin and Coke, Canadian Club, and the large variety of Scotch whiskies that were popular during those years.

Marion's "Twenty-Six" table was getting action from a couple of square Johns. I knew she didn't have time to talk just then. So, after weaving, bumping and elbowing my way through the crowd of funsters, I finally managed to squeeze into a corner at the end of the long mahogany bar. The ceiling lights had been selected with discretion, casting an intimate atmosphere over the scene. That atmosphere was further compounded by the smoke that floated upward to the low ceiling—mainly cigarette smoke, but mixed with the aroma that could only come from the intoxicating marijuana weed. Police never troubled any patron of the place for smoking it.

I was lucky enough to get the bartender's attention. I ordered a shot of Canadian Club whiskey with water on the side. I had just finished smoking a healthy stick of pot myself before I came in and the cool, serene feeling it gave me became more pronounced as the continuously playing vendor blared out with Nat King Cole's popular record of "Straighten Up And Fly Right." I was digging the sensuous sounds of the trio when I felt a tap on the shoulder. I turned and looked into one of the prettiest faces I'd ever seen.

"I like tall dark men like you," the vision said. "My name is Chris. What's yours?"

I had never seen this woman before and I was damn sorry that I hadn't. Her copper-colored skin was velvety smooth, a perfect background for the pearly white teeth that heightened her beauty when she smiled. Dark brown eyes, moderately contoured, and a dainty little nose combined with the rest of her features made a breathtaking picture. Eventually I found my voice. "My name is Trickshot," I almost stammered, "and I'm delighted to meet you, Chris."

Stepping back from the crowded bar, I offered her my chairless space which she accepted as I went about the task of getting the bartender's attention again. After he got her a drink, with a bit of fast maneuvering, I was able to get her a stool. That's when I got my next surprise. She mounted the stool and threw back her coat. Her luscious body came into view. Her breasts were straining at the fabric of her low-cut blouse as if they were trying to escape and her firm and shapely hips rounded into a slight bulge before tapering down to her well-proportioned thighs. Chris crossed her legs and they reminded me of a big leaguer's baseball bats. I found out later, Chris was thirty years old, but she really didn't look it; and that night I wouldn't have traded her for a teenager.

We began to chat, but as we rapped, every now and then, I would cast a furtive glance at Marion, who by now had rocks in her jaws. So when Chris suggested that we go to another bar, it was as though she was reading my mind.

I gladly excused myself and went over to Marion's "Twenty-Six" table. She looked at me with an evil eye. "I'll be right back, baby," I told her. "I'm just going to help the young lady find a cab."

Marion knew I was lying, but I didn't want to go to the trouble of explaining. It wouldn't have helped the situation anyway. I paid the bar bill and left.

I had graciously accepted the advice of two older pimps while hanging around the place. The knowledge I had received from Locke, the pimp, and Jim, the con man, I've maintained to this day.

We walked toward South Parkway and the jitney line. The advice that Lock and the other older fellows had given me was completely dismissed from my mind. The hundred dollars that was resting in the pocket of my sport coat was evidence that I had been paid. We headed for the Rhodes Hotel on Thirty-Fourth Street. There were no motels in the area during those years. When we arrived, Chris stood to one side while I went to the desk and rented a room under a false name, then headed for a rendezvous of pleasure—with pay.

The room was the usual setting common to transient

hotels that specialize in accommodations for couples who wish to indulge in sexual pleasures. There was a mirrored dresser with a make-up bench, two matching chairs and a writing desk. The plush green wall-to-wall carpet stopped at the door to the washroom, which Chris entered immediately, and the king-size bed had a nightstand on each side.

I didn't want to appear over-anxious, but my joint was so hard it damn near burst! Chris came out of the washroom in a jiff. In fact it was so fast that I wondered if it was she and not I who was over-anxious. I turned my back as I slid into the bed. I didn't want her to see my joint sticking out like I was deformed—especially throbbing and dripping as it was. Chris slid in beside me and snuggled up close. I rolled over and caressed her soft smooth body. We cuddled our bodies closer and entwined our legs. Chris spread her smooth thighs and I rolled onto her body. It engulfed me with a softness that was like processed cotton. She had no trouble helping me to enter her, because her own secretions had surpassed my leakage. My rod felt like it was buried in a kitten's fur, and being stroked tenderly to sleep. The feeling had my body trembling, but I just couldn't let it end. It was too wonderful, too fantastic, and too sexsational to allow it to end so soon. Then she seemed to open up a hidden door that permitted me to drop way down inside of her, deeper and deeper, so deep that the pressure was overwhelming and my whole body exploded, pouring my life substance into her. I was trembling and helpless when she gently rolled me over.

It was later that night. I had arrived home and was lying in my small bed when my mother told me that Marion had been calling the house from the time mother had gotten home from work. I didn't know how I was going to phrase it, but I grabbed the phone to do the job that shouldn't be put off any longer.

The little Jew answered the phone. I could hear the

mixture of voices and the blatant sound of the vendor in the background. An instant later, Marion was at the phone.

"Where have you been? Why haven't you called me?" Before I could speak, she had answered her own question. "I know, you've been with that out-of-town bitch!" Marion talked on and on. I started to hang up, but I would only be delaying my job.

Marion's nagging rap gave me a brief vision of what the "pimp life" had in store for me. I had chosen this life because I'd heard that a pimp only had to rest and dress. And of course, I had heard that it was necessary for pimps to beat their women and otherwise punish them severely sometimes, but I had never dreamt that it would be so nerve-racking and time-consuming.

Finally, I felt that I had stood enough. I could take no more. I blasted into the phone. "Bitch! Shut up and listen to me!" The shock left her speechless long enough for me to say, "I'll meet you after you get off, and then we'll talk." I hung up.

Time passed, and I relaxed thinking of the pleasures of the day and my beautiful Chris. Finally I drifted off to sleep.

The telephone shattered the early morning silence and a tap on the wall from my mother beckoned me. I lifted myself from the small let-out cot that served as my bed and went into her room to answer the phone. It was Marion, but this I knew before I had uncradled the phone.

"Are you coming down here, or should I walk up there?" she asked.

I looked at the clock that mother kept on the dresser. It was two o'clock on the dot.

"It'll take your boss a while to check up, so I'll slip on some clothes and walk down there."

I hung up the phone and went back to my midget abode. As I entered the door, a small mouse made his exit from my room to the kitchen and raced across the floor, finally making his escape through a hole under the kitchen sink.

It didn't take me long to get into my clothes and out into the refreshing night air. I took my time and strolled down Michigan Boulevard. Even at that late hour, people were scattered throughout the block. Some were perched on the front steps of the crowded buildings, others had chairs or stools, and then there were some sitting in upraised windows; all of them were enjoying the refreshing air that was so lacking in their over-populated apartments.

Marion was coming out of the tavern door as I neared the corner. She was telling the little Jew and the bartender goodnight. There was a large apartment courtway building just a few feet from the corner. It had a horseshoe entrance with well cared for grass in the front. I placed my foot on the rail that encircled the protected greenery and lit a cigarette. Leaning with my elbow on my knee, I awaited the inevitable controversy as Marion saw me and began walking in my direction.

"I'm surprised that you've taken the time to see me, now that you got a new woman."

Her opening thrust, though phrased as a statement, ended with a rising inflection, the sound of a question that awaited a much needed answer. This I was quick to give. "You told me that you wanted to help me get some money, so I'm sure you won't mind me helping myself."

"But why did you lie and say you were coming back? And then you took the telephone off the hook."

She was standing very close, staring up into my face. I turned my head from my leaning position and that's when I saw that Marion's big brown eyes were very watery and tears had begun to create a wet path along the creases of her pert little nose. At first my teenage masculinity faltered, but then I recalled some of my recent street schooling. (A woman will try to soften a man with tears.)

So I kept my face expressionless and remained phlegmatic as I responded with a tutored remark.

"You broads are always talking about the things you want your men to have. But every time he tries to get something that they can't give him, there's static and a lot of bullshit." I thumped the cigarette butt into the street and put my foot on the ground.

I was now standing up straight and looking down into her round face. She moved closer to me and buried her head in my chest. "Oh, Trickshot, I know you're right, but I just can't help it. I'm jealous, and I love you. Can't you understand that?"

It was then that the thought struck me! Maybe she was telling the truth. I had entered the world of pimping single-minded. Sure, I knew that Marion liked me, and I also knew that I liked her. But if she had come to me and said she wanted someone else, my pride might have been injured, or my ego might have suffered, but my feelings wouldn't have been hurt worth a damn! One of the first lessons Lock had given me was, "Cast aside your feelings because if you stay in the 'pimp game', eventually that will happen anyway. Nevertheless, practice. Time will allow you to handle it better." I figured that most girls had practically the same philosophy. If they liked the way a fellow talked or the way he dressed and liked the way he made love, they would give him money until they found another fellow that they liked better. At this early stage of the game, I actually thought I had it all figured. I surmised that it was a game of "Cop and Blow." Nevertheless, I couldn't allow this revelation of love to thwart me from my goal of pimping. I put my arm around Marion's shoulders and we strolled toward Garfield Boulevard.

I had never been confronted with a confession of love before—not even from some of my adolescent sweethearts. Our slow steps toward the Boulevard gave me time to think of something to say that befitted the occasion. I didn't want to fall into the sympathetic trap that Lock had warned me of, but I had an overwhelming feeling that this woman who out-distanced me in experience and age was very sincere. I decided to stay on safe ground.

"Marion, I appreciate the fact that you love me, but I don't want your love to cost me mental strain and financial loss."

I guided her to one of the vacant benches that was located on the green sod dividing Garfield Boulevard. We sat on the bench and watched the after-hours revelers as they sauntered by. A heavily built white woman, escorted by a tall, konked-haired black man, tottered out of the "It Club"; and staggered their way to the shiny LaSalle automobile parked at the curb.

The "It Club" had long been a famous gathering spa for the fast people of the night. It's legal closing hour was four o'clock, but this was often extended until the last patron had gone.

The following weeks brought about closer relations between Chris and myself. Some were good and some were extremely bad. Mainly because of my continued association with Marion: Chris naggingly wanted it to cease.

Giving all respect to the advice that I had acquired from Jim, the con man, and Lock, the pimp, quitting Marion would be professionally wrong; even considering the small bit of knowledge I had myself. However, Chris, as I see it now, could not allow herself to be stabled by a nineteen-year-old boy.

She quit me and returned to Detroit.

I satisfied myself by returning to my buddies in the pool hall; Ted and Ben, my childhood chums. Marion remained steadfast in her devotions and contributions.

## Chapter Two

SIX WEEKS LATER, Ted was in the Army and Ben had been rejected because of a heart ailment. I was lying on the small couch in my mother's room when the phone rang. It was Chris. I wanted to jump from the couch with joy. Lock, my trusted adivor, had told me that Chris would call eventually. He'd also told me to pressure her for more money when she did. A sort of penalty for staying away so long.

When Chris asked how things were going for me, I told her just fine. But this was a lie. Chicago at that time (1943) was under the administration of Mayor Kelly and was considered an "open city." But some civic groups, mainly consisting of housewives, had made quite a stir downtown at City Hall, claiming that the "Twenty-Six" girls were nothing but prostitutes in disguise who were "fleecing" hard-working husbands out of their paychecks. In turn, the obedient husbands had slacked off from their weekly escapades of fun away from home. This had cut Marion's income drastically, and made mine practically nil.

Chris asked me to meet her at the New Club Delisa. She had barely finished the sentence before I said, "O.K."

That night, I donned my most ostentatious togs: light blue sport coat, maroon colored slacks, white-on-white tab-collared shirt and needle-toed shoes that were shining like two diamonds in a black cat's head.

I arrived at the club at exactly ten p.m. Chris was seated at the bar when I entered. I strolled over to her side and kissed her lightly on her sponge-soft cheeks. Before I took my lips away, I whispered in her ear, "You look gorgeous."

Chris smiled, looked up with those beautiful brown eyes and answered in the loveliest voice, "Thanks. You look good yourself."

I asked the Maitre d' to get us a table and stepped aside as Chris lifted herself from the stool. That's when I noticed she appeared to be slightly taller. I looked down as she walked in front of me. Then I saw the new-styled shoes with the high-wedged soles and the very high-pointed heels and my eyes traveled upward to her familiar carved legs, her broad hips that the pink dress was protecting tightly. Her coal-black hair, as always, was neatly in place and threw off a bluish hue as she glided beneath the irridescent cabaret lights. The nightclub was packed and so were most of the customers' pockets. The country's industries had resolved to make the best war materials, while the customers present were drinking the best whiskey, Canadian Club, Haig and Haig Pinch bottle and V.O. Tiny flames flared and danced from the mouths of small brandy glasses, a fad amongst the cognac drinkers of that era. The pops of newly-opened champagne bottles made it sound like a gangster shoot-out. It was truly a fantastic feeling to be sitting at the table with a beautiful girl during this interim period of affluence. The floor show was enjoyable and the great Red Sanders' Band was about to come into prominence.

Chris gave me two hundred dollars, which was a Godsend at that time. The weather had begun to change and I needed a new top coat badly.

Chris stayed in Chicago about two weeks. She had come in to buy some fall clothes for her small son. It seems that Uncle Sam wanted to give me some new clothes, too, for it was during that time that I received my induction papers.

Chris had asked me to go back to Michigan with her and I had been willing, but the government changed our plans. I saw her a few days later and told her about my being drafted.

I didn't see Chris again until thirteen years later. She still looked good as she stood on a Detroit street corner trying to catch a trick.


I was inducted into the Army at Fort Custer, Michigan. After two weeks of processing, I was shipped to Camp McCain, Mississippi. The nearest town to the camp was Grenada, Mississippi.

At first view, I was really fascinated. There were rows and rows of Army tanks, with massive caterpillar wheels, resembling prehistoric dragons with long cannon tongues sticking from their hulks. The miles and miles of flat-top barracks looked as though a giant buzz-saw had sheared off the tops of their skulls. The autumn breeze had dominated the sun and swayed the trees at will. Leaves were snatched from their branches and fluttered to the ground like injured butterflies. Soldiers covered the terrain, dressed in identical garb, to remind them they were a family of one.

My basic training began immediately. And I was indoctrinated with this family into the latest art of killing.

I was lying on my bunk in the barracks when I began to think more seriously about what was happening to me. I thought about the country and how it was set up. I thought about all of the hypocrisy, and remembered the judge who had given me thirteen months for riding in a stolen car. I recalled that other judge who had sent me to the House of Correction. I wondered if things would change, if and when I returned. I also thought of the good times the older fellas were having with their big cars and fast girls on Fifty-Fifth Street.

I said to myself, "In what other country could a black man ride around in a big Cadillac car without working?"

Then I thought of the money my mother would be receiving for the duration of my time spent in the Army. What the hell! The country wasn't so bad after all.

My company was the "309 Railhead Quarter Master." It was made up of boys from Detroit, Cleveland and Chicago. Why they sent us down south, I'll never know. They say the Army has a reason for everything it does, so I imagined they had one. But I never could figure it out.

After I was in the camp a week, an incident occurred. A white woman was raped. Now, as those who have been in the Army know, generally there is a main street that runs from one end to the other through the military camps. They lined every black soldier in the camp along this route and the Provost Marshal seated the woman beside him in his Army jeep. They rode along this tedious strip for miles, viewing the multitude of features with shades of melting potted hue until, finally, this white woman picked out two soldiers, saying that it was one or the other who had raped her.

There is an O.D. (Officer of the Day) in each camp. It is his duty to know where every soldier is detailed. After looking at the O.D. book, they discovered one of the soldiers was on K.P. duty on the day that the rape was supposed to have occurred, and the other one was on the rifle range. I've often wondered what would have happened if there had been no O.D. book.

That, and other racial incidents changed my mind about the country and the system, even though we were in Mississippi.

I immediately went about assorted tactics to get out, whether honorable or dishonorable; the latter would not matter, since blacks were denied so many of their rights, anyway.

## Chapter Three

YES, I WAS HOME with an honorable discharge. However, it showed where I had lost ten days under some article of war. I don't remember the term they used. My mother was happy, Marion was happy, and Trickshot was very happy!

Marion didn't waste any time crowding me about marriage. We went to see her parents and I promised them we would get married the next day. That night, I went to Fifty-Fifth Street and won some money playing cards.

The next day I felt different. I didn't want to back out of the marriage; I just wanted to wait a while. Marion began to cry and remind me that I had promised her parents. We caught a train that evening and arrived in St. Louis, Missouri, that night. The next morning we walked into the city hall, found one of those "Quickie Preachers," and got married. I didn't feel any different. We caught the train and came back to Chicago.

My first argument with Marion as a wife happened a few days later.

I didn't realize that I had to live any differently just because I was married, and I was walking down the boulevard talking to a girl I had known for a few years when Marion saw me. She came out of the tavern and asked me what in the hell I was doing walking with Marie. I was so surprised, I was stunned for a moment. When I came to myself, I had left Marion laying in the street with a blow from the back of my hand.

It was the next day when Marion called me at my mother's house. I told her I would meet her at the Du Sable Lounge on Thirty-Ninth Street.

The circular bar was crowded and so were the walls. The conical lights of varying colors were placed in the ceiling with care. Most of the stools were topped by prostitutes, but if a person didn't know, they might choose a fag. There were pimps holding up the walls, while keeping sharp eyes on their property, and still other pimps trying to acquire new property.

The hotel which was operated upstairs over the basement bar made it convenient for all concerned. Snow or rain, they never had to go outside. It was truly a place of all the happenings within its own walls.

The food shop was located in the basement off from the bar. If you walked to the rear of the place, you would smell the aroma of the pot; but it wasn't always the one on the stove. There were questionable happenings occurring in every room. Years later when the place was torn down, some said "it was to prevent the walls from talking."

I entered the barroom before Marion arrived and elbowed my way to the bar. I ordered a drink from Rickey the bartender and then backed up to the wall and busied myself in conversation with a pimp I knew called Peg.

Peg was a local pimp with a fairly big reputation. He had

acquired his name because of an automobile accident that resulted in his having to wear a peg-leg. The rumor was that he had received a substantial financial settlement and this had launched him into his pimping career.

He was a well-liked guy, tall, with a toast-brown complexion, a very dapper dresser and he purchased a new Cadillac every year. However, the declaration of war had brought the manufacturing of new cars to a halt. The last models that were made were in 1942.

Peg was the kind of fellow that I liked to rap with most. The kind that I would listen to. He was the breed that I would watch and had the style that I admired. I intended to grasp all the knowledge I could get from these elders in this fascinating game of procuring.

I glanced over the crowd and saw Marion trying to squeeze her small frame through the constantly busy portal that led into the bar. Her pert, round face showed irate signs as she pushed her way toward me. She expressed her feelings. "Why would you have me meet you here? Couldn't you find a better place than this?—Oops! See what I mean?"

Marion has been jostled by "Minnie, the fag," who was arguing with his man.

"Aw, baby, don't be so grouchy. Say, I'd like for you to meet a friend of mine. Peg, this is my wife. Meet Marion."

"It's a pleasure. Hi, Marion," Peg responded cordially.

"Hi." Marion was sullen.

"What do you want to drink, baby?" I asked.

"I dunno. I guess I'll take a gin and Coke." Marion was still perturbed.

"What will you have, Peg?"

"Nothing for me, Trick. You know I quit."

"No, I didn't. How long have you been on the wagon?" I beckoned for Rickey the bartender as I spoke.

"I haven't had a drink since the accident, two years

ago," Peg answered.

"In this place, you can't even find a seat." Marion's disgruntleness was getting on my nerves.

Rickey fixed the drinks and I passed Marion hers. As I reached for my refill, my outstretched arm was bumped by Tall Jesse's whore, Libby, who had spotted one of her regular tricks standing in the portal and was pushing through the crowd to greet him before some other tempting dish caught his eye. My drink spilled on the shoulder of an obese lady who was sitting at the bar in front of me.

"Oops! I'm so very sorry." I tried to show contrition.

"Oh, that's all right. It's just a sprinkle. I was about to leave anyway."

The heavily-built lady was now standing and dabbing her shoulder with the napkin that Rickey had handed her.

"Here, allow me." I gestured with my hand.

"It's quite all right, now. It was nothing—really." The lady maneuvered her massive torso through the notorious gathering and left. I immediately steered Marion into the empty seat.

"I'll dig you later on, Trick." Peg was leaving. He'd been trying to cop the little red-head girl and she was walking out of the door.

"Do you feel better now, darling?" I was trying to calm Marion.

"Hum! Trickshot, must you always be around pimps and hustlers, not to speak of the whores?" Marion spoke naggingly.

"You knew that before you married me. Why should you squawk now?"

"I figured after we were married, you would change. Try to settle down and raise a family." Marion was looking down into her drink and stirring it with her finger.

It dawned on me! Like a flash of lightning opening up the night. This woman who topped me in years and experience was trying to change me, dominate me, penetrate my brain and cultivate it to her own choosing.

I had to show her my resentment, my anger, my determination; all of the older pros had advised me. "The way you start out is the way you end up." I intended to start out *right*.

"Bitch! I'm going to straighten you out now, so you won't forget it later. First, you or no other bitch is going to guide my life for me, and second, you knew when you married me that I liked whores and intended to have more whores. Why did you stay with me when you knew I had Chris?"

Her head still bowed, her gaze on her drink, Marion continued to rotate her finger around the mouth of the glass. "We weren't married then."

"Well, if marriage means that I must change my way of life and submit to a woman's will—fuck marriage." I called Rickey, I was ready to pay my bar bill and leave.

Marion guessed my intention. "Wait a minute, Trick," she said, putting a hand on my arm. "I'm sorry. Maybe I was wrong. Whatever you decide to do, I'm your wife and I'm with you."

I didn't answer. I was still thinking of the way she had tried to brainwash me. I glanced at my watch and decided it was time to leave the scene.

Marion and I were standing at the curb waiting for a cab when Baby Frank pulled up in his long Chrysler. He swaggered out of the car and walked around to the other side. When he opened the door, two lovely white ladies stepped out. It was a known fact that Baby Frank was the biggest black pimp in the city.

I watched him as he steered the young lovelies through the "Du Sable" door. I cast my glance back to the shiny car and visualized myself behind the steering wheel. This is what I needed, the key to the "pimp game." A pimp was nothing without a car. How could I drive around and pick up my money? How could I take my girls for a ride?

The toot of the cabbie's horn shook me from my reverie and Marion tugged at my arm. "Come on daddy, the cab is here."

When the cab pulled off, I was still thinking. Looking straight ahead, I uttered, "Marion, I've got to have a car."

"Where to, sir? Where to?" the cabbie asked.

I turned to look at Marion because she hadn't answered me. "Do you hear me? I've got to have a car!"

"Baby! Baby, the driver is talking to you." She was looking at me and pointing towards the driver.

"Huh? Oh, I'm sorry, man, take us to Fifty-Fifth Street."

The cab went out along Oakwood Boulevard and turned left at South Parkway. In a few minutes he let us out at Garfield Boulevard which was the same as Fifty-Fifth. I gazed down the long street of neons and we began our stroll into that long strip of illumination.

The night was hanging over the street like a coal black planet. Bright lights illuminated the jagged buildings that stood like rockets aimed at the sky, but that blackness in space hung as a barrier, a gigantic container of tar suspended upside down. I knew that some day soon, I would ride down this street in a car that was owned by me.

As we strolled past Dave's Cafe, there was a small gathering of people outside. I learned that they were waiting to glimpse the great boxer Joe Louis. Dave's was a favorite hangout of his. One of his best friends was managing the place.

As we walked further down the boulevard, I got an idea. I was going to call Ben the next day and put one of the con games Jim had taught me into operation.

The hotel clerk woke Marion and me up the next morning telling us it was checkout time. I got in touch with Ben immediately and told him of the plan I had in mind. After hanging up the phone, we checked out of the hotel.

Later that day, I met Ben and explained what I wanted him to do. I wanted him to find a greedy sucker who had money, but the mark had to be a stranger to me in order to pull this caper off successfully.

About a week later, Ben called and said, "I've found a sucker."

The stage was set. I had given Ben the same expert schooling that Jim had given to me. I gave Ben some money and told him, "Go and buy some hair rollers, but make sure that they're metal and the same width as a dollar bill." I had borrowed some money to use in this caper. There was no chance for a slip up.

Ben produced a little Jew from the north side. The Jew thought that Ben was white and Ben had sold hot whiskey to him many times. Playing the part of "cap man," Ben had introduced the Jew to me.

We had rented a hotel room along with a small electrical heater. I told the Jew that I had just gotten out of the penitentiary where I had met this old man, a part-time scientist who upon his release was being deported for his unsavory actions in this country. The old man had taken a liking to me and told me how to perform this intricate operation. I went into my spiel after Ben had told me that the little Jew had brought along two thousand dollars, all in hundred dollar bills. I turned to the little guy and said, "If I had a bankroll, I wouldn't need you. I had told your young friend here," motioning toward Ben, "to bring along nothing but large bills, since only a certain amount of the original ink can be drawn out of the two authentic bills."

He listened with interest.

"Now give me one of your smaller bills and I'll give you

a demonstration.

I extended my hand; the little black-haired Jew with the glasses hanging over his small hook nose reached into his side pants pocket and freed the rubber band from a small roll of fives, tens and twenties. While he fumbled with the bills, I stuck out my hand and grasped two ten dollar bills from his roll of money.

"This will do," I said.

It would have been wrong if I had accepted two five dollar bills, since I only had ten and twenty prepared rolls concealed within my sport coat pockets. (Jim had said a coat should always be worn during this operation.)

"Now watch closely, sir." I gave the little Jew a furtive glance. "A certain kind of paper must be used in this operation," I told him as I placed the thin layer of paper between his two ten dollar bills. "Always make sure that the prepared paper is cut evenly with the authentic bills. I say prepared, because I've bathed the thin layer of paper with this special chemical which is the secret to the entire operation."

I held up the small bottle of colored water that I had produced from the outside pocket of my coat. The little Jew's eyes and head followed the movements of my hands as I held the small bottle in the air.

I placed the bottle onto the nearby dresser and went back into my performance. I rolled the two ten dollar bills which had the layer of paper in between around the metal hair roller.

"This is a specially prepared alloy. After becoming heated, it throws off heat with terrific speed, therefore the chemical reacts from the tremendous heat and the chemically soaked paper draws the ink from the authentic bills." I had completed the job of rolling.

"Will you pass me that bottle, please?" Ben sat motionless as the little Jew retrieved the bottle.

Standing at a pre-prepared angle, I made a move to my left inside coat pocket, switching the roller with the layer of paper for the pre-prepared roller that contained three ten dollar bills. I also had the cigarette in my hand as I received the bottle from the little Jew and asked him for a light.

Jim had always instructed me to place the ten dollar roller in the left pocket and the twenty dollar roller in the right pocket, plus, always place a loose cigarette in each roller pocket. If the sucker is fortunate enough to catch your movements, you can always declare you were merely reaching for a cigarette.

The switch had been made, the sucker was back in position, leaning forward, hands rubbing each other with clammy dampness, eyes peering over bifocaled lenses and twitching feet spread widely apart.

I knew I had my victim wrapped up. I had to tighten him. I said, "Now watch this, because it's very important."

I removed the cap from the bottle of colored water and began to dab small amounts of its contents on the similar looking hair roller than had always been rolled with *three* ten dollar bills.

"I've got to be most careful and not use too much of this chemical because it reacts very pronounced when brought into contact with heat." I said this while casting a stealthy glance toward the little Jew.

His reactions were satisfying, eager, interested and anxious.

I placed the hair roller into the small electric heater and then sat back to tell of the days, months and a few years I'd spent with the never forgettable old scientist who had been deported to Yugoslavia.

At a given time, I looked at my watch and said, "Well, I think it should be ready now."

I reached into the small electric heater and carefully snatched out the hot roller that had been wrapped in a protective layer of tinfoil with Scotch tape to keep it intact. I juggled the hot roller in my hands, then gave it a few minutes to cool off. Then, I peeled the outside protective wrapper away from the roller. The green of the crisp hot money appeared. I freed the bills from the hair roller and spread them out on the dresser. Instead of the two tens that the little Jew had given me, there were three crisp ten dollar bills.

The little Jewish fella almost burst with excitement. After calming him down, I went into my tightener. "Now you see, this is an iron-clad operation. There is no counterfeiting involved. No plates are necessary and there's no obscure markings to worry about. Every bill is identically the way the government had sent it out."

The little Jewish guy was hilarious! He wanted to buy some of the chemical. (Which gave me an idea I hadn't thought of.)

Ben was acting as instructed—enthusiastic, but not overly. I asked Ben to go out and bring some sandwiches and coffee while I got down to the business at hand. (Namely those hundred dollar bills that were folded in the little Jew's pocket.)

While Ben was gone, I told the little man what a tedious job it was making sure everything was correct, such as making sure both bills are faced with their heads in the same directions. Making sure that the bills face to back, thus getting a front and back print on the blank paper.

He was really fascinated as he spoke. "But Bennie, he tells me that you have a machine. The money-making machine he calls it."

"Yeah, yeah, I know, but let me explain. That's just a name. It really means nothing." I reminded myself to tell Ben to use another term. It's true that the underworld called the con game the "money-making machine," but Ben should've just told the guy "about a fella he knew who could reproduce money."

The little man was looking at one of the hair rollers, and said, "You know what? This looks like any ordinary piece of metal to me." He was rolling it around in his fingers. I had to plant an illusionary thought before his mind would become set on the factual.

"Do you think an ordinary piece of metal could produce heat the way this one just did and we'd get the same results?"

He smiled. "By jimminy! That's right. Oops." He had dropped the hair roller and, lo and behold, when the little Jew bent forward to pick up the roller, I saw the butt of a gun! He had the small pistol in a shoulder holster. By not having a breast string, it swung free when he bent over. Now this is a bitch, I was thinking to myself. Here I am within a few minutes of my first car and the sucker has a gun.

I knew I had to take him for his bankroll, but I didn't want to do it in the rough. I was planning on becoming a top pimp and I'd learned that pimps don't rough hustle unless the chips are down. I was perturbed. I had demonstrated for him the good part of the game. What would he do a few moments later when the bad part comes up and he sees his money has gone? My mind was racing. Where in the hell is Ben? I thought to myself. Should I set this guy up for another day? I wasn't afraid of losing him, his own mother couldn't have discouraged him now. He had seen the performance with his own eyes. In fact, I doubt if he would have stood still and waited another day.

I heard a knock on the door. It had to be Ben. He winked at me when he passed me the sandwiches and coffee. I felt good knowing he had done what he was supposed to do. However, I didn't get a chance to tell him about the gun that was holstered under the little man's shoulder. My God! What will he do when this thing happens to him? He didn't appear to be a violent man, but still, he had a gun. I'd never heard that the Jewish people were violent. In fact, it had always been the opposite, I thought. I recalled reading it somewhere that one or two of them had joined the Mafia. Holy gees! What if the little guy's a killer? Shit! Killer, Priest, Mafia or Saint, I had to have a car. With determination surging up inside me, I exclaimed, "All right! Let's stop messing around and get down to business. Did you bring some money to work with?"

I looked at the little fella with questioning eyes. I pretended to have no knowledge of his concealed wealth. The little man wasted no time flashing the two grand, all in hundred dollar bills.

Ben gave me the eye before he spoke. "I got that damn mustard on my hands." He was striding into the small bathroom. I knew what Ben was going to do.

I went through the same procedure with the hundred dollar bills as I had done with the tens, only this time the hair roller had to increase in size.

Ben came out of the bathroom and gave me the signal that I was waiting for. He said, "That face bowl is leaking, or either I'm just plain sloppy. I got that damn water all over me."

I flashed the package of evenly cut paper slips and put them back into an inside coat pocket. I then stretched my hands to the bottle and put it back to my outside pocket. I asked for a match for my unlit cigarette, put the unused roller in my pocket and reached for the paper slips again. I made all of these unnecessary moves to confuse him and make him become familiar with my hands going to my pockets. I knew that the hundred dollar roller would be more difficult to switch than the previous one which had held the three tens.

Ben had told me about the face bowl and I knew what he meant. I had to get the message to him about the little man's gun. It was hell working under this strain, this pressure, and the unpredictable reactions of this man. To relieve him of the small fortune held in his pockets meant a glorious giant step toward my main endeavor. The acquisition of a "pimp wheel," thus attracting the desires of fast girls, as free with their purse strings as they were commercially with their bodies. I couldn't falter here.

The little Jewish guy had put his money on the coffee table. Ben was now sprawled on the large black leather couch as if the ham sandwich and coffee had made him drowsy.

I finished my cup of coffee and threw the cardboard container into the shabby wastebasket that rested beside the green fabric lounge chair where Ben had previously sat.

"I'd better wash my hands before I start rolling up the bills."

I walked into the small bathroom; as soon as the door was closed, I looked beneath the face bowl. The fake roll with the money-sized paper slips was in the spot where Ben had planted it. I stashed it inside my shirt, rinsed my hands and went out of the bathroom to begin the operation where I'd left off. The little man watched me until I'd rolled up the last bill.

*Crash-h-h!* The floor-stand ashtray turned over and hit the floor with a spill. Cigarette butts were scattered. Ben had kicked it over! He sprang from the couch, hands moving in perpetual motion, brushing off his pants.

"Damn it! Looks like I'm trying to burn myself," Ben exclaimed.

The switch had been made. The distraction caused the little man to turn his head, and that was just long enough for the switch to take place. I began to dab the expensive roll with the final touches which was the contents of a similar-looking bottle, but this time it wasn't filled with colored water.

Realizing all of his dreams of easy riches were about to explode, I handed him the hair roller with the cut paper slips rolled around it and said, "Well, my friend, this two grand is the beginning of a profitable association."

I placed the fake roll in his hand and motioned towards the electric heater. "Go on, you place it in the heater."

The little Jew handled the roll as if it were the Hope Diamond, then he laid it in the heater as though its fragility was that of an egg. He backed away from the heater, eyes constantly on the small heat-thrower that held his vision of enrichment. The edge of the green fabric chair touched the back of his leg and he felt his way into the chair seat. He was so busy watching the roll that was lying idle in the now red hot heater that I don't think he saw or heard me when I said, "I think I'll take a crap. How about that, Ben? I never thought I'd pick up money after throwing crap out."

Ben laughed. I stepped into the bathroom again, only this time it was to stash the hair roller that was surrounded by the twenty crisp hundred dollar bills. With that gun in his holster, I didn't want him to find those hundred dollar bills on me.

After flushing the toilet, I walked out and into the room again. Ben looked at me and winked. He nodded his head toward the little Jew. My head and eyes followed his nod. The little guy's appearance was that of a zombie, unwavering eyes, glaring, staring, fixed straight ahead, as though obsessed by the now glowing crimson coils.

Then it happened! *Boom-m-m!* There was an explosive sound from the small heater that echoed throughout the room. Ben leaped from the black leather couch. The little Jewish man was on his feet, shocked, befuddled, hands outstretched, eyes on the small dying flame that danced and wavered its last signs of life, amidst the rubble of charred black ashes that were once twenty crisp one hundred dollar bills! He jerked his head around and fixed his bewildered eyes on me. "Wha ... what happened?" He was now in front of the small heater, bending over, threatening to grasp the charred ashes. He turned to look at me again. "What happened?" He was pointing, a frown on his face, with finger still poised.

My face was an excruciating mask. "Too much, damn it! I used too much."

I stepped in front of the little man, cut the heater switch off and began to paw with my ballpoint pen into the rubble of charred black paper ashes. I lifted the hair roller that had now turned black, holding it on the ballpoint pen. I said, "Yep, that had to be it. I used too much chemical."

I turned to face the little Jew. I showed remorse in my face, and spoke with contrition. "Well, you can see what I've done. However, I'm willing to put myself at your disposal. Whatever you want me to do—just name it."

My arms were at my side, hands turned up, palms open. The little fella had moved back to the heater. He was gazing down, just staring, silently. I looked over at Ben and winked. The latter was playing his part to perfection, showing reaction, but remaining silent.

I knew what was going through the little man's mind. I had told him I didn't have any money, so he knew reimbursement was out. There was only one thing left for him to do, get some more money and try to make up his losses. Yep, my fish was on the hook and he couldn't let go.

The Jew turned around and spoke. "I'll have to go home and think about this. I just don't understand it."

He twitched his head again and glanced at the scattered ashes that now showed a grayish hue within its smokey blackness. The little man reversed his head and spoke to me again. "As I said before, I'll go home and think things over. Where can I get in touch with you?" He was reaching for his writing pen.

"Oh, since I've been home from the penitentiary, I've

been staying with my aunt, but she's on relief and she doesn't have a phone. However, your friend knows where to find me. I'm at that pool hall on Fifty-Fifth and Prairie most of the time."

Then I saw it! Jim had told me to always watch the sucker's eyes. The little Jew looked at me and then he glanced at Ben, then back to me again.

Good Lord! Was this it? Was he going to reach for that gun? Whatever he was thinking, I knew that it meant me no good. I had to distract his concentration. I popped my finger and said, "I've got it! I know what I can do."

The man's face relaxed. He pushed the glasses back upon his nose. He was gazing up at me, waiting for this new hope that sounded in my voice. I gave him fresh thoughts of enrichment to block his intentions of violence, if that's what was on his mind.

I reached out and put my hand on his shoulder and said, "If you can pick me up tomorrow, I'll give you the formula to the chemical, although I would appreciate it if you'd give me a chance to make a little money for myself, because as I told you before, I'm flat broke."

His face lighted up again, as he spoke. "Yeah! That will be fine. That's a lot of money to see go up in smoke." He seemed more relaxed as he turned to speak his thoughts. "Say, what about that special paper? Will you show me where to get it, too?"

I knew I had him back into my net. "Oh, sure. That's no problem. I'll tell you what to do. If you pick me up at the pool hall about three o'clock tomorrow, I'll take care of everything."

I threw a glance back at the small heater and shook my head with despair. "The old man always told me to be extra careful with that chemical and never use too much."

I was still shaking my head and staring at the floor when the little man spoke up again. "This old man you speak of, he must have been quite a guy?"

"Without a doubt, he definitely was. He'd often told me of an idea he'd had that would change silver into gold."

"Holy Christ! I wish I could have met him before he was deported." He looked at his watch and spoke again. "I guess I'll get back to my place. Oh, by the way, what's your. . . ." He stopped. He remembered the agreement he'd made with Ben that he wouldn't ask any name and I wouldn't ask his.

As he headed out the door, Ben called to him. "Wait a minute. I'll go to the car with you. I need some cigarettes anyway."

The little guy slowed and threw a last glance at the puddle of ashes, although he never knew that the last small bottle was filled with *gasoline!*

At three o'clock that next day, I had completed a car deal at Twenty-Second and Michigan with another Jewish gentleman who sold Oldsmobiles.

The war had inflated the prices on everything, but I was still able to put four hundred dollars down and drive away in a 1941 Olds. I could have gotten the latest model which was the 1942, but that would have cost me three or four hundred dollars under the table.

I had fun telling Marion about the caper, including the reactions of the little Jewish guy. She would ask me stupid questions such as, "Did you meet the little guy the next day?"

"Oh, I could have met him and possibly beat him again, but it wasn't worth the risk." I also explained how Ben had prepared the large fake roll when he went out to get the sandwiches.

"Well, baby, I'm thinking of going to California. Do you think you'll like it out there?"

"Trickshot, you're kidding!"

"Like hell I am. Ben's got another sucker set up. After I take him off, that'll be enough bankroll for the trip."

I drove down Fifty-Fifth Street, but I didn't stop at the pool hall. I knew the little Jew hadn't forgotten so soon.

Ben was in the clear. All he did was bring the guy to me. The little Jew thought I had run out on him and Ben. He would have known better if he had seen the gobs of new clothes that Ben had recently purchased.

Ben and I separated the new sucker from his $1500 bankroll that following week. I now had almost a grand for expense money to California. I called Marion and told her to pack her bags, we were ready to leave.

We were on Route 66, heading west. "Why were you so anxious to leave?" Marion was still asking questions.

"Damn it, Marion! Don't be so damn dumb. Did you want me to stick around Chicago until they found my black ass in an alley? That little Jew was soft, but Big Henry, that last dude we beat, was plenty rough, plus he had some mean guys working for him."

## Chapter Four

WE HAD LEFT THAT MORNING and the little bronze Olds was spinning its large whitewall tires down the winding highway. It was wonderful, getting away from the city, the monstrous-sized buildings, with sweltering heat and offensive smells.

Fleeting landscapes amazed me as the little Oldsmobile gobbled up the highway. The spacious meadows resembled a masterpiece painting drawn by a renowned artist with a magic brush. Rolling hills of green spotted with trees and foliage, provided proper background for the galloping horse, the grazing cow, and occasionally a barking dog.

Our first stop was St. Louis, Missouri, the place of my birth. We had dinner with some relatives, checked into a hotel and left the next morning. My next place of rest was Oklahoma City. Here I found one of the many amazements of our trip. As we passed the capitol building, surrounded by a rangy yard of green grass, a gigantic oil derrick of grotesque appearance was sprawled on the beautiful sod. Resembling the head of a giant grasshopper, the massive pump was going up-down, up-down.

I was in the heart of town when I stopped at a filling station to get directions to the black neighborhood. It was unthinkable of acquiring lodgings in a white hotel—really unthinkable.

We stopped at the Little Cecil Hotel, a clean, two-story structure with a storefront below and a few decent rooms planted above. After resting and showering, we ventured to find a nice place to eat. A young soul brother pointed me to supposedly the best place in town. It was a whitewashed frame shack with a tendency to lean. A worn-out linoleum floor with a few scattered holes were topped by a wooden counter and eight or ten stools. We sat in one of the two unsteady, wooden booths. The collard greens and hamhocks were the best I'd ever eaten.

As we headed towards the highway, we passed through the residential areas and here I was surprised again. On most of the beautiful lawns, those monstrous oil derricks could be seen. I even saw one on a church lawn as we headed on Route 66, going up-down, up-down.

It was another day when we arrived in Los Angeles, California. I had heard that Mooky D., a friend of mine, was out there. We checked into the Central Hotel that was situated on Fifth Street and housed a bar and restaurant downstairs. The street held the scenes of the average ghetto, barbecue joints, wine parlors, liquor stores and record shops blasting the latest war-time hits. It was 1944. The war was going strong and California was one of the country's main ports of embarkation.

There were uniformed servicemen everywhere you looked and the war-time money flowed like the rippling waves of the giant Pacific Ocean.

I didn't know how to contact Mooky D., but I was told that he came to the hotel quite often. It was two days later when I saw him enter the hotel lobby, looking very much the pimp that he was; medium height, brown hair, partially round faced, slightly wide nose, medium-sized thick lips, and evenly placed white teeth. His small black Spitz dog was leading him on a leash. When he looked up and saw me sitting on one of the lobby couches, his face cracked into a big smile, showing those white teeth. "Well, I'll be damned! Trickshot, when did you show on the scene, man?"

He moved the dog leash to his left hand and extended his right. We exchanged greetings, sat on the lobby couch and began to rap.

"How long have you been out here and who did you bring along?"

"I've only been here a few days. I married Marion—remember the little round-faced girl that worked down on the 'Twenty-Six' table?"

"Aw, yeah. I remember now. She worked for the Jew who had the bar at Fifty-Fifth on Michigan Boulevard."

"That's right. I brought her along with me. She's upstairs sleeping because she works at night."

"Yeah, I can dig that, but let me pull your coat about this town. There's a lot of money out here, considering the servicemen, the large industrial plants and one of the biggest aircraft factories. But you've got to be damn careful. These Louisiana and Texas hoosiers that comprise the police force will bust a nigger's head then try to send his black ass to San Quentin Penitentiary." Mooky D. tugged at the dog leash as the little Spitz attempted to follow a rust colored Doberman Pincer that was leading a lady out of the lobby door. "Say, man, why don't you leave this crib and shack with me? I've leased a Japanese temple down on First Street."

"A temple! What do you mean—a temple?"

"Well, when this damn war started, the government rounded up all of the Japanese-Americans and put them in some kind of camp. The government couldn't take the legally owned property away, so they leased it to anyone that was interested."

The little Spitz was in heat upon my knee. Mooky D. pulled him down and continued to rap. "I've got eight living quarters that I rent out. However, I've got an extra bedroom and we can share the kitchen. I'd like to have you and Marion. It would be company for me since Evelyn is away so much."

"Oh, yeah! That's your ole lady isn't it? How is she?" I had forgotten about Evelyn.

"Oh, she's fine. She works in a house up in Frisco. I'm planning on moving there soon. It's more of a hustlers' town—more like back East."

"Look man, I appreciate this offer. You can hip me to what's happening, plus I'll save some money. These damn hotels will kill a man's bankroll."

Mooky D. gave me his address and telephone number and I moved the next day.

The temple was located at the far end of East First Street. It was a two-story brick building with a pointed dome. A long hallway was situated on the first floor with four-unit living quarters on each side. The second floor had the same arrangement, only the front unit had been converted into a room of worship. At least, that's what I surmised it to be. There was a fair-sized platform with an altar on top. Old expensive drapes of red velvet hung heavily from the windows. There were long velvet strips about two feet wide. These also hung from the wall with dragon designs and little fringes dangling on the end.

It wasn't long before I familiarized myself with the neighborhood. First Street wasn't very long, but it was a busy street. I hung around First and San Pedro. On the corner was the Civic Hotel, underneath was a jewelry store and coffee shop. On the opposite corner was a large nightclub and farther up the street there was another club, complete with dancing girls, twelve-piece band and other expectants that go along with nightclub gay-larity.

All of these establishments were previously occupied by the Japanese-American people. The vicinity was called "Little Tokyo." Like other streets throughout the nation that had fallen prey to ghetto dwellers, First Street had its share.

The nightclub bars had their share of prostitutes. The hotels rented rooms to transients and permanents; they were occupied by hustlers, whores, and pimps from all parts of the country. If degrees were given to this categorical group of people, here you would find the holders of the Ph.D's.

I had found Marion a spot in a whore house on the outskirts of the city. I spent my time smoking pot and in and out of various bars. There was a chance I might find a new prospect that would increase my status in that fantastic game of pimping.

It was a night when I wandered into the hotel and got involved in a crap game with a couple of young dudes. Alec, the tallest of the two, was married to a cute little whore called Lily. I found out the two guys were jewel thieves. It was the beginning of a nightly occurrence for me; that is, every night that they would score and had some jewelry that I might win.

This went on for a couple of weeks. One night, I was shooting for a point and dropped one of the dice which I had concealed under the money in my left hand. All hell broke loose in that hotel room. Lily, the cute whore, with the wide hips, small waist, light skin and small eyes, yelled, "I warned both of you about that slick ass Chicago nigger. I'll bet he's been cheating all the time."

Alec jumped up from the floor and rushed to the dresser drawer. Eddie snatched the third dice up from the floor and began to inspect the spots.

"I'll be a dirty motherfucker," Eddie said. "This dice

doesn't have any deuces or fours on it."

Eddie was medium height, black skin, cold brown eyes and as muscular as a giant. I'd rather face Alec with the gun that I was sure he was about to retrieve from the dresser drawer. But Eddie the muscular misfit was advancing toward me with mayhem in his cold eyes.

Aw, shit! It was as I had figured. Alec had the snub-nose thirty-eight in his hand. He turned from the dresser and advanced toward me. I didn't know which one of them would reach me first.

I backed up against the dingy papered wall. I threw up both of my arms, grasping the money in my left hand. I would have gladly given them the money. But the mate to the fallen dice was still concealed within the crumpled and sweaty money.

"Hold it, fellas! I can straighten this out if you let me." I was rapping for my life and that's no shit. "It won't do you any good to off me. Man, I can show you how we can all get rich."

Eddie, the stocky-built guy, had reached me first. He was holding me by the neck. I could hardly cop the plea that I wanted so badly for them to hear.

"Let him go, so we can hear what he's got to say. It better be good, motherfucker, or your ass is finished." Alec was talking while holding the gun over my shoulder and the mouth of the barrel was in my ear.

"Man, I've got a game that I rip off every week and they're all a bunch of squares. I could take you dudes along and we'd split the take." I tried to look as scared as I really was.

"What about the money you've beat us out of already?" Eddie was bristling.

"Yeah! What about that ring that you won last week?" The whore screamed, hands on her hips.

"I sold it, but I've still got the dough. I'll make it up to you dudes, if you just give me a chance." I had lowered my hands, waving them as I talked.

Alec had taken the gun from my ear. He was holding it pointed down toward the floor. "When will we get the money for that ring?" Alec waved the gun toward me when he asked.

"The money is in the bank, but you'll get it tomorrow. I'll give you what I've got to prove I'm not stalling."

I went to my pockets with the money in my hand. I released the dice that was concealed under the money, then brought all of the money out again.

"This is all I've got. Here, you can search me if you'd like." I patted both of my pockets and moved forward with outstretched arms. I counted on them not searching me, figuring I was too frightened to tell them a lie. If they had found the other dice, it might not have been so bad. But I knew it wouldn't have looked good.

"How much money do you have there?" Eddie stepped forward and snatched the money from my hand.

I was going to make it. I was nervous and scared. I was also lucky and knew it. I promised the two young dudes that I would bring the money for the ring that following day. They let me go with a warning, that I'd better not forget to keep the appointment. When they let me out of the door, I was gone, gone—like vanished.

It was a week before I saw Alec at the supermart. He pulled his cart behind me as the clerk was checking me out.

"I thought you were going to bring our money." His face was hard and his voice was the same.

"Oh, I didn't see you. How've you been?" An amiable smile showed my teeth.

"Damn how I've been. Where's our money, man?"

The clerk had finished ringing the register. She was waiting for me to pay her. I came out of my stupor. "I'm sorry, here you are." I paid my bill from a small roll of money and replaced the roll in my pocket.

I could see Alec's eyes staring, straining, following the money. The clerk was checking out the few articles in Alec's cart as I moved on. I wasn't too scared. I had been carrying a small thirty-two revolver that Mooky D. had gotten for me. There was no need to run from the trouble that I knew later on I was bound to face. Hurriedly, he went to his pocket and paid his bill. I continued, arms filled with parcels and walked slowly towards my car.

"I'm not going to ask you again. What about our money, man?" The youth had followed me to the car and placed his few groceries on the pavement.

I opened the car door and rested my groceries on the car seat. Then I turned to face my adversary.

"Look, man, you caught me cheating and took all of my scratch. I think we should forget the whole deal." I stepped back a few feet. We were facing each other.

Alec made a step forward while clawing at his pocket. His right hand came out of his pocket with a shiny object. His fist flicked sideways and I heard the click. I was back-peddling and watching his hand that now had a gleaming knife up-raised.

My hand zipped to the thirty-two revolver that was concealed beneath my shirt. He was coming closer and I continued to back up. His knife glittered in the glare of the sun. I was tugging desperately to free the gun that was now entangled within my shirt. I stumbled and fell. But the fall half-freed the gun. Alec was now bending over me. He froze. He was looking into the barrel of the small missile launcher which I aimed up at him. Somewhere, a lady's voice shrieked! I could see Alec grit his teeth and tighten his body as his hand emptied and the glittering knife clattered to the pavement. The expression on his face told of the expectant death that a squeeze of my finger could deliver.

Computerized thoughts dashed through my mind. I didn't want this kind of trouble. I couldn't stand it. I was two thousand miles away from home.

I lifted myself from the ground, and glanced at the crowd that had gathered. People were looking out of the supermart windows. A small silver-haired old lady was standing in the entrance of the store. She was trembling, hand up to her mouth, biting her nails. I surmised that someone had called the police. Without a word, I hurriedly went to my car and drove off.

When I arrived at the house, I told Mooky D. what had happened. He asked me, "Did they get your license number?"

"I don't think so. No one had noticed us until he pulled his knife."

"Well, you'd better be careful. You don't know what to expect in the future. What about that ring you won from them? Did you really sell it?"

"Naw, I've still got it, but I gave it to a jeweler so he could change the mounting."

"That was a smart idea, especially if the stone wasn't large enough to be identified."

"Oh, it was a fair-sized stone, about a karat and a half. It was originally in a yellow-gold mounting, but I told the jeweler to put it in white-gold with a fancy design."

"Boy! I'll bet it's gonna look good. When do you think it'll be ready?"

"Any day now. I gave it to him two weeks ago."

"Well, I'm sure you'll let me see it when you get it out . . . I'm gonna take my dog for a walk in a few minutes. Remember what I told you—be careful."

It was two weeks later when I heard that Alec and Eddie were busted in a downtown department store trying to score for some jewelry.

## Chapter Five

I HAD BEEN AVOIDING some of my regular haunts, thus heeding the warning that Mooky D. had given me. I had just left the Dunbar Hotel, very popular during the era, located in the black neighborhood at Forty-Second and Central. It contained a nightclub that was sometimes frequented by the top white movie stars—especially when they felt like slumming.

Mooky D. walked through the kitchen into my small adjoining bedroom.

"Here, man, try this dynamite. A friend of mine just got back from Mexico and gave me a can of it."

I accepted the two reefers and placed them under the dresser scarf. It was only a short time before I heard a knock at the door.

"Who is it?" I yelled.

"It's the police, Trickshot, open the door."

The voice was complacent in tone, so I thought some of the fellas were having their little joke. I opened the door.

"Aw, man, why do you guys—"

There, before my eyes, were the biggest and tallest police I'd ever seen. They stepped into the room and gazed around at the regular-sized bed pushed up in the corner with the small lamp resting on the miniature table beside it. A small window was hung in the wall with brown polyester drapes for a cover. The outdated dresser decorated the far wall and two wooden chairs divided the room.

The tallest detective with the red hair and pointed nose reached for the closet door that was in the opposite wall from the dresser. His sharp features modulated when he spoke. "These female clothes undoubtedly belong to your wife Marion—right?"

I was slightly shaken that they knew about Marion. However, I answered, "Yes, they do."

The other rangy detective, though not as tall, ran his fingers through his brown hair. His beefy face cracked when he asked, "Yeah, we hear that she's out of town working. When will she be back?"

They were letting me know that they krew all about me and it would be useless to lie.

"I really don't know. She hasn't called to tell me yet."

The husky bare-headed man strolled to the dresser and yanked at one of the drawers. The drawer was partially out when he turned. His rubbery jaws moved. "You know what we're here for. Do you want to tell us or will we have to find it?"

"I don't know what you're looking for," I answered.

"O.K. If that's the way you want it." The tall one spoke.

They proceeded to snatch out the dresser drawers, throw the clothes out of the closet and on the floor. They felt along the edges of the drapes and pulled the shade down, unrolled it and inspected the pole that it was rolled on. I knew then they were looking for dope.

Mooky D. had heard the disturbance. He came through the kitchen and stopped at the dividing door.

"What's the trouble, gentlemen? Why are you tearing up the place?"

The detectives were distracted momentarily. The tall sharp-faced policeman was the first to speak. "You're the landlord, huh?"

"That's right," Mooky D. answered.

"Well, we're police officers and we've received information that this fellow has dope and stolen merchandise concealed on these premises."

"I just rent to him. I don't know what he has." Mooky D. was blocking the door to his apartment.

A thought opened up my head like a shot of smelling salts. Stolen property, they had said, and dope. Alec and Eddie had gotten busted. It all began to add up. They had told the detectives about the ring. I felt the weight of it on my little finger. I wanted to pull it off, to hide it, throw it away, anything but have it found in my possession. But they had placed me in one of the wooden chairs and told me not to budge. Oh my God! Another thought of despair penetrated my cranium. The reefer! The two sticks that Mooky D. had just given me.

I threw a furtive glance towards the dresser. The husky man with the reddish face was lifting up articles, first the cologne tray, the clock, a picture of Marion and me, then the jewelry box. He dumped everything out of the box and pawed amongst Marion's earrings and other sparkling objects. His brown mane turned and his frosty stare targeted on my folded arms. He took two massive steps that made his giant frame tower over me.

"Let me see your hands." His voice was crisp-stern. "Aw ha, look at this, O'Malley."

He grasped my left hand and was showing it and the ring to the other detective.

"Pull it off." The tall guy's nose seemed to twitch when he spoke.

"Is this the ring that you won from Eddie?" My calculations had been correct. The two young punks had talked, probably after being beaten half to death.

"I didn't win this ring from anyone," I answered, as I handed him the gleaming object.

The husky detective flexed his meaty fingers and pawed the ring. He sauntered across the small room and stood under the ceiling light.

"When did you have the mounting changed, Trickshot? We were expecting it to be in yellow-gold."

"Here, let me see it. Yep, this is the ring all right." The tall redhead had interrupted before I could answer. Small flashes of hue infiltrated the room as the ceiling light contacted the ring. "Well, it doesn't make any difference. We'll get a make on it anyway." Husky had spoken again.

I was perspiring badly. I wanted them to hurry and take my black ass to jail. I could beat the rap for the ring, even if they were fortunate enough to find its owner. But, if they had found those two sticks of pot, I would have been a new inmate at San Quentin Penitentiary.

"We know you smoke grass, Trickshot. Save us the trouble of finding it and we'll see that things go easy for you." The tall guy spoke and his nose twitched again.

"I don't know what you're talking about," I answered, as I felt the perspiration trickling down my neck.

The husky detective had just thrown the mattress on the floor, when the tall one attempted to push past Mooky D.

"Do you have a warrant to search this part of the house?" Mooky D. asked him.

"What about it, Sarge?" The tall guy was looking at Mooky D., waiting for his superior to answer.

"Aw, screw it, we've got the ring anyway." The tall detective gave Mooky D. a long cold stare before he turned away.

"The next time I come here, I'll have a warrant for you." He finally turned and walked over in front of me. "All right, stick out your arms."

He fastened the handcuffs on my wrist, and turned to speak to the husky detective. "Looks like we've blowed on the 'pot' thing."

"Yeah, but we'll take him down and find out who owns this ring."

So, the big guy was a sergeant, and they were both probably assigned to burglary or robbery. I thought of the sergeant's last remark and wondered if they had in mind for me the same beating I figured they had given to Alec and Eddie.

I maneuvered the handcuffs and locked the apartment door. The two brawny detectives sandwiched me as I was escorted down the hall to the outside where there was waiting an unmarked police car.

The air was brisk as I looked up to the sky. The night was hanging like a bin of coal with stardust sprinkled within. They placed me in the back seat, and I saw the tall detective turn the ignition. The motor answered its call to duty and the long and joyful ride had begun. The car went to First Street and turned left. I visualized Mooky D. scurrying into my room and retrieving the two sticks of pot from beneath the dresser scarf. The ride down First Street brought on the familiar sights. A luridly dressed couple were holding each other up as they shuffled out of the noisy bistro. The police car crossed First and San Pedro Street. Conical lights over the nightclub entrance gave assurance that the place was inviting. Melodious sounds escaped into the night as a funseeking patron was entering the nightclub. I saw Guzzle Bird Willie talking to a prostitute.

He leaned on the light post and shook his finger in her face as the black unmarked police car moved on.

Minnie Lue was coming out the Civic Hotel. Her high-heeled, needle-toed shoes made a sonorous sound when they attacked the sidewalk. The massively made-up face and her hip-swinging stride showed that she was now at work.

The car cruised a couple of blocks and turned right. It wasn't long before the black police car pulled into the ramp of a tall white, gigantic and peaceful-looking building. It had barred windows that appeared to keep intruders out. This was the Los Angeles Police Department, central headquarters.

I was escorted to an elevator that sped us to the designated floor above. I was taken to a room and there relinquished all my personal belongings. I was then taken to another room where my picture was snapped and I was fingerprinted.

The next stop was to be my home for the following three days. It was a six by ten feet cell with upper and lower bunks together with a face bowl and stool taking up most of the space. I was fed twice a day and could buy cigarettes if I chose. All of the cells faced outside windows and had it not been for an officer who worked the midnight shift, I think some of us prisoners would have caught pneumonia.

I had no idea how long the detectives intended to keep me locked up. The agony of not knowing was worse than the confinement. It was late and I had been in jail almost two complete nights. A scream aroused the whole tier. I expected to see the officer who was on duty appear at any moment. The scream was heard again, only this time it was more pronounced, more terrifying—and slightly sickening.

The angry felons expressed their rage with verbal shouts of obscenities and then shoes were banged against the bars.

The scream was heard again, but jeers and other shouts had now joined together, accompanied by tin cups clanging against the bars. Eventually was heard the voice of authority and the patter of running feet. Accompanied by two men in white, the night officer had finally arrived.

The deranged prisoner was taken from his cell kicking and screaming, another candidate for the "funny farm." Like other prisoners, I wasn't able to go back to sleep. My thoughts turned to Marion. I knew Mooky D. had called and told her what had befallen me. I wondered at the time why I hadn't heard from either of them. I had no idea how long the two giant detectives planned on detaining me. However, I calculated that they were trying frantically to find the owner of the ring. That is, if Alec and Eddie hadn't told them already. If that be the case, there was nothing that I could do anyway.

It was the morning after the third night. I was vengefully angry; angry at Marion, angry at Mooky D. and most of all, angry at the two monstrosities who had brought me there. It was after we were served our first meal that my name was called.

I was taken from the cell and led to another part of the building where there were a long string of offices divided by a long hall. The man took me into one of these offices and sat me before a desk. There wasn't very much in the room except a typewriter on the desk, a telephone, a tall four-pronged hat rack, another chair behind the desk, a wastebasket and a large map on the wall behind the desk, with an overhanging flourescent light.

Very shortly I was confronted by my two captors, ole "twitch nose" and his boss "Husky." The sergeant seated himself behind the desk, then gave me a cunning stare. "Trickshot, how would you like to have this back?" He was balancing my ring between two of his obese fingers.

The tall redhead interrupted as usual. "Yeah, we'll give

you the ring back if you want to take out some insurance." His damn nose was twitching again.

"What kind of insurance? I don't understand."

"Well, you're new in this part of the country. But, if you want to stay out of trouble, you'll put a little protection on yourself."

Husky let the ring fall to the green blotter that partially covered the center of the desk.

"I still don't know what you mean."

But there was one thing I did know. Evidently they couldn't find the owner of the ring. I contributed this to the changing of the mounting. Even if Alec and Eddie had confessed to every crime in the city, the owner couldn't swear that it was the same ring.

"We don't want to give you or your wife a hard time, Trickshot . . . I'll tell you what . . . you tell us where you get your pot and we'll see that you get the ring back—plus, your stay in Los Angeles will be more pleasant."

Ah, ha. So there it was. Me, they wanted to turn into a stool-pigeon. I had to restrain myself from laughing. The bastards wanted me to believe that they were returning the ring to me for services rendered. But I knew they had to return the ring to me anyway. It would be best to play along. I rubbed my chin and looked down at my ring, which was still resting idly on the massive green blotter.

"I think I can handle it, but you'll have to give me a few days to set it up. This guy that I buy my grass from works out of a tavern. I'll have to make sure when he's got it before I can let you officers know."

The tall detective looked at his superior as if to say, "Do you think the prick is lying?" The sergeant picked up the ring, looked at it, and passed it to me.

"Now don't think you can duck out on us after I've given you the ring. Hey! What was that guy's name that moved and tried to hide from us?"

The sergeant had turned his head to call the tall detective, who was standing in the hall talking to a uniformed policeman. The redheaded detective walked back into the office. "Now, what was that again?" He looked at "Husky" questioningly.

"You remember that nigger that was out of New York City. The one that had that white tramp.

The tall redhead seemed to recall. "Oh, yeah. That little guy with the slick hair. You don't have any white girls, do you boy?" His nose did a tremendous twitch as he reversed his head and looked at me.

"Aw, naw, I was recently married and my wife wouldn't go for that." I tried to look as sincere as my voice sounded.

I was given a card by each of them with the telephone numbers printed on each. Then I was released with instructions to call them whenever I had the information that would lead to the pot dealers arrest. This happened in the month of February, 1944, at the Los Angeles Police Department.

Mooky D. was glad to see me when I arrived home. He told me that he called Marion, but he had also advised her that it would do no good to leave her work. She wouldn't be allowed to see my anyway.

Mooky D. also explained to me that no one could have seen me because the detectives had left my charge open. I felt ashamed about the anger that had aroused in me while sitting in my cold cell. I explained to Mooky D. about the two tall detectives and assured him that I would have to leave. He agreed that it would be best, otherwise I might some day be stopped and searched by them and they'd find a stick of reefer that they'd know I actually never had.

I called Marion and told her why we had to leave. She said she would be home that night. It was early the next morning; our bags were packed and we told Mooky D. good-bye.

We took the same Route 66 back home. I was told that the northern route was slightly rough at that time of year. As we had noticed before, 66 was a wonderful and scenic tour. The sun was rising and resembled a piece of round cheese, casting rays of seasoning to the vegetation below. We would pass meadows of green as far as the eye could see, interrupted by mountains of gold, a hue caused by the glare of the sun. Route 66 stretched out and wound around the gigantic mountains like the body of a giant python, though I admit it wasn't as smooth.

Marion had done pretty well. I began to think how lucky I had been to find Mooky D. and get the connections at the whore house. I recalled Lock telling me how important it was for a pimp to have connections. I turned my attentions to Marion, but kept my eyes on the highway.

"Say, baby, how much did those girls get from a trick at that whore house?"

"Oh, it would vary, but the lowest was five dollars." Marion's head was turned, looking out the window.

"Five dollars! You mean a guy would only give you five dollars and then you'd have to give up half of that?"

Marion snatched her head around. "You're damn right! And I'd see twenty or thirty guys every day. I'm glad we're going home . . . at least you can get ten dollars from a man and you don't have to split it with some bitch of a madam."

Marion had placed her chin in her hand and her elbow on the door armrest. She was looking out the window again.

"Damn, baby, don't get so riled. What about those girls years ago that were working on Forty-Seventh and Calumet Avenue in Chicago? I've heard that they used to get fifty cents from every guy that they turned."

I slowed the car to a cruise. The sign ahead said "Deer Crossing." Marion raised her chin from her hand. "Well, you can bet your sweet life, I wouldn't have been amongst them. Fifty cents! Hump!" She crossed her legs, knee over knee, and her chin went back into her hand—leaning.

"But everything weighs out the same. Just think, in those days a pimp could get a Cadillac for fifteen hundred dollars. Boy! I sure wish it was like that now."

Marion was ignoring me. Mooky D. had told me that it was a tough whore house, but the house madam was paying off so a pimp didn't have to worry too much about a bust.

"Well, baby, it's good you're hip to the Vaseline. I hear that the grease makes it much easier."

"Ain't that a bitch! Let twenty or thirty men continue to punch in you and, Vaseline or not, I'll bet your ass would have a black eye. Vaseline . . . hump!"

I shut up and took in the scenery. We stopped and got some sleep in Gallop, New Mexico, and two days later, we were home.

## Chapter Six

THE STAY IN LOS ANGELES had only lasted two months and the quick return home was as much a surprise to my mother, to Ben and the rest of my associates as it was to Marion and me.

My first endeavor was to check with Ben and see how safe it was to make my presence known. Ben assured me that there was no danger from the little Jew. It seemed that the government had apprehended him for receiving a truckload of whiskey which had been stolen out of state. I asked Ben about Big Henry, the other sucker we had swindled, and was told that he had gotten killed at Fifty-First and Michigan Avenue by some white gangsters who were taking over his policy operations.

The news of Big Henry's death had the effect of sadness, though, I must admit, my freedom would have been hindered had he been alive on my return home.

It was two weeks later when Marion's grandfather died.

Among his estate was a tavern which Marion's mother had inherited. It was no more than was expected that Marion should help in the operation of her mother's newly-acquired establishment. However, expectations and responsibility did not cease there. I was given the position of head bartender. My only subordinate just happened to be my wife. This arrangement had the sanctioning of my mother because it represented a job, something which I had never had. I noted a tinge of family connivance, but the plan was laid with a veneer that was hard for me to compete with at the time.

The tavern was not a showplace, just a scattering of distillery donated pictures and ordinary wooden booths. The long plain bar was the background for the moderate leather-topped stools. The clientele was local, working class, middle-aged, and the average laymen. Occasionally a few of the younger set would appear, thus livening up the place.

It was on one of those long, dreary and first of the week rainy nights. I propped my foot upon the empty beer cases and gazed out of the large window into the turbulent darkness. Frequent flashes of lightning divided the blackness and the crystalized raindrops became transparent.

Across the street, a sign hung precariously above the shoe-shop entrance, loosened by the violent winds and now was a hazard to the hurrying, huddling figures that passed underneath. Two headlight beams penetrated the night and silhouetted the rain drops as the blue sedan pulled in front of the door.

A short, pudgy form dashed from the car and entered the tavern. He stood inside the door and shook his shiny black coat which looked to be water-repellant. His eyeglasses were in need of windshield wipers and his graying head of hair was in need of a towel. He looked down the bar at the row of empty seats, then laid his dripping coat across one stool while he situated his blubberish frame across the other. He had very light skin and a wide nose. His gray mustache moved when he said, "Give me a bottle of beer."

I scraped my brain trying to recall where I had seen this face before. I retrieved a bottle of beer from the cooler, opened it and placed it in front of the obese man.

"You're Trickshot, aren't you?"

"That's right. Have I met you before?"

"Naw, but I've seen you in my place." He gulped a glass of the cold beer and it left traces of suds along his gray mustache.

"Your place, where is that?"

"The gambling joint atop the barber shop on Fifty-First. That's my place."

"Oh, yeah, now I remember. I came through there a couple of times last week. A friend of mine hangs out there."

I remember seeing this oversized man at the crap table. But I took him to be just another gambler. I could tell there was something on his mind.

The constant patter of rain on the tavern window and vibrations from the claps of thunder verified my thoughts.

"That last one shook the whole building." He was speaking of the latest clap of thunder as his small eyes glanced out into the night. He turned to face me and his puffy jaws moved. "I wouldn't have been out in this weather, but it was urgent that I talk to you."

"Yeah, well, what's on your mind?"

He gulped his last glass of beer and leaned his massive elbow on top of the bar. "You can get something, I hear, that the white boys want." His small unwavering eyes were staring at me.

"That depends on what they want."

His bloated body shifted and then he spoke. "If you can get some gas stamps, I know people who will pay well for them." He shifted his body again and I felt sorry for the stool.

"I'll see what I can do. Why not leave your phone number and I'll call you tomorrow."

I had heard rumors about the gasoline stamps, but I really didn't have the connections for them. The fat man wrote a phone number on a tiny white card, then maneuvered his corpulent body from the stool. He put on his coat, making sure he'd raised its collar, then disappeared through the door into his waiting car.

That next morning, I called Ben to find out if he knew anything concerning the stamps. He told me to meet him at my mother-in-law's bar and he would tell me what he knew. It was about noon when I entered the bar. Ben had already arrived and was occupying one of the booths while drinking a bottle of beer.

"Hi, I didn't expect you so soon."

"Well, I didn't have nothing to do, so I figured I'd have a bottle of beer until you showed up." Ben downed a swig of beer and lighted a cigarette.

I yelled across the bar to my father-in-law, then slid into the seat. The booth table separated Ben and me. I ordered some more drinks from my father-in-law who had been tending bars most of his life. His last place of employment was for a Jewish fella who owned a tavern directly down the street.

I turned and faced Ben. "Say, man, tell me about this gas stamp gimmick. I've got a dude that's interested in buying some."

Ben duffed his cigarette and said, "I know two guys who are getting them, but I'm sure they've got connections already. You see, Trick, since they've been rationing gas, all these small gas stations have been doing land office business."

"Give me the rundown on the prices. You know I've

been off the scene and I don't even know how much to quote."

"Well, you see, it works like this. The government has been hiring a lot of Negroes at those distributing houses. There's a large one located near the outer drive, just as you cross over the bridge."

My father-in-law had set the drinks on the bar and was about to walk around and bring them to us. I slid out of the booth and got the drinks, thus saving the old guy a trip. I returned to the booth and seated myself again. "Go ahead, man and finish telling me about the stamps."

Ben duffed his last cigarette and continued. "Well, these guys that work at the distributing houses have coffee breaks and lunch periods. Whenever they take a break, they bring out some stamps. It's a simple—"

"Wait a minute. What happens to the stamps before the guys go back from their coffee breaks?"

"Aw, that's no problem. They either have someone waiting to get them or they stash them until they get off that evening."

I stirred my scotch and water, then downed a big gulp. "Are those stamps that easy to get?"

"Oh, they're just ordinary stamps. In fact, they're smaller than a postage stamp."

"Smaller than a postage stamp! Damn! A guy could put a whole roll of them in his socks and no one would ever notice." I lighted a cigarette and waited for Ben to tell me more.

"That's just what happens. Oh, I don't say they all bring them out in their socks—some of them wear jockey straps, false hat linings and many other ways that the whiteys are not aware of." Ben patted his pocket, forgetting he had smoked his last cigarette.

"Here, man, take one of these."

I produced a pack of Luckies. Ben started to get up, but

the tavern didn't sell cigarettes and there were no machines in Chicago at that time.

He accepted one of mine and continued. "See, all the stamps are the same size, but the different colors represents the amount of gas that can be purchased with that stamp. Some stamps are company stamps, and one of these might purchase a hundred gallons, while another stamp that's used by the public, might only purchase five gallons."

"Ain't that a bitch! You mean a guy can walk out of the place with a roll of stamps that might run into the thousands of gallons?"

"Not can, they do it every day."

"Shit, man, we've got to get in on that hustle. Why haven't you got a job down there?"

"I've been trying, man. I've got an application in. It's been there for three weeks. I don't know why they haven't called me."

I had to light another cigarette. "Now tell me, how much do they pay per stamp?"

"Aw, shit, Trick, don't be so dumb. They don't sell by the stamp. They sell by the amount of gallons the stamp can purchase, and the going price now is five cents a gallon, but that's big dough when you figure up five or ten thousand gallons a day."

Ben was mashing his cigarette out. I offered him another but he refused.

"Shit! No wonder Fat Mouth and the rest of those guys are driving those late model '42 cars."

"Yeah, Fat Mouth has been working there about three weeks now."

"They weren't hiring guys before I left for California. How long has this arrangement been going on?"

"Oh, about six weeks—or maybe seven at the longest."

"Isn't that a bitch? While I'm out in California trying to get a whore, every motherfucker and his cousins are back here getting rich!"

Ben slid out of the faded wooden booth. "I'm going to the corner drugstore and get some cigarettes. Do you want a pack?"

"Naw, I'm straight." I patted my pocket and felt my almost full pack.

While Ben was gone, I exercised my brain. I had to find a contact for some stamps. I went to the phone and called Marion. It was a difficult task explaining to her why I wouldn't be to work that night. That jealous streak was aroused in her, and she could visualize me shacked up with a strange broad. I couldn't picture myself arguing with Marion all day, so I decided it was best to hang up the phone.

I looked in my wallet and got the small white card. Without a doubt, I should call the fat man. The number he had given to me must have been for the gambling joint. A husky voice told me to hold the phone and I could hear the stick man calling the rolls of the dice.

Ben came through the door while I was talking. Finishing the conversation, I hung up the phone and rejoined Ben in the booth and then called to my father-in-law to prepare another drink.

"Well, Ben, when you came in the door, I was talking to the fat man."

"Oh, yeah. What did he say?"

"I told him, for six cents a gallon I would deliver the stamps."

"Yeah? And what did he say?"

"He said, O.K."

Ben was smiling. "I think I know where we can get some."

A smile of elation attacked my solemn face and I said, "Spill, man! Tell me where?"

"Well, it's like this. Crummy Joe has been working down

there for about a week and he hasn't found a steady connection yet. At least, he hadn't two days ago. He's been peddling the stamps to different people. I don't think he knows any gas station connects." Ben looked at his watch. "Most of the guys are off work at five o'clock. We may catch Crummy Joe at the '411 Club' on Sixty-Third Street."

Ben saturated his throat with the last glass of beer and then we left to find Crummy Joe.

Three days later, Ben and I made our first delivery of gas stamps to the Fat Man. Crummy Joe was bringing us all the stamps that he could steal. It wasn't long before the news had spread that Ben and I had a "Boss" connection for the outlet of the stamps. I was introduced to a white guy from the north side. Just before closing time, Marion and I were checking the register after an unexpectedly busy night. A tapping on the window captured my hearing and I sauntered to the door.

The large white bulb over the entrance had been switched off, a nightly habit at closing time. I pressed my face against the glass door, then cupped my hands and peeked out. The Fat Man was perched in front of the door, his roly-poly figure was outlined by the distant street light and his gray hair that topped a wide forehead; and horned-rimmed glasses straddled a pointed nose, thus dividing an oval face that carried a medium-sized mouth.

I opened the door and let them in. The Fat Man had on the familiar black water-repellant coat. The white guy was dressed in a dark green herringbone coat. This topped a toast-brown double-breasted suit. His white on white shirt was strangled by a tie that had the same hue as his dark green socks. I led them to one of the back wooden booths.

The white guy, who was about six feet tall, was the first to sit down. The Fat Man wiggled himself into the other side of the booth while I made myself comfortable next to his white companion.

"What's on your mind, fellas?" I asked.

Adjusting himself in the cramped booth, the Fat Man spoke up. "This is a friend of mine, Trickshot. I want you to meet Dino."

I turned sideways and extended my hand. "It's a pleasure to know you, Dino."

Dino extended his hand which was very soft, and his voice, like his dark blue eyes, was friendly. "Glad to know you," Dino said.

"Would you guys care for a drink?" I asked.

"I never touch it," Dino refused.

"I shouldn't, but I'll have a beer." The Fat Man licked his lips after ordering his drink.

I yelled to my wife, who had just cleared the register of the night's receipts, and told her to bring the beer, plus a scotch and water for me.

Fat Man scratched his silver-gray mane and his round jaws stretched as he said, "This is the man I delivered the stamps to, Trickshot."

"Oh?" I reversed my head to look at Dino, who was lighting a cigarette.

"As you know, that gambling joint keeps me pretty busy, so I just don't have time for other things. I figured it was best to introduce the two of you and then both of you could make your own arrangements concerning the stamps," Fat Man said.

Marion was placing the drinks and the Fat Man was licking his lips again. The little conference didn't last long. Dino gave me a number to call with an understanding that he would buy all of the stamps that I would bring. It was later when I learned that it was Dino's idea that the Fat Man should continue to watch the take from the gambling, thus satisfying Dino who was really the boss behind the scene anyhow.

I let Dino and the Fat Man out the door, then turned to look at my wife. I knew that she was tired because it had been a busy night, but I could also see that inquisitive gleam in her eyes. "Who was that white fella, Trickshot?"

"Aw, just some guy that I'm doing business with."

"What kind of business?"

"None of *your* damn business! Damn it, why are you broads so fucking nosy? A man can't turn without a woman wanting to know which way he's going!" I was tired and upset.

"What do you mean broads? I'm your wife and I think I should be told."

Our clandestine action in the far wooden booth had created suspicion in Marion's evil soul. The argument between us continued until we reached the apartment.

I had moved most of my clothes from my mother's house over to Marion's apartment. I unlocked the apartment door and the couch was the first stop, where I took off my shoes, then stretched my legs and sprawled out. Marion had gone into the bathroom to run my bath water, but her constant jabbering was spoiling my relaxation.

"Bitch! If you don't stop that nagging, I'm going to leave this house and then you can talk to yourself."

I heard her yell back, "I thought you were so damn tired? You must have one of your bitches waiting for you somewhere!"

Her continuous flow of rhetoric had inflamed me. I sprang from the couch and dashed into the bathroom. Marion was bending over the tub. Evidently she was testing the temperature of the water. The running of the water and the sound of her persistent prattle had obviously drowned out the sound of my approach.

I spread my hand and grasped the back of her neck. With all my strength and weight, I plunged her head downward. Marion gurgled, grabbed, and splashed, then her feet clawed the air. With no intent of murder in my mind, I released her water-soaked head. Her head resembled the mop that the porter had often used around the tavern.

She was holding her throat as her dripping head was arched over the tub coughing. I went back into the room and put on my shoes, then I threw a parting remark as I reached for the door.

"Maybe that will stop you from yakking so damn much."

I slammed the door and faced the chill of the night.


The following day, my mother's phone awakened me. It was my father-in-law saying that a man was waiting to see me. Still groggy from the much needed sleep, I raised up on my elbow and said, "Put him on."

It was a few seconds before I heard the lucid voice. "Hi, Trickshot, this is Fat Daddy."

"Who?"

"Fat Daddy! You know, the cab man."

"Oh, yeah! How've you been, Daddy?"

I was coming out of my tranquil sleep and raised up farther in the bed with a pillow propped behind my back.

"I would like to talk to you about some business," he said. "I'm sure you can imagine what it's all about."

"Yeah, I've got an idea. Why not meet me at the bar tonight. I'll be there about eight o'clock."

"Will do." Fat Daddy was brief.

I cradled the phone and reclined back on my pillow. Only a fool would not have recognized the objectives. Fat Daddy owned a fleet of cabs and the cabs needed gas to operate. I had what he needed, gas stamps.

When he entered the tavern that night, he was about two barrel slats larger than the Fat Man who ran the gambling house. I pondered momentarily about the two, then threw the coincidence out of my mind.

My favorite wooden booth was occupied by a drinking party from around the neighborhood, so I invited Daddy into the midget office that had now become a sort of storeroom. Fat Daddy's mammoth frame caused the small room to be overcrowded. A gathering of beer crates and tavern supplies accentuated the decor of the enclosure. I placed myself on two stacked boxes and propped my foot upon an empty beer case.

"Trickshot, I hear you have a good outlet for some gas stamps. If that's true, I think we can do a lot of business."

"Yeap, just meet my six cents a gallon price and you'll have all the gas you need—stamps, that is."

Fat Daddy uttered a grunt which almost was a laugh. "Naw, Trickshot, you've got things figgered wrong. You see, I get all the gas stamps I need. In fact, I get more than I can handle. That's why I'm here to see you."

It goes without question that I was most surprised. I knew that this man owned a fleet of cabs. What would seem more logical than he needing stamps for gas? "Oh, yeah, well run things down to me so I can dig what's happening."

"Well, it's like I just said, I get more stamps than I need. I ask a nickel a gallon; if you can get six cents, that will enable you to make money too."

The fat man shifted his corpulent body and disturbed a perched case of beer. I flinched—"Oops! I'm sorry," he said.

"That's all right," I answered, "no harm done. Now tell me, Daddy, when will I get these stamps and how many will there be? It has to be enough to make the effort worth my time."

The big man pulled up his baggy trousers and remarked, "Oh, I'll have one of my boys drop them off to you later tonight. Do you think you can off five grand worth right away?"

I was jubilant, though calm. "Why sure, that'll be no big thing. What time will your boy come through?"

"Aw, it will be around midnight, I imagine. Just you stick around the place." Fat Daddy reached for a cigarette.

"Here." I clicked and steadied my cigarette lighter.

"Thanks," said Fat Daddy, as I guided him from the small enclosure.


It was the following morning when I called Ben. "Hey, man, wake up!"

"Hi, Trick, what's shaking?"

"Everything is cool, man, I received that package I was telling you about."

Ben's voice was now more lucid. "You did! That's mellow. What's the figure?"

"Five grand," I calmly stated.

"Five grand! Damn, that's really mellow."

"I tell you what; I'll call Dino, the 'white boy,' and set things up. Then you meet me at the lounge later on."

"Crazy! Later—" Ben hung up.

Later that night, Ben and I were in the wooden booth rapping.

"But look, Trick, we have never had a chance to cop this kind of bread before, man. We've got to take it off."

"But figure it this way, Ben. If we play it straight with Daddy this time, he might give us twice as many next time."

"Man, fuck next time. There may not be a next time." Ben was adamant.

Greed and want so often go hand in hand; therefore, it was plainly unnecessary for Ben to press me. "Yeah, well, all right. I told Dino that you would bring the stamps to him this evening."

"Crazy!" Ben was elated.

## Chapter Seven

TWO WEEKS PASSED, and I continued to stall Fat Daddy. Finally I stopped receiving his calls, which was obviously a stupid move.

A month had gone by and it happened one night while I was in the tavern. I heard the telephone ring and Marion answered, "Hello ... No, he isn't ... Who? ... D.D.? ... Hold on a minute."

Marion called me and extended the phone, "It's D.D."

"Hi, dude, what's up? ... No shit, when?" Noticing the excitement in my voice, Marion looked up. "O.K., D.D., meet me at Sixty-Third and South Parkway." I hung up the phone.

"What's wrong?" Marion asked.

"D.D. just got a wire that Fat Daddy and his boys have got Ben stashed somewhere."

I went behind the bar and lifted my father-in-law's pistol. After pushing it down in my belt, I turned to Marion. "If things turn out bad, I want you to call Donaldson, the bondsman."

"You be careful," Marion warned, knowing other words of advice would be of no use.

I drove to South Park Boulevard and turned right. There was a slight emptiness within my stomach and my hands were almost wet with sweat. I was coming into the 6200 block on South Park. As I neared Sixty-Third Street, I saw D.D. standing on the corner. I guided the car close to the curb and leaned over and opened the door. "Come on, hop in. I want to beat the red light."

D.D. leaped into the car and the traffic light changed to amber as the car lurched across Sixty-Third Street. We rode along and turned at Sixty-Fourth Street, just riding and trying to think what to do next.

"Did you get any lines on where they might have him stashed?" I asked.

"A broad that I've been fucking called after I talked to you," he said.

"Well, what the hell did she say, man? You act like this is a question and answer show!" I shouted nervously.

"They might have him in that old garage on South Park and Sixty-Sixth Street. Her husband runs with that outfit, and she heard him talking on the phone. She said they mentioned your name, too."

Pangs of unexpected fear attacked my already nervous stomach as I felt for the rod that was in my belt. I turned the corner and realized how sweaty my hands were on the steering wheel. I didn't intend for them to catch me off-guard, like they had caught Ben. We drove by the old garage. Sure enough, there were two or three cars that we both recognized, parked in the graveled lot next to the old deteriorating garage.

"There's Bob's car. I know you recognize it; as many times as you've waited for him to drive off, so you could run up and stick it in his wife," I said, looking at D.D. and smiling.

"Can I help it if—" His voice broke off.

Someone was coming out of the garage. It was Samson, the dude who had delivered the stamps to me.

"Let's follow that motherfucker, and make him tell us what's happening in there," I said.

Now D.D. was a schoolmate buddy. He wasn't into anything too much. Every now and then he would sell a few bags of pot or have a few crap games in his father's basement, but he was a loyal friend when it came to trouble. He had been a street fighter ever since we came up. Weighing about two hundred pounds and only five feet eight or ten inches tall, he was built for rumbling.

We tailed Samson to a snack shop, and waited for a few minutes until he paid for his sandwiches and a few cups of coffee. Before he could drive off, D.D. got out of my car, sneaked around and came up on the driver's side of Samson's car. The lady was just bringing his change.

"Hi, Sam, old buddy," D.D. said. Looking up at D.D., Samson was half smiling, but you could see the fear in his eyes. By that time I had moved in on the other side and was sitting next to him. The waitress gave him his change and left.

"Sam, you should always lock your car doors, when you're driving by yourself," I said casually, but my stare was more sinister.

"What do you guys want?" he asked, damn near shaking.

"Remember when you told the teacher about us breaking into the gym?" D.D. asked him. "Well, that beating was nothing," said D.D. before Samson could answer.

"How many's in there and what have they done to Ben?" I asked, looking at the sandwiches.

"Pa... Pa... Pa... Pat shot him by mistake," he stuttered, showing obvious fright.

Ain't this a bitch!—My mind was racing. What to do? I knew I couldn't sit there all day thinking. I told D.D. to follow us in my car. After giving him my keys, I told Samson to drive. The bastard was shaking so bad, I thought he was trying to get the attention of the prowl cars that would pass us occasionally.

We drove to D.D.'s father's home. Seeing the rod in my hand now, Samson almost fainted. I didn't want him to panic and start running and screaming, because I had no intention of going to jail for shooting a punk like him.

"Listen, Samson, I'm not going to hurt you. I just want you to stay with D.D. until I come back."

Samson was really a weakling. A little over six feet, he was skinny like a stringbean. He wore big horn-rim glasses, but this sonofabitch could steal the glitter out of the stars.

I put a little pressure on him, when we got him downstairs in the basement. He told me Fat Daddy, the big taxi owner, had gotten him the job. That's why he had brought all the stamps to Fat Daddy's place.

I thought back a bit and remembered when Fat Daddy and I made the deal. He'd told me a fella would drop the stamps off to me. When Samson had brought the stamps, I figured he was just a runner.

I told D.D. to keep an eye on the punk until I returned. I didn't worry about it too much. D.D. had put Samson in the hospital when we were kids in school for snitching on him, and I knew Samson had never forgotten it.

As I left, I drove Samson's car to the back of D.D.'s father's house. I didn't want the car to knock the cover off of us. After hiding the car in back, I took the sandwiches and put them in my wheel, and put the rod in the center of my back, tightening my belt a few notches.

I didn't expect it to come to violence, but you never know. If they searched me, they might miss the rod having it in the center of my back. Anyway, that was better than not having it at all.

As I drove, I thought about Pat, the fella who Samson said "had shot Ben." I believed him when he said it was an accident, because Pat was not a killer, and was probably trying to frighten Ben. Well, in a few short minutes I was going in the lion's den, but I held all the aces. They still wanted the stamps and thought we still had them.

Driving up to the old garage, I honked the horn. It wasn't a second before the door was opened. I knew they had dug my wheel as I pulled up. Pulling to the rear of the garage, I turned the car around heading it out. I didn't know what was going to happen, but I knew I could drive through that ragged-ass wooden door, if I had gotten a chance.

There must have been eight or ten of them; some sitting around on cans, a couple sitting on the old wooden stairs, and over in a far corner was a cot with an old table standing beside it. I looked further and saw a form in the cot. It had to be Ben.

A tall lanky dude was playing solitaire on an old wooden bench along the wall. I knew the voice before I turned around. "You've got a lot of nerve, motherfucker!"

Holding the sandwiches in my hand, I said, "I think you ordered these."

"Where's Samson?" the fat bastard asked, looking kind of shitty at me.

"He's all right, that's more than I can say for Ben. I was told Pat shot him. How bad is he?"

"Aw, it's just a slug in the thigh," Fat Daddy said, pointing to the cot. "I didn't want to croak him. I just wanted the money or the stamps." He pulled up the baggy pants that encircled his barrel-like figure.

Well, here was where I was to play my best role. If he went for my spiel, we'd have no more trouble. If he didn't, we'd go a long time looking over out shoulders if we were lucky enough to get out alive.

"Fat Daddy, you talk like a sucker and you think like a sucker," I said. "I gave the white boys the stamps personally. I think we've all gotten burnt. I hate being played for a sucker myself, but I can't go over to the northside fucking around too tough. You know how I would come out if I did that. I was going to call you and tell you what happened, but I still had hopes that the whitey would buzz me. You know, I wouldn't just take your shit and think you'd do nothing about it."

Jim had told me a long time ago, always watch a sucker's eyes to see how he's going for your spiel. If it isn't working, switch to another line until you hit the right one.

Fat Daddy seemed to be thinking; he was rubbing his first chin. (I had hit it!) Flattery was this funky bastard's weakness. I went to work on him. I saturated him with flattery, as though he were "Caesar."

"Just look around," I said, pointing to the funkies. "Anyone of them would croak me if you just said the word."

"You're damn right they would," he spoke up. His ego was showing.

"Look, Daddy, I'm not ready to leave town, and that's what I'd have to do if I crossed you." My arms were stretched out palms up. "But tell me, why did you put the snatch on Ben? You sent the stamps to me."

He pulled up his sloppy trousers and looked at me, cunningly. "I knew he was your partner, and I've heard that he makes a lot of contact for you, seeing as he can go in a lot of places over north that you can't," he said.

He was right. A lot of times Ben would go in big hotels

downtown, and I would wait outside. Him looking white, and me being black would cause nothing but stares, especially in those days, if we were seen entering some of the places together. I saw a chance to get Ben off the hook for good. I figured I could take the ball from here on in. I remembered Jim's lesson about instilling the factual in order to conceal the unseen.

"I told you, you think like a sucker, Daddy. Why would I let Ben meet my connections? If I did, then he wouldn't need me! You know about those mink coats and diamonds that he gets. Well, who do you think gets rid of them for him!"

The fat freak was coming around. He must have weighed three hundred and he wasn't six feet tall. He picked up one of the sandwiches, which was cold by now, and began to add more poundage to his already stuffed frame.

"You know, Trickshot, I've always liked you. That's why I called when I heard you had an outlet for the stamps. You've got connections, but you don't know how to put protection on yourself." His lumpy jaws exercised as he mutilated the cold food.

I thought to myself, why do you think I'm holding Samson, you boob?

"Now if you would cut me in to a connect where I could dump some stamps at a nice price, I'd forget about this loss."

I had him. He had stopped chewing and was waiting on my answer.

"Listen, Daddy, I'll cut you into some dudes over north, but you'll have to look out for your own merchandise. After what they've done to me, I don't trust any of them." I reached out and rested my hand on his meaty shoulders.

He began to smile. I remembered again what Jim had told me about the cross. The fat slob. He'll never see the people I did business with. If and when I introduce him to a whitey, it will be with the understanding that they should keep the stamps and split the take with me. I knew time would wear him down. A lot of things can happen in time. The first time I look at the paper and see a white hoodlum that has gotten himself washed, I'll tell Fat Daddy that this was the dirty sonofabitch who took our stamps. He could never check it out, because he didn't have any contact over north. He finally got around to speaking of Ben.

"Who're you going to get to fix Ben up?" he asked.

"I'll call old Doc Smith."

"Better be careful, I hear they're watching his pad on account of those abortions," he warned.

"Say, that's right. They did bust him when that little white girl died," I recalled aloud. "Well, Doc Blake is still around if I can catch him sober."

With that I walked over to the corner where the cot was. Ben looked up in surprise as if to say, get out of here you fool! I assured him everything was all right. I asked to use the phone, then I called Marion, and told her to be ready when I blew the horn. I wanted her to check into the hotel with Ben.

"What about Samson?" Fat Daddy asked.

"I was wondering when you were going to ask," I answered.

"You know, he's the only one I've got working in that joint now," he said.

"I know. I heard Ralph got fired," I replied. He was surprised that I knew of the other flunkie he had gotten a job.

"Trickshot, you're a card. I guess if he'd been working, you'd have him stashed somewhere, too."

The door, with its rusty hinges, was opening. Ben had gotten himself as comfortable as possible, in the rear. As I leaned back in the car seat, the rod pressed against my spine bone. It was a secure feeling!

I got Marion to check in the hotel with Ben while I went for a doctor. After that we didn't get any more action. The grapevine news travels fast. When Crummy Joe stopped bringing us his stamps, we knew the word had gone out on us.

I had been at the tavern for quite a while and this was not my shot. It's all right to help your in-laws and yourself, but I never liked *having* to be somewhere if I didn't want to be. I told Marion I was going back to the streets the next day.

## Chapter Eight

IT WAS 1945.  Rumors were circulating that the Allies were well into Germany and victory was near.

Two southside, well-known black sportsmen had recently purchased the Pershing Hotel from its previous white owners. The Elgrotto Night Club that was located in the basement of the hotel headlined the apex of the black entertainment world, including the fabulous talents of the great Peal Bailey. Located at Sixty-Third and Cottage, it was in this colorful night-spot of magnificent tones that I met Wanda.

A girl of copper complexion and medium height, her friendly face displayed a pair of serene eyes that showed of hazel browness under the ceiling lights. Her proportions had the measurements that would force men to take notice. She could have easily become a contest winner. At the callow age of nineteen years, her freshness was that of newly plucked fruit. Like myself, Wanda was a product of the ghetto; born of parents who had a limited education and they were common laborers in a society that promised them no advancement, due to their lack of scholastic achievements and the pigmentation of their skin.

Wanda had been a school dropout at the adolescent age of sixteen, during which time her attractive appearance had enticed older men into offers of money and gifts, thus luring her into a life of tinseled dreams and prostitution. She also was a girl with a penchant for excitement and adventure, plus a daring to live life to its fullest.

I had reached the legal age of twenty-one and our youthful acceptance of life seemed to entwine. Wanda was so much more enjoyable than Marion, who was my senior by a few years. When I would express the urge to attempt the foolhardy, such as speed along the outer drive at 100 miles an hour, Wanda would always spur me on with a vibrant glare of anticipated excitement and encouraging words that expressed confidence. Her strong healthy laugh and the flexibility with which she moved her body entranced me to no end. Of course, there was another contributing fact. Wanda was an outstanding moneymaker, too. It was open knowledge, which I had no intention of concealing from Marion, that Wanda was my whore.

There were unforgettable scenes of name calling and insinuations between Marion and me. But this had no effect on the relationship that was destined to continue between Wanda and myself.

It was 1946, the war was over and new life was pumped into things that had been dead during the war. The previously closed race tracks were now opened and everyone was speculating for the Kentucky Derby favorite. Joe Louis, the boxing champion, had returned to the ring and an explosive rematch was in the making with a boxing specialist called Billy Conn, who had once come within seconds of dethroning the great "Brown Bomber." New cars were rolling from the assembly lines for which orders had to be placed; due to the limited production, they couldn't meet the public's demand.

The big fight between Joe Louis and Billy Conn was scheduled for New York City. Wanda wanted me to take her and likewise did Marion. Knowing my duty was first to my wife, I told Marion we would leave three days before the posted fight.

It was my second trip to New York City, and it was here that I met a young singer named Carmen McRae who had no idea of her own greatness, but the coming years were destined to reveal her unique talent.

I met a fella at the fight named Red, a name I will cherish the rest of my life. Like me, I'm sure other folks will also agree, because in the later years, his name and good deeds in the underworld became famous from the east coast to the west.

It was in this fabulous city of steel and stone, with its pointed structures and mingling traffic like maggots on potted flesh, that I sat back and meditated about my impending future. I had started out my pimping career with that traditional thought of the ghetto implanted in my youthful brain (kick a whore in the ass and make her get money). Surrounded by all the gigantic splendor and magnificence of this, the country's largest city, a change of strategy entered my mind as I sat alone and pondered. No longer would I filter back my entire resources into the ghetto. With some of this money I intended to travel and meet people, people who would be an asset to me in my climb toward the summit of the pimp game.

While traveling to these fashionable resorts, I'd better my chances of meeting well-to-do ladies that might well afford the follies of my fancy. I realized that in mixing and mingling among these persons, even though I'd fail in my intentions, some of their class would rub off on me. Oh yes, there was an inner feeling of inferiority that was mixed with a haunting desire and want of the multitude of affluence that my seeking eyes were forced to observe.

I came out of my reverie and called Marion who was in the shower of the room that we had rented when we checked into the Theresa Hotel. "Hurry up, woman. I don't want to be late for the fight."

I received no answer from the splattered enclosure and busied myself reading the sports report in the daily paper.

An hour later, I parked the car and hailed a cab, a precaution for convenience amongst New York fight fans. The distance to the fight was short, but the trip was long and tedious. It seemed that all the traffic in New York was headed towards the Yankee Stadium.

When we alighted from the cab, we encountered the expected crowds of pugilistic fans. Marion and I elbowed our way towards our seats and then I was blocked by a little hunchback man selling booklets containing the history of the champion and his opponent. After being stymied by several souvenir hawkers, we finally reached our seats.

Marion had brought along her binoculars and she would nudge me when amongst the thousands of faces she'd recognize an acquaintance from some other distant city.

It was two minutes and eighteen seconds of the eighth round when Bill Conn hit the deck. He was counted out by the referee, and once more the great Joe Louis had retained the Heavyweight Crown on June 18, 1946.

There was gaiety throughout Harlem that night, and the woes and confinement of ghetto life, for the time being, were forgotten. There were parties in the taverns, and the kitchenette apartments had their celebrations, too.

I had promised to meet Red at one of those parties in a

basement on 124th Street. The long homemade wooden bar was built atop the green tiled floor. Two basins that were used by the tenants to wash their clothes were situated at the far end of the basement. These were now filled with ice to keep the bottled beer cold. A crap table was placed in the center of the encrusted floor. Stools were strewn along the makeshift bar and chairs along the walls.

I placed Marion in one of those chairs while I ventured to the crap table. There were hustlers and pimps present from all parts of the country. Ernest and Walter from Frisco were drinking at the bar, J.J. and Phil had flown in from Detroit, Babe and Rabbit had King David in a huddle, while Big Time was trying to get their attention so he could have the light-skinned barmaid prepare another drink for them.

Red went behind the bar and gave the shapely barmaid a cigar box. This was for the depositing of money from the drinks. His pockets provided a cash register for the proceeds from the crap table.

I yelled for the barmaid to give Marion a gin and Coke, then I proceeded to indulge in the game of chance.

The party lasted until the wee hours of the morning. Other top-notch players from across the country made their appearance with all the flair and flamboyance of a Hollywood extravaganza. Strong Jones from the "Windy City" made his late appearance—a technique that's sure to get attention—escorting a handsome middle-aged woman who was wearing more diamonds than she was clothes. It was whispered around that she owned the largest whore house in the mid-west.

There was an attractive brown-skinned girl sitting at the end of the bar alone; her girl friend who had entered with her had left with a guy from New Jersey. I had noticed, each time I walked past her our eyes would meet.

Roy, a dealer from Cleveland, had broken up the crap

game for the time being. This, I figured, was as good a time as any to introduce myself to the lady. Her red peroxide-dyed hair was styled in the latest fluffy curls and this fitted the contours of her round puppet face. I slid atop the vacant stool which was beside her and said, "Could I buy you a drink?"

She looked at me with tiny eyes and smiled. "Are you sure your wife won't mind?" Her small eyes glanced toward Marion.

"How do you know I have a wife?" I was standing very close to her now with a stale drink in my hand.

She reversed her crossed legs, knee over knee, and answered, "I've noticed you send her drinks. I've also noticed how her eyes continue to follow you. In fact, she's watching you this very minute."

I was leaning on the home-made bar and my back was facing Marion. I could feel her glaring eyes as the microscopic hairs on my neck began to tingle. I resented Marion's obvious show of dominance, her ostensible display of possessiveness. I turned toward the light-skinned barmaid and was about to order some more drinks.

"Are you going to order for me, too?"

Marion had come up beside me. I think she would have walked between the girl and me if it hadn't been such a squeeze.

"Sure, I'm also ordering you a drink, but you'll have to go back to your seat and then I'll bring it to you." My voice was cold and my eyes relayed the virulence that I held within. There had been times when I would have exploded into the unwritten code of the ghetto. Chastise her physically, reprimand her verbally, thus blatantly proving to this group of renowned procurers that I was worthy of their respect. However, I had resided myself to class and to the century-old adage of rhetoric without physical display.

Marion could sense the deadliness in my voice and the

hostility in my eyes as I stared at her. She promptly obeyed and returned to her seat.

The cute red-headed girl accepted her drink and told me her name was Penny, that she had flown in from California for the fight. I was glad to find out that she knew some people in California whom I had met when Marion and I were out there.

"Say, Penny, why not give me your number? The next time I'm out that way, I'll give you a buzz."

I waited for an answer and couldn't help noticing her reluctance to take the ballpoint I was offering her. She had thrown a furtive glance toward Marion who's jaws were puffed out like balloons filled with chafe.

"I asked *you* for the number—not my wife." I held the pen extended, openly, boldly, toward her.

As if she had reached a decision, Penny grasped the ballpoint and scribbled her telephone number on a small card. I pocketed the card and pen, then I was beckoned for by Pee-Wee, a player from my home town, Chicago. I excused myself and followed him into the small toilet that contained only a commode.

Pee-Wee seemed excited. "Say, man! I hear that the girl you're talking to is a top whore from out California way."

"Yeah, I know. I found that out while we were rapping." I was phlegmatic.

"It's too bad that you don't snort cocaine, you might have a chance to pull her." Pee-Wee gave me a friendly, sympathetic look.

"Snort cocaine! What does that have to do with it?" I was serious.

"Well, man, you know how it is with broads. They like to do things with their men, such as smoke pot, drink, snort cocaine and other pleasures that they might enjoy." Pee-Wee was rubbing the ends of his process down as he talked to me.

I felt that he was telling me right—that is, as much right as he really felt himself.

"To hell with her! I know a number of fellas who are pimping and they don't snort cocaine." My resentment was ostensible.

"I know what you're saying is true, Trickshot. But, from what I hear, snorting cocaine is one of Penny's main amusements. I just can't see you copping, unless you can get groovy with her. It's as simple as that."

"Well, thanks anyway, man. But I'm not going to get a dope habit just to satisfy a broad. I don't care how good a whore she is." I was adamant.

"A habit! Man, you don't get a habit with cocaine." Pee-Wee turned his head and looked at me.

"It's dope, isn't it?" I was belligerent.

"In the sense of the word, yes. It's characterized as such, but so is marijuana." He intended to enlighten me.

"Look, man, if it is or isn't, I won't be finding out. If I don't cop, at least I'll be straight." I turned around and straddled the commode; the feeling of relief was enjoyable as I released the consumed Scotch and water.

Pee-Wee and I left the midget latrine to join our former associates. I glanced at the seat that Marion had so faithfully occupied, and to my dismay, it was vacant. My sweeping glance settled at the end of the long bar. There was a small gathering of people displaying voices of confusion. A computer I did not need to tell me what had happened. I saw Red as he was restraining Marion. The light-skinned barmaid was beckoning for me, as my quickened steps accelerated me toward the perplexing scene.

When I arrived at the spot of the excitement, Marion's round face was distorted in anger, jaws puffed, hair in disarray, and her verbal insinuations were directed at Penny who was still perched atop the stool, calmly, though reinforced by two male protectors.

In the heat of anger and humiliation, I almost blew my cool. I grasped Marion's arm and spun her around. "What in the hell do you think you're doing?" My voice was strident and cold.

Marion blurted, "That bitch should get her a man and leave other people's alone."

"Come on, you're getting your evil ass out of here," I said. "This is the last time I'll be drug by you in front of my friends." I paid my bar bill, shoved Marion in front of me and we both headed for the door.

Marion said, "You speak of me dragging you—hump—it was a drag for me to sit like a damn wallflower while you were at the bar with that little whore."

We were outside the door and Marion had slowed to wait for me so she could speak her mind and that was her greatest mistake.

The basement door opened on the side of the building with a small sidewalk separating it from the adjoining building. This miniature path would take us to the street beyond. Red had slammed the basement door briskly, either to keep the noise from floating out or probably glad that we had gone. It was easily a hundred feet before we should step out on the main thoroughfare. Marion and I were alone in the small passageway. I could afford, at least for a minute, to drop my newly acquired class.

She had just finished her words of anger; I grabbed her by her freshly done hair and began to pepper her face with open-handed slaps. Marion tried to evade the perpetual blows, but I had her hair twisted amongst my fingers in a vise-like grip. I controlled her bobbing head, and her repeated attempts to scream were interrupted by my successive blows.

A late sleeper in the adjoining building opened a window and flung down a derogatory remark. I answered him in his same language and continued about my task.

## Chapter Nine

WE WERE ON THE TURNPIKE and New York was many hours behind. It had been raining when we checked out of the hotel and the downpour had stayed with us, even into the state of Pennsylvania.

I looked at Marion who was fast asleep beside me. The drudgery of packing and traveling had finally taken its toll. The chance to escape from Marion's womanly chatter and the constant, flapping motion of the wiper blades dragged my mind into thoughts of my present marriage.

I knew Marion would never become a docile person. It was obviously not in her sphere of thought to relinquish to me my necessary freedom. Nor was it in my fancy to go cavorting. However, my intended strategy would involve the acquaintance of many women.

I mused past the sweeps of the wiper blades; thus rallied a plan that I thought was unique. When I returned to Chicago I would take Wanda and flee—California, yes, that's where we would go. California would be ideal. My marriage had not proved out—at least, not the way I had intended it. No kids were involved, so I cared less concerning a divorce.

The rain had abruptly stopped and the smell of damp foliage was in the air. The sun showed its early face over the mountain tops and color blended the forestry as only nature could. The wet highway reflected like a mirror, an illusion caused by the celestial globe.

My thoughts gave me an urge to stop in Detroit and see

my friend Jesse Cupp, then my thoughts reversed back to Wanda. Dear, wonderful, lovable Wanda. How nice the trip would have been if I had brought her along instead of bringing Marion. But then, Marion was still my wife; something about the vibration of it began to ring sour. I had to hurry and get back to Wanda. We had talked three times during my short stay in New York and each time she was her usually gay and vibrant self. But the last time, I sensed something was wrong—she sounded too happy. I had gotten those well known pangs in my stomach, warning me that something had gone amiss. Yes, I had to hurry back to Wanda. There were too many temptations in this asphalt jungle, too many procurers like myself, always stalking, always ready to pounce upon prospective prey the likes of which Wanda herself presented.

The hours fleeted by as did the passing scenery and the resumption of the accelerated speed had awakened Marion.

We made one stop in Indiana to get a bite to eat and the next stop was home in front of Marion's apartment. After settling ourselves, I uncradled the phone and dialed the tavern number. My father-in-law informed me that Ted was home from the war, and had asked about me. I pushed the button down and redialed the phone. Ted answered. He had been staying close to his family's tavern ever since he'd arrived home. I asked him if he'd brought any souvenirs of the war back home with him.

"I was lucky to bring myself back," he jokingly said, "much less some damn souvenirs."

We laughed and had a reminiscent conversation about the youthful things we had done before the war. Ted had married one of his school days sweethearts before he was drafted into the service. The uniting bond of this marriage had brought about his partnership in the tavern. Ted told me that he had gone out on the town a couple of times with Ben and they had had a drinking good ball. I told him how sorry I was that I had missed the reunion, but we definitely would get together real soon.

I rested the phone and my thoughts fled back to Wanda. I wanted to call and tell her that we had arrived back home safe and sound, but Marion's presence had forced me to hesitate. The mentioning of Wanda's name would fill Marion with vexation and a tirade from her at the moment I felt I couldn't endure.

I reclined to the bed and decided to complete my rest, but there was no rest for me. The fatigue from my long road trip and the verbal confrontation I would no doubt have with Marion—these things meant nothing. I had to see Wanda. My mind reflected and recalled some of Lock's revered advice, "One your heart gets a yearning, your pimp game's a failure." The yearning was more pronounced than Lock's advice.

I slid out of bed and went into the bathroom. The running of the water attracted Marion. "I knew it wouldn't be long. You've got to go and nurse that bitch. At least you could get some rest. You'll be worn out enough when you leave her."

The tirade had begun. I ran the water faster, more forceful, hoping to drown out the insinuating rhetoric which I wanted so much to avoid. But my efforts were useless. Marion had freed herself from the bed and was now standing in the bathroom door. Her face was a waxing movement.

"What's wrong with you? You act like a love-sick cow. Has that bitch got your nose open or something?"

The deliverance of her words had hit the target dead center. My resentful exposure of guilt could not be restrained. I wheeled, holding the large bath towel, and with an unexpected movement jammed the fluffy fabric into her chattering face. Marion was taken aback by my unpredictable reaction. Her expression showed surprise, then her round face took on anger.

"Ain't this a bitch? You've gone and gotten hooked by a whore who's got a pretty face and a pretty shape and you claim to be a pimp!" Marion's face then broke up with laughter, and this did more to pierce my armor of masculinity than did her previous words.

I made a step toward her, then refrained and slammed the door. I stepped into the bath tub and pulled the shower enclosure.

When I came out the bathroom, Marion had left me a note saying she had gone to her mother's tavern. I turned the record player on and hurried into my clothes, with thoughts of more pleasurable things as soon as I could reach Wanda.

I had locked the apartment door and was sitting behind the steering wheel of the car when I saw Marion returning down the street. Her well-kept body presented a luscious view and her stride aroused a slight sexiness as she strolled toward me. I hastened to start the motor in order to avoid more virulence. She watched the car lurch from the curb. I glinted out the side of my eye and saw her stop, hand on hips motion and her head followed the direction of the car as I drove down Prairie Avenue, then crossed Fifty-Fifth Street. A middle-aged lady with framed eyeglasses dropped a loaf of bread and some other packages from her overcrowded grocery bag. I braked the car while she hoisted them, then proceeded on my quest for Wanda.

I turned the car east on Forty-Seventh Street and couldn't resist the vision of the feminine species leaving Payton's Lounge. Musical notes filtering through the closing door tempted me to park the car, but, of course, the vision of Wanda was more tempting, more magnetic and definitely more unyielding to me. I curbed the car in front of a large courtway building at Forty-Sixth and Drexel Boulevard, got out and hurried into the vestibule. Want and anxiety made it seem like hours before her mother buzzed the door and the news that Wanda was out almost shattered me. Vanity prevented me from inquiring if she had been home last night. I returned to the car, trying to control the butterflies that were playing tag inside my turbulent stomach.

I looked at my watch. The dial showed two o'clock. Maybe she had gone to see a movie, or maybe on an errand for her mother. No, her mother would have told me. I had driven the car five blocks, maybe she'd returned by now. I pulled into the filling station and eyed the outside phone. It was occupied by a little haggard-faced man. Damn it, didn't he know I had to find Wanda?

I screeched the car out of the filling station driveway and threw on brakes to avoid the passing traffic. I drove a few more blocks. She had to be home by now. My eyes targeted on an empty phone booth at Fifty-Third and Cottage Grove. I curbed the car and dashed into the cubicle, reaching for the receiver and some change simultaneously—no dimes, just two quarters. I pressed one of them in the quarter slot. While waiting for the first ring, I wondered why the phone company had a system so obsolete. Wanda's mother answered and the situation was still the same, Wanda hadn't been home! All of Lock's teaching had been deleted from my mind. It held no room for codes, traditions and other procuring antiquities. There was just one thing that loomed vital to me and that was the whereabouts of Wanda, my Wanda.

I thought of the Elgrotto Club, the place where we had met, then I realized what time it was. The place wasn't even open. Maybe she was at the Du Sable or Joe's 315 Club, then the 411 Club on Sixty-Third Street and Herb's on Fifty-Fifth Street, along with many, many more.

When I arrived at the apartment it was three o'clock in the morning and Marion's jaws were puffed out as if foul air was trying to escape out the wrong end. I was so tired that her continuous flow of recital failed to ward off my sleep.

It was noon when the phone awakened me. My mother called from her job to tell me that Wanda had called just as she, my mother, was leaving for work that morning. Marion was in the bath tub, I could hear her splashing the water.

I dialed Wanda's number with eager anticipation and her sleepy voice was music to my ears, sweet music indeed.

"Where have you been?" I tried to make my voice sound only mildly concerned.

"Oh, I got in about seven this morning," she said. "My mother told me you were by. Why didn't you tell me you were coming home? I would have been waiting for you." Wanda's voice had lost its tinge of slumber. It was now very healthy and lucid.

I allowed the conversation to remain on an even keel, but my mind was still on her absenteeism. I had to be careful and not display the jealousy that had suddenly taken over within my whole being.

"Listen, Wanda. I've got to stop at the tavern, then I'll be by to pick you up. Maybe we'll have dinner together. I'll call before I come. That will give you time to dress."

I cradled the phone and reached for a cigarette, then heard Marion opening the bathroom door. It made a popping sound, the kind of sound a door makes when it needs resetting.

She was sitting in front of the dresser mirror, combing her hair, when she spoke. "I'm starved. Let's go to Geneva's place for dinner."

"I've got something to do. You'll have to eat alone today."

I dabbed the cigarette in the ashtray while giving Marion a furtive glance. The verbal onslaught she directed at me was not unexpected, not unexpected at all.

"I know what you have to do. You've got to go and play nursemaid to that bitch Wanda. When are you going to wake up to the fact that you're making a damn fool of yourself?"

I leaped out of the bed and dashed across the room. I had picked up one of my house shoes while I was enroute.

"That's right, go ahead and hit me, beat me. You want to kill me if I so much as mention her name."

Marion had turned from the mirror and was now staring at me with a coldness that I could not reckon with. I had momentarily become an umpire between impulse and conscience. The assignment had caught me unprepared mentally, as I stopped and spoke with guilt-ridden rhetoric.

"How do you know that I'm going to meet Wanda? You have no damn crystal ball—and besides, what if I am? You can bet she'll be waiting for me with some money."

My show of virulence didn't cause Marion to flinch one bit. Indeed, she was quite the contrary, lips pressed together tight as a bear trap, jaws firmly set like hardening concrete and eyes throwing flames that could ignite a forest blaze—a real large blaze—one that she could picture me in the center of.

Such hostility I decided not to compete with. Turning away, I headed towards the bathroom to avoid the range of Marion's displeasure.

I had completed my bath, left the apartment and was on my way to pick up Wanda. The sun was shining—not too hot, just right, and the drive through Washington Park showed the newly sprouted grass, providing a stage for autumn-colored trees with skeleton branches that were finally showing buds of green—green that would soon be foliage to magnify the beauty of this public domain.

I drove across Cottage Grove and entered Drexel Boulevard, then viewed the antique buildings which showed fading signs of affluence, buildings that at one time had housed middle-class whites, buildings now being cut up into cubicles to confine thousands of blacks.

## Chapter Ten

I CROSSED FORTY-SEVENTH STREET and saw Wanda standing on the sidewalk displaying that delicious beauty to all who would dare behold—medium length curly hair that glowed of brownish tint in the rays of the sun, sheer, knee-length yellow dress, squeezed at the hips by a thin brown leather belt, and those disturbingly attractive legs that traveled down into a pair of brown and yellow shoes. She reached inside the brown alligator purse and pulled out a Kleenex as I slowed at the curb.

Flinging the door open, I said, "Gee! You look good, lady." And, of course, I was not lying.

When Wanda leaned over and planted two small lip-prints on my right cheek, I received the aroma of the expensive cologne, which most definitely heightened her femininity to the apex amongst all womanhood.

"Thanks, daddy, you look good yourself—if you don't mind, let's ride a bit before we have our dinner." She was groping into the low-cut front of the yellow dress and low-cut it was. "I know you spent all your money while you were in New York. This will help you some, I hope.

I took the roll of bills and continued down Drexel Boulevard, then turned at Thirty-Ninth Street towards the outer drive. I peered over towards the Du Sable Lounge and saw Peg's car as it pulled away going out Oakwood Boulevard. I put the money in my pocket without bothering to count it.

"Let's go out on the lake, I've got a joint I'd like to smoke, then I'll have a good appetite."

Wanda had turned to look at me. She didn't know it, but she could have asked me to go to the moon and I would have tried to oblige.

"O.K. baby, I feel like I could stand a smoke myself. You know, they didn't have any decent grass in New York."

"They didn't? I've heard they have everything in New York that a person might want."

"Well, that didn't include good reefer, you can take my word for it."

"What about cocaine?" She was just talking casual, watching the passing scenery, but the inquiry about dope coming from Wanda, my Wanda! I found my voice and answered, "I saw some dudes with some, but I don't know how good it was."

There was silence as we crossed the outer drive bridge and proceeded to the gigantic rocks overlooking the lake and parked the car. The small rippling waves seemed to create a soothing breeze, the kind that gave you the urge to sit on the edge and dangle your bare feet into the crawling blue water below, thus reassuring the maintenance of fast fleeting youth that we all cherish so clutchingly.

Why had Wanda asked me about cocaine? I had never known her to indulge in narcotics of any form, and yet she had asked with the expression of an old hand at the game.

We got out of the car and walked among the huge boulders perched atop the lakeshore embankment.

"Here, light this, daddy. It'll give us both a good appetite." Wanda reached the cigarette-sized stick of reefer to me and reclined on a giant white rock, white as the molecules of sand drenched in the splashing water beneath.

We gazed out across the desert of bluish-green water and spoke to each other in words of deep admiration. There was no doubt about my feelings for Wanda. It was a glorious and fantastic feeling. If this be love that had engulfed me, then in love I was—because I had never felt the yearning and want for any other woman that I now felt for Wanda.

I had forgotten about her absence from the house when I returned. Whatever doubts or suspicions I had enhanced were now gone like the bubbling white suds from yonder waves.

I reached to my pocket to get my cigarettes. I wanted to cocktail the roach. I felt the roll of bills that Wanda had given to me. I would count them later; right now I was too happy to bother.

The pot had brought on those familiar hunger pains. Glancing at my watch, I said, "Well, baby, don't you think it's time to leave. I feel like I could eat a horse!"

Wanda responded by lifting herself from the palor bulk of stone. "Where are we going to have dinner? I'm not in the mood for soul food. Let's go downtown and maybe take in a movie after we eat. Okay?"

"That's fine with me, baby, but remind me to call Ted. I told him I'd be by his tavern sometime later on."

"Well, that's okay; we could drop by his place after we leave the movie."

"Yeah, that would be crazy. Do you have anything in

mind that you would like to see?" I asked.

"I was looking in the paper this morning and noticed something at the Woods that I think I'd like. Damn, I can never remember the names of pictures. I'll get a paper when we get downtown."

We had entered the car. I was backing out to turn it towards the outer drive.

"Oh, yeah, daddy, give me some money. I'll get some make-up while we're downtown."

I retrieved the roll of bills from my pocket and began to count. "What do you need?"

I had stopped counting and was hesitantly holding the money while waiting for Wanda's answer.

"Just give me twenty dollars, that will take care of the things I've got to buy."

I thumbed off two ten dollar bills and passed them to Wanda, and a small red object dropped into my lap. Though it didn't make a sound, my eyes caught the reflection of its descending fall.

"What was that?"

I spread wide my legs and bowed my head. I had stopped the car, then opened the door to inspect the car seat. There in the creases of the leathered upholstery was a red capsule which I had seen the similarity of at Red's party in New York. I picked up the red capsule and looked at Wanda. It was a look that carried surprise, disappointment, hurt and finally anger. The capsule must have been mistakenly given to me within the roll of bills that I had received from Wanda. I got back into the car and held the capsule in front of her.

"Well, tell me about this."

Her beautiful profile had taken on a slight palor—not frightened, just shaken up a bit—and then, in the space of a second, her expression modulated. "Oh, I wondered what had happened to that cap of blow." It was as if she had mislaid a cigarette—or something.

"Blow? You mean this is cocaine?"

I was still holding the red capsule up in front of Wanda's toast-hued face. Her walnut colored eyes showed with surprise that definitely was not counterfeit.

"What did you think it was?"

Isn't this a bitch? Now she had put me on the defensive. I recalled Pee-Wee's explanation at the party back in New York. "You don't get a habit with cocaine." However, in my opinion, it was all dope. But I didn't want to appear as a complete square.

"It could be anything, that's why I'm asking you what it is." I was pragmatic—pressing.

"I've told you once, daddy, it's nothing but cocaine. If you doubt my word, try it and find out for yourself."

There it was, the challenge, the dare, the confrontation, that I knew I would have to face some day. Pee-Wee's haunting words were stalking me relentlessly. " 'A woman likes to get high with her man'." Wanda knew I drank and smoked pot, but she had never seen me do anything else. I pushed my hand toward her with the capsule between my forefinger and thumb.

"Here, take it. If you say it's nothing but cocaine, I believe you. There was nothing wrong in my asking, was there?" I was trying to put her on the defensive.

Wanda let out one of those healthy laughs—head back, throaty and real lucid. It makes the other person feel obtuse.

"What in the fuck are you laughing about?" I showed tiff.

"Oh, daddy, you look so strange. I actually believe you're afraid."

Wanda removed a portion of the capsule and put it up to her nose, inhaled deeply, then turned her smiling face to look at me. The remaining part of the capsule, she extended to me.

"Here, take it, daddy. It won't hurt you. In fact, it'll make you feel better." Her voice was challenging.

I grasped the gelatin container, peered at the snowy white powder that glistened brilliantly from the mouth of the capsule. I knew I was going to snort this magical dust that induced stimulant feelings of sex and lust, but why was I hesitating? Why were my fingers poised, holding this miniature object as though it weighed a ton? Maybe it was the demanding sound or the challenging impact of her voice that brought about my reluctance?

I discarded the ambiguity of her rhetoric and raised the capsule within the opening of my nose. My body took on a movement of inhalation, wherein I felt a foreign thrust of pollution flow through the passages of my cranium and the strange sensation was electrifying.

Wanda's attractive face took on creases as she displayed a big smile and asked, "Well, how was it? I told you it would make you feel better. Does it?"

"Oh, I figured it was all right, otherwise I wouldn't have tried it." I spoke casually.

I tried to eliminate the fact that I had been influenced by Wanda, but we both knew that it had been her whole idea—and her's alone.

I started the car engine again, then proceeded to the outer drive. It wasn't long when I realized my appitite was gone and I became very talkative.

Wanda cast a sly grin at me and said, "What about taking in the movie first and then we'll have dinner, okay?"

"That'll be okay with me," I said, "I've suddenly lost my taste for food anyway." I later found out that my hunger was quenched by the cocaine I had snorted.

I turned onto the outer drive and joined the traffic which flowed like a healthy artery with a multitude of corpuscles, heading into the heart of the city's functionings.

Turning at Randolph Street, I entered the jungle of massive giants towering above each other with grace and poise, thus displaying the skills of man's architectural genius.

The lurid marquee at the Woods Theater was the first to catch Wanda's eye. "There it is! That's the picture I want to see. You know how much I like to see Bette Davis in those domineering roles." Wanda was excited and pointing.

I turned right and parked the car in the Dearborn Street parking lot. We entered the show and watched the fabulous Bette Davis go through those antics which had made her famous. I was also noticing the many trips that Wanda was making to the ladies' room—frequent trips, as though she had been drinking beer.

At the conclusion of the movie, I asked Wanda, "Are you ready to eat yet?"

I was taken aback when she said, "Oh, I guess I'll wait a little while. I think the excitement of the picture might have taken my appetite."

I was surprised at Wanda's reluctance to eat, but I was more surprised at myself. Suddenly, without my noticing, my craving for food had vanished, too.

"I don't feel like eating either. That's funny, not too long ago, I felt as though I could have eaten a bear."

Wanda gave me that sly grin which I had recognized before.

"Damn it! What are you constantly grinning about?"

"Oh, daddy, you really don't know, do you? It's that cocaine that you had back there on the beach. Didn't you know that it takes your appetite?"

Her laughter at my ignorance made me feel inane. Besides, who was she to laugh at me? I was her man and she was my whore, which made me the boss. Wasn't I twenty-three years old, while she was only twenty-one.

"Damn it! I'm not supposed to be a connoisseur on dope, and wipe that silly-ass grin off your face."

Wanda showed contrition as she modulated her face and spoke with words that dripped of pure honey. "Daddy, you know I would never make fun of you. But I honestly thought that you understood the effects of cocaine."

"Sure, I've heard what other people say about it, but it's different when you feel the reaction personally. I was a wee bit tired, but now I feel a strange new energy."

Wanda started to laugh, but somehow maintained a straight face and said, "Yeah, I know just what you mean."

I said, "Say, baby, I know you haven't got a weak bladder. Why so many trips to the ladies' room?"

"Aw, I was just taking a little blow so I could enjoy the movie better."

"How much of that stuff do you have? I've always heard it was real expensive."

"I've got another cap, why? Do you want some more?"

"I didn't ask because I wanted some more, I asked to find out how you came by it?"

We were leaving out of the lobby and I held the door for Wanda as she answered me in that honeycomb voice. "I got the blow from a trick, but, daddy, you've never asked me where I got money, jewelry or things such as that before. I thought you always knew that some john was doing the giving."

Wanda was talking as we maneuvered our way through the strolling pedestrians. Though she wasn't looking at me, there was a look of puzzlement on her youthful face. We were running across the street toward the parking lot, but my mind was running faster than my feet. I had to check myself, that unseen monster of jealousy had perked its head again, and now I had to deceive Wanda and myself, though it was impossible to fool the latter.

"I'm supposed to look out for you since you are my woman, isn't that true?" Before Wanda could answer, I continued, "I don't want anyone to give you the wrong thing. A young girl can get crossed up real easy in this concrete jungle. Can you tell the difference between heroin and cocaine by merely looking at it?"

Wanda had that blank stare which I had seen many times before; times when she had to look to me for guidance; times that made me proud to extend it.

"No, I couldn't tell just by looking at them. They're both white in color, aren't they?"

"There, you see what I'm trying to tell you? There are thousands of young girls—girls just like you—tricked into a life of misery and degradation due to their lack of knowlege about such things. Things that appear glamorous and exciting, proved to be pitfalls of entrapment, thus leading to a road of destruction from which there is no return."

Wanda was listening intently as I moved the car out of the parking lot into the moving traffic.

"But, Daddy, I don't associate with people who handle the heavy stuff."

Wanda had turned her head to look at me, displaying all the sincerity that she could muster.

"You don't huh? Who did you get this blow from?"

"Willie. You know Black Willie, the guy with the blue Caddy that has the wheel on the rear. He gave me the cocaine and five hundred dollars to spend the night with him. That's where I was when you arrived in town and came by my mother's house and how I happened to have the eight hundred dollars."

I had been driving down Lake Street, heading east toward the outer drive. The overhead el train made its rumbling sound as I pulled the car to a corner vacancy which read "No Parking. Bus Stop."

"What eight hundred dollars?"

"The money that I gave you was eight hundred dollars. Oh, that's right, Willie gave me a five hundred dollar bill. Look at your money and you'll find it there. I think he was trying to impress me by giving me the large bill."

While Wanda was talking, I was busy tearing at my pocket and recalling that I had forgotten to count the money when I discovered the red capsule. I skinned the bills apart and, sure enough, there it was. President McKinley's solemn face peered out at me and I gave him a big smile in return. Why should a President of such distinction maintain company with others of such low denominations? I took the five hundred dollar bill and placed it in my wallet. In truth, I was afraid I might absorb too many drinks and give it away by mistake.

A policeman, saddled above a large brown stallion, clopped up beside the car and instructed me to move out of the bus stop area. (Chicago had a Mounted Division at that time.) I stepped on the pedal. The car lurched across Wabash Avenue and continued east toward the outer drive.

I knew of this man Black Willie who had given Wanda the money and cocaine. I surmised he had a hidden motive for being so generous with his finances and I knew his motive, whatever it was, meant me—Trickshot—no good.

Black Willie was a dope dealer and I was sure that Wanda was not aware of this. Secondly, like other dealers, Willie enjoyed the pleasures of choice girls and Wanda was definitely in that exclusive category. And finally, Willie had a reputation for being most deadly amongst the cross artists in the ghetto—like a rattlesnake he was.

I decided not to indulge in rhetoric against his character at this time for fear of Wanda sensing the jealousy which was constantly becoming harder for me to conceal. However, I knew that I had not heard the last of Black Willie.

I guided the car south along the outer drive, turned west at the midway and then headed for Ted's tavern by way of Jackson Park.

Like my mother-in-law's place, Ted's tavern was an unglamorous, small, neighborhood bar which catered to the middle-aged people of that locale. Ted was sitting at the recently shellacked wooden bar when Wanda and I entered. He got up from the chrome-plated stool which was cushioned with a leather top, then vigorously shook my hand with a grip that expressed maturity since the last time I had seen him.

A tall six feet two inches with copper-brown complexion, Ted's sharp features were minus the acne pimples of his adolescent youth. His handsomely carved face now showed the strong smooth sculpturing of early manhood.

I introduced Ted to Wanda and the three of us occupied the far corner wooden booth which also reminded me of the booths in my mother-in-law's place. Ted spoke of the many places he had been while serving in the Army. I ordered a round of drinks for the three of us, then devoted my full attention to Ted's descriptions of the countless foreign lands.

I looked into the face of this man whom I had known since childhood. It was a face that showed strength and trust. It cast off no warnings of the hidden layer of resentment that was concealed underneath. The resentment that would show its true self in later years with all of the virulence and connivance of a cold-blooded politician.

Wanda excused herself and I, of course, assumed that she was dusting her nose again. The hunger pangs began to attack my stomach, then I decided to ask Wanda for the remaining capsule of cocaine. When she returned to the booth, I went to the men's room and returned. We had another round of drinks and left.

The day had not been a trying one, but when I opened the car door for Wanda, the appearance of her up-raised thighs presented the idea that I wanted to relax. The drive to the Pershing Hotel didn't take long and the registering at the desk was quite brief.

We entered the room and it was one of those select

vacancies which the hotel kept until a celebrity came along. Of course, it cost me a five dollar tip. However, I cast the bribe off as a pittance when Wanda began to disrobe.

The decor of the room was in colors of blue and white. The carefully hung drapes were white to match the provincial furniture and the sky blue carpet matched the bedspread and walls. The massive lamps that topped the nightstands on each side of the bed had large white shades—white as the inviting sheets which Wanda had now exposed by folding back the king-sized blue spread.

I tuned the wall radio to a station which brought in Daddio Daly who had recently launched his disk jockey career after retiring as a bartender from the Elgrotto Club.

Wanda's panties seemed to be filled with a vibrator as she sauntered to the washroom and her golden brown body was a wonder to behold. It was only moments before the two of us resembled a pretzel, entwined with acts of sex and lust that even Freud or Kinsey could not imagine. Wanda had a way of making love which made all others to me seem childish and her climactic screams of passion brought out the sadistic beast in me, sadism that left teeth marks throughout her delicious body; sadism that would bring from me repeated orgasm.

## Chapter Eleven

I WAS LYING IN BED with Marion when Chink, a friend from my childhood days, knocked at the apartment door. Donning my robe, I opened the door and could see that all was not kosher.

"What's happened, man?"

"Ben just got killed!"

I was numbed, staring at him, petrified, hand still holding the door knob, but his words sounded clear as a bell, a bell so blatant that there was no question of its authenticity. I could hear Marion burst out in tears. She had overheard Chink's message of disaster. I pulled him inside the apartment and closed the door.

"What happened?" I repeated.

"It was a fight. As much as I could gather," Chink said, "Ben was at the bar arguing with a fellow and they decided to go outside and settle it. While Ben and this guy were on the ground scuffling, the guy's brother came out of the bar and kicked Ben in the neck. That was it. Ben died on the spot."

Chink's emotion-filled voice quieted and his eyes displayed the burden that the verbal task had placed upon him.

"What bar? Where did it happen?" I had sat back on the couch, still in a state of fogginess.

"It happened in front of the Show Bar on Sixty-First Street. Ted and a few of the fellows are still out there. They were watching the police remove the body when I left them."

I finally put my wits together and dressed. "Was Ben alone when the argument started?" I just couldn't picture Ben getting killed in a common tavern brawl.

"I'm not sure," Chink said, "but I think I heard someone say that his girl friend was with him."

After getting dressed, I joined Chink in his car and in a few minutes he braked the car at Sixty-First and King Drive. Being the tallest in the group present, Ted's lanky frame was the first one that I recognized. All hell had broken loose inside and outside of the tavern. The word had spread like a forest fire out of control, and cars loaded with friends of Ben were arriving in insurmountable angry moods. Stools were overturned and the mirror behind the bar was broken by a flung whiskey glass. The police, who had answered the call of confusion, put through another frantic call—the last was for urgent police assistance. The final result was a dozen or more of us locked in jail.

A noisy and congested few hours later, we were released, after promising the District Commander that we would all go to our homes and create no more trouble.

Back at the apartment, my despondent thoughts thrust Ben's image before my eyes. No more would he and I sit and plan fantastic capers. No more would he be around to settle Marion's and my arguments. This spontaneous loss of Ben was unbearable, so unbearable that it hurt, real deep. Marion cried as though she'd lost her brother, because like a brother to her he had been.

I spent the night answering the telephone. Marion closed the tavern and joined me with the last few drops of the depleted bottle of whiskey.

Three days later, the cemetery was emptying of mourners, friends and family. Ted and I had been pallbearers, so together we had ridden to the cemetery.

"Just think of all the daring things he'd done," Ted said, "and he'd never gotten a scratch."

"It's still hard to believe," I answered.

"I think he was going to marry that little girl he was sweethearting with," Ted said. "He'd mentioned it to me just the other day."

"Yeah, he'd only known her a short time, but she seemed like a nice person. I'd only met her once myself."

"Drop me at the tavern. I'm suppose to meet a fellow concerning a business deal. Why don't you come in and have a drink, too?"

"I've got some business to take care of myself. I'll catch you later on."

I didn't want to tell Ted, but my business was Wanda. I hadn't seen much of her in the last few days because Marion was ever-present and that included the funeral which Wanda would not attend.

I dropped Ted off at his tavern, then hurried the car to Wanda's house. Marion had ridden to the cemetery in Ted's wife's car, so I figured they'd stop at one of the bars and have some cocktails.

I wanted to see Wanda because I'd heard she'd been seen in Black Willie's car a couple of times. I got those funny pimp pains in my stomach again as I pulled up in front of

Wanda's house. I rang the bell and received the same words that I had gotten in the past. "Wanda wasn't home." It felt as though a prizefighter had suddenly punched me in the gut.

I returned to my car and began sleuthing a trail which would eventually lead to Wanda. When I curbed the car in front of the Pershing Hotel, Buddy Walls was standing in the entrance talking to Strong Jones. I intruded upon their restricted conversation.

"Hi, fellas. What's going on? When I catch you two dudes' heads together, I know that something is about to happen."

Both of them showed a toothy big grin and their humor helped me to forget momentarily about Wanda.

"Hi, Trick," Buddy said. "I didn't see you drive up. I was just telling Strong about the party last night. By the way, where were you? Man! It was a sho-nuff ball!"

"He thinks everybody can party like he does," Strong said. "I was telling him that I had other things to do."

"Man! What else is there to do when your game is going good?" Buddy answered, while extending his hand, palm up.

I slapped his hand and said, "I guess you're right. When your pimp game is going good."

Buddy's last remark had reminded me that my own game wasn't going so well at the present time. I couldn't even find my woman.

"Come on inside and let's have a drink," I said. "That drive to the cemetery sort of tired me out."

"Yeah . . . it was too bad about Ben," Buddy said. "Did they ever catch those two brothers who did it?"

"Oh, yeah. They caught them the same day," I answered. "They're both in the County Jail awaiting trial."

The three of us entered the long box-shaped bar room and gathered at our favorite corner near the portal that led into the hotel lobby. I had just told Sam, the bartender, to pour our drinks when Wanda and Black Willie entered the door from the Sixty-Fourth Street side. Wanda's hand was locked in Willie's bent elbow. Buddy looked at me and Strong Jones nervously tried to avoid doing the same.

I walked around the corner of the bar and blatantly said to Wanda, "I would like to speak to you."

Wanda, instead of stepping towards me, moved intimately closer to Black Willie.

"I think you want to talk to me," Willie said. "You weren't at the tavern when I called, so I left a message with your wife." Black Willie had stepped in front of Wanda and was now defiantly facing me.

I looked at this man who had obviously accepted the possession of my woman—my Wanda. I say accepted because I had learned early in life that a woman could not be taken unless she, herself, was willing, and the movements that Wanda had made, sliding behind Willie and perching herself atop the stool, told me that my learning was correct.

My humiliation had lasted long enough and I decided that it should end. I stared at this black devil and in the molecule of a second, everything that he represented appeared immensely disgusting to me. The perimeter of his coal black face enclosed small piercing eyes which hovered above two high meaty cheek bones and his wide flat nose sat atop a thick mustache that was guardian over two massive lips. The barroom's revolving ceiling lights reflected pastel colors from the diamond pin that decorated his arrogant chest.

A glimmering thought told me to try his chin, which I will admit appeared very strong, but his well-built frame, though not quite as tall as me, warned me that I would probably be the loser. I decided not to follow my first thought as I said, "The conversation won't be necessary. I've gotten the message." I turned and approached the bar.

"How much do I owe you, Sam?"

The words came out smoother than I had expected because I was filled with emotion. Those familiar pains in my stomach had given out with their all.

Of course it had occurred to me that some day Wanda would leave me. But it was never in my imagination that it would happen like this. At least to tell me over the phone would have cost her only a dime. I could feel the furtive glances throughout the bar and the rhetoric of the whispers I was forced to imagine. The humiliation of the whole affair made me feel simply stupid. The hurt, the anger, and most of all the pride, had twisted my entire mental structure. I tried to resist the temptation that was gnawing at me. God only knows how hard I tried. But resistence never has been a competent adversary for love. I retrieved my change from the bar and gave in to my whim of damnation and, of course, before I departed through the door, I was forced to take a despondent and parting look at Wanda—Black Willie's Wanda.

I can now imagine that Ted had tired of listening to my unfortunate tale of grief. I had been seated at his bar ever since I'd made my exit from Black Willie and Wanda and it was now near closing time. I had drunk myself into submission and was trying to force Ted to do likewise. There were a few hangers-on still at the bar and for the last few hours, they had all been my guests. The little brown man with the pushed-in face had adopted me because I looked like his son who had been killed in the last war. Intoxicated as I was, it was still obvious to me that it was the free drinks which he had adopted, and I doubted if he even had a son.

"Why don't you go home and sleep it off?" Ted asked. "Things are sure to look better when you wake up."

I could hear what Ted was saying, but it just didn't seem to make sense.

"I can go home anytime. Let's go some place that we're not suppose to go," I blurted, while groping for Ted with one free arm and securing myself on the stool by grasping the bar with the other.

"My partner is off tomorrow," Ted said. "I'll have to open up this morning, otherwise I would join you."

"Well, let's stay right here and drink until morning," I said. "Then you won't have to come back and open up. How about that. Pretty smart thinking, huh?"

The little brown man had bowed his head, face down on his folded arms, and Ted was busy trying to arouse him.

Unknown to me, Ted had slipped to the phone and called Marion. It was to my utter surprise when I felt a constant tugging at my shoulder and I struggled around on my stool to face her.

"Come on out of here," Marion said. "Don't you see it's past closing time, or do you want Ted to blow his licenses?"

I blinked at Marion through alcoholic stupor, then turned towards Ted. "Hey, Ted, here's Marion. You know Marion. Marion's my wife. Come on, sit down, baby. I'm going to buy you a drink."

Ted had finally gotten the tipsy, flat-faced man outside the door and Marion was patiently coaxing me towards the same.

"Come on, baby, it's way past closing time and we've got to get out of here." Marion had put my arm around her delicate shoulders and we were proceeding slowly towards the door.

Ted had put all of the lights out except a large one in the window and a smaller one that hovered over the open cash register.

"Are you coming with us, Ted?" I asked. "We're going

some place and get some more to drink." I had slowed at the door, head twisted, looking back at Ted.

"You go ahead," Ted said. "I'll meet you later, after I lock up the place."

Marion was having a difficult time helping me to maintain my balance as she guided me, and just before the door closed behind us, I almost pulled Marion down. I twisted around and yelled back at Ted, "Don't forget to meet us."

Performing a miracle that was beyond my imagination, Marion had seated me in the car and to me the ride took on illusions of alcoholic subconsciousness.

I was atop a gleaming white stallion, and my polished armored suit glistened in the sun. I carried a large shield that bore an emblem of knighthood and a long shiny sword dangled from my side. Wanda was perched atop the horse in back of me and her grasp around my waist made me feel proud, but, suddenly, from out of the hills of rolling green moors, came a man of more modern design. The face shield of his head armor was raised and I could see his black, sinister face, as he steered the lurid Cadillac directly at us. He swerved alongside and swiftly swooped Wanda away from me and the white stallion shied at the sight of this unfamiliar dragon, thus throwing me to the fertile sod of greenish hue. The blue Cadillac sped away over the spacious meadow as I lay on the grass entangled in shiny armor.

"Wake up! We're home. I've got to open up the tavern this morning so I can't fool with you all night."

Maybe it was the morning air or maybe the awakening realization of Marion's chattering voice that partially sobered me. I fumbled my way out of the car and recalled the dream which my alcoholic stupor had produced. I knew the face in my dream had belonged to Black Willie and, even if my horse hadn't thrown me, I couldn't have caught him. And of course, if Marion had not awakened me, I would have yet been lying on the grass.

The dream brought new thoughts to my still groggy brain. How could I expect to keep Wanda with the same old car? My Oldsmobile still ran good, but it was ancient compared to Willie's up-to-date Caddy. I thought of his diamonds and the way he spent money. Those things I had to compete with if I wanted to recapture Wanda.

Marion and I had come to the top of the steps and she was unlocking the apartment door and, once inside the apartment, I began to undress. Marion sat on the side of the bed and looked up at me. There was a sound of glee and triumph in her voice.

"I hope you're sober enough to understand the message I have for you," she gloated. "Black Willie called and told me to tell you 'that Wanda had chosen him for her man'." Obviously Marion didn't know about the confrontation between Black Willie and me.

"So what? She's just one woman in a world of many," I said. "There was a time when I didn't even know her name." My response was quite an obvious shock to her.

Marion continued to stare at me as she spoke. "Oh, you may pretend to me that you don't care," she said, "but I happen to know that you are weak for her. I also know that you were running all over town looking for her the other day."

Marion's words of truth were cutting deep inside of my half undressed body. But I could not give her the pleasurable thought which she would eventually express, "I told you so." I sat down on the long brown couch and cast her a look which carried nothing but contempt.

"Just what makes you think I'm so weak? And that goes for Wanda and any other broad." The words were only half complete when I recalled that I had blurted out practically these same words to Chris.

Marion's expression suddenly became ominous. "I'm glad you've told me how you feel. Now I can make the decision that's been bothering me." Marion's big brown eyes took on a deadly stare, then she sauntered over to the couch and stood up over me. She said, "I've decided that I want a divorce. You can move your clothes whenever you wish."

She continued to stand and look down. I imagined to watch my reactions to her cold-blooded announcement. I was about to slip my undershirt over my head, but Marion's words caused my arms to freeze in mid-air—hands toward the ceiling as though I was being robbed. After a second of mental clarification, I lowered my arms, undershirt still up around my shoulders and Marion still standing boldly gazing down at me.

Her words fell like an avalanche on my already weakened shoulders and the realization that Marion was sincere served as the aftermath of small boulders that tended to bury me deeper into the humiliating void of despair. I had taken Marion's position in my life for granted. True, I had thought of going off with Wanda, but somehow I had never figured things could work in reverse. Of course, I had heard that the life of a pimp was immensely cold, but why should I get the chilly part so soon? I hadn't even gotten started good, plus it wasn't fair—no, not fair at all. Fate had taken a hand in this conspiracy to deprive and discourage me from the magnificent things I had planned. But I refused to relent to this gathering of forces. I must have looked inane as I sat there with the undershirt up around my shoulders and the lingering smell of alcohol constantly oozing from my pores. Losing Marion hadn't upset me emotionally. Those feelings had long ago been reserved for Wanda. It was my prestige, my vanity and my status in the pimp game which actually bothered me. Whoever coined the phrase of 'rats leaving a sinking ship,' undoubtedly had a pimp's life in mind, for I was to learn in later years that this was a standard procedure among girls in a pimp's life. When one girl leaves, the others may soon follow.

I pulled my undershirt down into my shorts again and then reached for my pants. "Well, there's no need in delaying something which eventually I must do anyway. You say you've been thinking of a divorce for quite some time. What caused the delay?" I forced myself to remain phlegmatic. I was determined not to allow Marion the pleasure of seeing me wilter.

"Just how long," Marion said, "did you think I'd let you make a fool of me? You let that young silly bitch make an ass out of you, but I wasn't going to let you do the same thing to me. Oh, I tried to hang on because I figured you'd eventually come to your senses. But instead, you've actually gotten worse."

I was swiftly getting into my clothes and the sooner I vacated the apartment the better it would be for the both of us. Marion was continously talking and it helped me to realize that parting with her wasn't so bad after all. Her jaws continued their up-down motion.

"I know you'll probably tell all your friends that I'm no good, but I'm quite sure everybody knows how you've treated me since you've met that young bitch."

I was completely dressed again and my ears were fatigued from Marion's constant recital.

"I've tried to be a good wife," Marion continued. "I've stood aside and watched you chippie with no-good broads. I've even hustled for you, hoping you might take the money and put it to some good use. But no, all you wanted to do was chase that silly young freak. Well, I'm tired of the whole damn affair, including you."

Marion's breasts were heaving with angry passion and I could see that unmistakable hostility in her eyes.

I reached for the door and prepared to make my exit, then turned and made my last remark. "I'll return later and get my clothes."

Marion was standing in the doorway when she hurled her answer at me. "Don't make it too much later. If so, you might find them in the alley."

The woman's words most harshly flung tempted me to retrace my steps and chastise her, but the thought at this time would have been mere folly and I continued along the hall and down the stairs.

As I drove toward my mother's house, my entire structure was replete with anger and humiliation. I was angry with Black Willie and Wanda for the humility they had cast upon me, angry at Marion for the humility she had forced me to accept, and finally angry with myself because there was certainly nothing that I could do about either.

## Chapter Twelve

IT WAS TWO DAYS LATER and I was in the Cadillac sales room on Rush Street on Chicago's near north side. The small paunchy salesman with the neatly pressed blue suit was reciting to me the optional features of the green fishtail two-door Cadillac coupe. To make the purchase, I was forced to pawn my ring and watch, which was in the mediocre class. My endeavor took me to Ted's tavern and there I received a well-told tale of the crap game that had taken all of his finances.

The Fat Man who operated the gambling joint on Fifty-First Street made it possible for me to give the impeccably dressed car salesman a cashier's check plus my well-used Oldsmobile as a trade for the new '48 green Cadillac coupe. It was General Motors' first year of introducing the fishtails to the public, inasmuch as the people had become satisfied with the new Hydromatics which had been previously tested on the more attainable Oldsmobiles. This same series Cadillac had cost only $1800 before the war, but now the price had doubled due to the post war inflation and the country was steadfast in its refusal to return to the lesser economy and of course, this interim of prosperity was most satisfying to me for I had never realized such freedom of affluence.

As I pulled into the mass of cars on the Lake Shore Drive, I adjusted the car seat as far back as it would go and fitted myself in a slightly sideways position—kind of slick, you know—and propped my elbow out the window. I could barely await the opportunity to drive alongside of Black Willie while Wanda was with him and pretend that something had captured my attention in the opposite direction.

The occasion presented itself three days later, and as I crossed 47th on South Parkway Boulevard, I saw that well-known rear wheel extending from Willie's blazoned blue Cadillac trunk and I could see the outline of a female's head next to him. Primarily, I was going to turn at 46th Street, but this was too good to pass up. I raised my foot from the gas pedal and slowed the car, then timed my stop at the approaching light, and I was sitting alongside of Black Willie's car when the red light stopped both of us at 43rd Street.

I had turned the car radio to a roaring peak and its melodious sounds could not possibly go unheard. From the side of my eye, I saw Wanda turn her attractive head in my direction; and I became busy lighting a cigarette from the dashboard lighter and I most certainly took a long time lighting it. The stop light changed to yellow and when the green light appeared, I thrust the green coupe forward with a lurch and gave the both of them a rear view of my fishtails turning at 42nd Street.

Three weeks later I had taken all of my clothes from

Marion's house over to my mother's apartment and the phone rang. I could tell from the accent of the first "hello" that it was the call that I had been expecting as Wanda so brazenly expressed to me that she had ceased her relationship with Black Willie. I did not delude myself that I should play hard to get and thus adhere to the age-old rules of pimpology for which I gave less than a damn now that I had a chance to rekindle our association.

The past three weeks were merely a make-believe world for me and the girls with whom I had been seen were actually showpieces which served the purposes at the given times. There were times when I would get into my car and ride. My eyes would be pragmatically seeking Black Willie's garish blue Cadillac and there was always the chance that Wanda might be with him. I had lost interest in the game of "cap and blow." Other girls did not concern me, and it was only when I wanted sex or female companionship for appearance sake and that alone, that my thoughts would deviate to other girls.

For finance, I had resorted to my previous game of selling slum jewelry and this had proven to be vastly profitable now that the war was over.

Wanda's voice was slightly raspy, though thoroughly convincing, as she continued. "I imagine you're still angry with me because of Willie, but I can explain it if you'd care to listen."

She didn't know it, but it was a pleasure for me to be condescending.

"I'll listen," I answered.

"Well—first of all, it was easy to accept Willie as my man because of the financial arrangements. I never had to give to him. It was always the other way around, and there was always the presence of your wife Marion. So many times when I wanted to see you, not to make love or get wrapped up into something way out, but just to see you, and be able to rap—just the two of us—you know. But after a few sarcastic remarks from your wife, she would make me feel so cheap that it was rather humiliating. I just got to the point that I wouldn't call. I'd rather wait until you called me, and if you didn't call, I'd usually go into the streets to find other outlets. Some of those times I'd run into Willie, and I'll admit, after a period of time, I would call different bars and some of his hangouts trying to locate him, but it was always after failing to get in touch with you.

"Now I don't need to tell you that he was repeatedly pressuring me to become his woman. You knew that he went for me by the large sums of money he laid on me. All of these things made it easy. When one night he found me in one of those low despondent moods, and it was easy for me to say 'yes.' I remember it clearly. I had called your house and no one answered. I then called the tavern and your wife answered. She made me feel so common, so small, and then I became angry."

There was a pause. All of this was news to me. Of course, I hadn't seen Wanda to talk to her and it was understandable that Marion had not told me.

"What did she say?" I asked.

"Aw, Trickshot, I called to explain about myself," Wanda said, "and not about her."

"But I would understand you better if you would tell me what Marion said."

There was a small pause of silence and Wanda spoke again. "Well, she said, 'How in the hell do I know where he's at, I'm only his wife.' Then she hung up the phone. I was so humiliated and angry. I caught a cab and rode to the 411 Club and ordered a double shot, and it wasn't long before Black Willie came in. He could undoubtedly see that I was angry and extremely upset. He gave me two hundred dollars to go to the hotel with him and we stayed there until you saw us the next day at the Pershing Hotel bar.

The rest you know."

My mind reflected and I recalled Marion giving me Black Willie's message, but she never told me that Wanda had called. Willie must have called when Wanda and he were at the hotel. Wanda didn't know it, but I was repletely thrilled to learn that I had temporarily lost her through surrounding circumstances rather than lack of affection. Though it mattered little now, the thought of Marion withholding Wanda's message brought on a surge of umbrage.

"I guess you've heard," I said, "that Marion and I have broken up?"

"Oh yeah. I heard it last week. I started to call but I just couldn't find the nerve and I'm sure I felt guilty."

Wanda's voice had lost its raspiness. It was sounding as it had in the past, feminine, youthful, and I could have sworn that I detected a delicious sound of contrition. You know, when the words become softer as though they're difficult to get out, and it wasn't hard for me to visualize her beautiful brown eyes with their dainty, made-up lids, which provided cover to conceal a childish guilt.

Wanda was saying something into the phone, but our words became intermingled as I was telling her to meet me at her earliest convenience. We both let go with simultaneous laughter and Wanda spoke first. "How about that?" she asked. "I was trying to say the same thing to you."

"Well, that at least shows our thoughts are still the same."

I was holding back on Wanda. Why couldn't I express the way I actually felt? I really wanted to tell her that our hearts had become intermingled the same as our words. Oh how I wanted Wanda to love me as much as I loved her.

"Well, tell me. Where shall we meet?" she asked, invading my thoughts.

It was Sunday night and the Club Delisa's Monday morning breakfast dances were a summit affair. "I'll pick you up this morning and we'll go to the breakfast dance. Okay?"

"That'll be crazy," Wanda answered in the most magnificent voice. It really was!

After an exchange of past reminders, we postponed. It was five o'clock Monday morning as my green Cadillac coupe fishtailed its way through Washington Park. The freshly fallen dew had polluted the green leafage with a fantastic aroma and the crickets were singing their last songs before the crack of dawn. I had chosen my finest threads, consisting of houndstooth blue sport coat, deep sky blue slacks, white-on-white roll-collared shirt, and a multi-colored blue tie, the same hue as my socks, which were protected by needle-toed blue suede shoes.

As my car poured onto Drexel Boulevard, I began to receive those awful stomach pains and this time it was a different kind of fear. Would I look good enough to stabilize within Wanda the love she once had? I braked the car in front of Wanda's house and adjusted the rear-view mirror so I could see my tie, my youthful face and my recently straightened hair.

I was ringing the bell in the vestibule. Wanda buzzed the door and yelled to me that she was coming down, thus saving me a walk up. I waited at the bottom of the steps and I could actually hear my excited heart. I heard the door slam from above and the sound of feminine steps descending on me. I reached for my handkerchief and gave my jet profile a final pat and when I brought my handkerchief down, I wouldn't have traded places with a king.

The snugly-fitted white dress was clinging to all the pores of Wanda's statuesque body and her always beautiful eyes were competing with the vestibule lights as I stepped forward and met her on the next to last step. She was now taller than me. My upward gaze caught a face minus all blemishes, a mouth with lips so daintily placed, yet so naturally hued with rich youthful blood that they might have burst and bled if the kiss wasn't placed just right. Her smile portrayed those uniquely even-placed teeth and her large breasts seemed to heave when she spoke.

"Gee, daddy, you look good."

I extended both my hands; steadied her on the steps and kissed her on the depth of her elevated chin. The scent of her fantastic cologne drove sensuous shocks through my entire being and finally I got around to answering her.

"If you stood next to a dead tree, you'd make it look beautiful."

Her face cracked into another smile and I helped her down from the last step.

We arrived at the Club Delisa just before the floor show began. Big Boy, the maitre d', spotted me and, I imagine he visualized the five dollar tip I would so frequently give him for a preferred ringside table.

My status amongst the persons in the fast life was now rising toward the top and quite a number of heads were turning and bowing at the notice of our entrance. It seemed like only last night's dream when I entered this same place of entertainment with Chris even though I knew many a moon had passed and Wanda was like a new day for me now. Every white clothed table was topped with varieties of fantastic drinks and surrounded by figures of mixtured hue. It was confusing to distinguish whether the rainbow colors were coming from the assortedly placed lights, or the expensively jeweled patrons.

Big Boy, the maitre d', had made a place for Wanda and me in the ostensible second row of tables. I had often told him of my dislike for the first row because the waitresses would often pass and some had been known to spill drinks.

We had been seated and the lights were dimmed for the gala beginning of the colorful floor show. It happened just before the obese comedian mounted the stage. Black Willie and one of his dope runners, whose name I did not know, were making their way toward my table and the ominous look on Willie's black face forewarned me of trouble. I felt Wanda's hand grasp my upper arm when her eyes caught sight of Willie and his haggard-faced companion. They were now within arm's reach of our table.

Willie stopped and cast his eyes down at Wanda's glorious figure, thus ignoring me as though I was invisible. He said, "I would like to talk to you outside—and alone."

Willie's eyes gave evidence that he had been drinking and his wide nose expanded noticeably as he breathed.

The fat-bodied comedian had grasped the microphone just as Wanda answered. "There's nothing for us to talk about. I'm sure my note explained my intentions."

Wanda never raised her eyes. Her stare was transfixed on the roly-poly entertainer as though she was obsessed. The skinny companion looked at Black Willie, as if to ask, "What will we do now, man?" A few people at the tables behind us began clamoring with their souvenir knockers, and their voices joined the clamor. "Down in front! What do you think you're made of—glass?"

"What do you mean the note should explain everything?" Willie said. "You're coming out of here and talk to me."

I had given Wanda the chance to disassociate herself from Willie, using her own words, but this he did not want to accept. I urgently found that his dislike for me was possibly the reason for this entire scene. I had to make my presence known.

"She has explained herself," I said. "There's really no need for further discussion."

If the man had baited a trap to lure me in, it couldn't have been more proficiently done. Willie immediately reversed his virulence toward me and it was now obvious that I was the intended target from the very beginning.

"Motherfucker, I didn't say anything to you, so keep your damn mouth shut."

Willie's words were so voiced that the pear-shaped comedian's repetoire was noticeably unraveled and persons at the tightly surrounding tables were pushing chairs back in frightened anticipation of the impending dangerous scene.

I freed Wanda's grip from my upper arm and pushed my chair back from the small circular table. It was then that Big Boy and two of his heavies approached and escorted Black Willie and his rail-faced subordinate out of the club room. Before Willie left—which was a delight to everyone present—I could see the look in his deadly eyes, which forewarned me of future trouble. I recalled the vow I had made to myself during my trip to New York, that I would endeavor to maintain class, and avoid common notoriety, but incidents like this, of course, were unavoidable.

The remainder of the oncoming floor show had been profusely marred by Willie's unpredictable appearance; that is, as far as I was concerned. And anyhow, before the show was over, I'd decided to leave, thus avoiding to answer the sure to be asked questions concerning the previous loud incident.

Wanda was in full agreement as we raised ourselves from the small circular table. I left the waitress a satisfying tip and we headed for the long hallway to the exit.

The voluptuous shake dancer was winding up the show, but she lost some of her ogle-eyed audience as Wanda glided along ahead of me, and of course the stares were not for me.

The morning that was previously jet was now a refreshing gray. Persons who had earlier slept were wide awake with their lunch pails and content to start another week.

## Chapter Thirteen

TWO WEEKS LATER, on a Saturday night, I had dropped Wanda off at her mother's house. I told her to be dressed and ready at midnight, then we would join the other weekend funsters.

I looked at my watch as my car leaped from the curb. The hands were closing in on ten o'clock. I adjusted the automatic pistol in my belt, a loan from a friend who had returned from the war, and a precaution I had taken ever since the unforgettable scene with Black Willie.

The night was as lovely as a Saturday night could be—that is, for a summer night—and it looked as though everybody was out trying to enjoy it. There were people with formal attire. Some were complete with the tall hats and the coats with the split long tails. I'd often wondered how difficult it would be if a lady had to run while wearing one of those extremely long evening dresses. Ladies were wearing their dresses long anyway; a style primarily called "the new look," a fad however, that didn't last long.

I drove past Joe's 315 Club on Fifty-Fifth Street (formerly called Buddy Coleman's Lounge). Firebrand, Drawback, and Jab were there, also Joe, the owner of the place, standing out in front watching the feminine scenery. I hadn't seen too much of these fellows lately, some of whom were my old friends. I decided to park and chat a while.

The familiar boulevard had changed only slightly. The favorite pool hall had moved down the street. The Garfield Hotel now looked old and drab. White's Cafe de Society had closed long ago, and the small restaurant downstairs had disappeared too. Otherwise, everything was still the same except, of course, the guys had gotten a little older. I shook hands with all of them and accepted the flattering praises of my pimping endeavors most modestly.

Joe, the owner of the lounge, walked over to look at my car and said, "Hot damn! When you were just a punk shooting pool downstairs, I'll bet you never figured you'd be driving a car that look like this."

The other fellas followed him, craning their necks and asking assorted questions about the different optional features on the car. Modesty, I must admit, was very trying to maintain.

"Aw, I'm just trying to keep pace with most of you guys," I said. "One of these days I may catch up."

"How many girls do you have now, Trickshot?" Drawback asked. "I hear you did pretty good when you were out on the west coast."

Before I could answer, Jab spoke. "Yeah, I heard that you took a dude's girl and he tried to stab you—or something like that."

I reached back into my memory bag and though it was

ages ago, the singular incident of violence was most vivid. To inform them that I had been caught cheating in a cheap hotel crap game would not have helped my growing status in the pimp game—it would have been dumb, really.

"Yeah, I had a small misunderstanding with a guy out there," I answered. "But it was all straightened out."

"Your name has been popping up kinda regular," Drawback said. "They tell me you had some trouble with Black Willie over at the club a few weeks ago. You know you've got to watch out for him. I hear he plays kinda rough."

Long before we had met, Black Willie's reputation had preceded him, which was the reason the gun made a slight bulge under my shirt.

"A few of the fellas have informed me that he is quite dangerous," I said. "So all I can do is stay on my toes."

A few years earlier, I would have verbally boasted of my readiness but I had past learned the valued rules of the ghetto.

I glanced at my watch and the time told me to split. "Well, I'll catch you guys later on," I said. "I've got to make a run." I made a double-step to avoid bumping into a youngster who had just gotten off the el train and had come running down the steps.

I pointed the car towards South Park Boulevard and decided to light the small roach that was concealed in the top of my sock. To be caught smoking the illegal reefer would mean the loss of my car, so adjusting the rear-view mirror and locking both car doors provided me psychological security.

Wanda and I would want a snort of cocaine later, especially after we'd hit a few bars. Heading for Bo-Bo, the dealer, who hung out at a tavern on Fifty-Eighth Street, I threw the finger-burning roach out the window, and that's when I caught view of the massive Cadillac grill in my outside rear-view mirror.

It was shining. It was blue. Yes, I was sure it was Black Willie's car. My free hand automatically went to my waist. The ever-pressing pistol had put pressure on my stomach and I had readjusted it when I sat in the car. My hand on the steering wheel had a pronounced kind of dampness. I shot my stare up to the rear-view mirror because I didn't want to move my head. I turned the car west on Fifty-Eighth Street, though I had no intention now of stopping to see Bo-Bo.

The sleuthing lights that were hanging in my rear-view mirror turned, too. I rolled my eyes upward again. I could only distinguish the figure of one person in the trailing car. It was a relief to know that Willie's skinny companion wasn't accompanying him. Primarily, I was going to turn down Prairie Avenue, but Michigan Boulevard, then a two-way street, would be better under the present conditions. It was wider with more room to maneuver and the conditions were mine to choose. I released the gun from the inside of my shirt—thanks to the haunting memory of the California scene—and placed it on the leather-upholstered seat beside me.

At a normal rate of speed, I crossed Indiana Avenue, then turned right on Michigan Boulevard. The lights in the rear-view mirror were dogmatically stalking me. In the middle of the block ahead, I saw a large parking space. The two cars now were in the 57th block just opposite old Carter School, the school which Ben and Ted had attended. But I had not time for the God-given right to reminisce. I had to make sure that I was going to live to see another day—and of course, live to see Wanda.

I felt those terrible pains arriving in my gut. They were really having a ball—like a chain untying itself without enough space—and my hand was so awfully damp, I had to regrip the wheel.

I normally guided the car to the curb and alighted on the

opposite side near the grass. The trailing blue Cadillac had pulled abreast in the center of the boulevard. There was no mistaking the outline of Willie's inky black profile. The blue Caddy speeded forward with a thrust and stopped abruptly in the space ahead of me.

I left my car door open purposely—under certain conditions, it could act as a shield. Black Willie bounded from his Caddy and started toward me with quickening steps. I was now standing behind my open car door with the gun down by my side. My eyes were on his hands as he hurried toward me. I couldn't believe what I saw. As I gave his husky body a speedy visual check, there wasn't a bulge anywhere. The man was almost abreast of me. Could it be possible that he was completely unarmed?

I stepped back and shut the car door. The man was obviously blinded with rage as his foolhardy actions so presently proved. He stretched out his powerful arms as if to grab me, strangle me—truthfully, I don't know which—and with no intent of murder in mind, I swung the gun forcefully upside his head. Though staggered, his strong hands had formed a tightening grip on my neck. Whether he was crazy or blind was a decision. Couldn't he see that I hovered a small missile launcher?

The man was strong and this is truth that I speak. Fearful visions of him disarming me, beating me, disfiguring me, and with those strong arms and hands, he could no doubt kill me, I began to back up as my sweaty hands tightened on the pistol and there was a loud explosion heard above the quiet of the night; heard by Willie, heard by me, and I'm sure heard by the housed persons along the boulevard.

I pointed the pistol low, with intentions merely to wound this man, this man who possessed the strength of a gorilla and a hatred which brought him forward. The bullet had caught him in his thigh, but the grip on my neck which he refused to relinquish was now tightening. I continued to back up and squeezed the trigger again—this shot was aimed at the other leg.

Through pants of breath which were strong, yet tired, he uttered, "You pimp sonofabitch!"

The fear of being subdued, thus having the gun turned on me, brought on a self-preservating decision. I was going to kill him! I was now aiming the mouth of the pistol toward his upper body. My hand squeezed the pistol for the third time; however, his leaking body was forced to yield, as the third shattering crack echoed through the night. Willie was falling as I was back-peddling, and his falling arm hit the gun just as it fired.

A murder charge I did not want to face. I began struggling to place Black Willie's bleeding body into the rear seat of my Caddy. A friend of many years, who was a narcotic detective, happened to be passing at the time. He helped me place Willie's body in the car and I recall the officer lifting a Panama hat from the ground. If it belonged to Willie or me, I don't remember.

There had been quite a few ogle-eyed neighbors, but not one came upon the scene. Nevertheless, an old lady did give a later testimony. I had no trouble driving Willie to the Provident Hospital located on 51st and Vincinnes Avenue. My police friend later told me he thought I was going to dump the body when he allowed me to drive off.

This happened in the summer of 1948, and after months in the hospital, Willie recovered and though so intended the last bullet was not fatal. It had landed in his stomach when his falling arm had struck the gun. I was glad he recovered. I really was.

During Black Willie's recovery, I was free on bond and the charge was attempted murder. Somehow, the police had arrived at the hospital with me. I submitted myself to them willingly.

I hired the expertise of a successful young lawyer, Claude W. Holman, who at this writing, is the President Pro-Tem of Mayor Daly's powerful Chicago City Council. The lawyer quoted me a liberal service charge, which I did not have at the time, thus forcing me to seek financial aid. Of course, my first stop was Ted. Knowing the seriousness of the charge, I was shocked when Ted refused me.

Wanda put forth super efforts and a gambler on Fifty-Fifth Street made me a loan. I was advised that Willie would be in the hospital for months and the case might not really be heard for at least a year, during which time I was hustling—I mean real hard hustling. I don't remember anyone telling me that I wasn't allowed to leave town, though I imagine it was a statement forgotten by the professional bondsman at the time.

I began to make trips to and around Detroit, Cleveland, Pittsburgh and quite often New York. Wanda was maintaining her usual fast pace. In fact, she met some big money spending dates, one of them a white dope pusher whose name she would never divulge. It would do me no good to delve into her professional business.

The money, however, just would not stay with me. I was leaving no stone unturned.

One day, I made a trip to my wife's tavern, hoping she would remember some of the good days we'd had. Her response was one with deep unforgiveness. "You've chosen your bed of rocks," she said, "now you can lay down in them. I might help you, if you didn't have another woman, but I just can't see myself being used again."

"The favor would be for me, not her," I answered, "but if that's the way you feel, fuck it."

Had I been a contortionist, I'd have kicked my own ass. To ask and be refused is humiliating to the average man's pride, but, of course, I had brought the scorn upon myself. I needed money and I needed it badly. Maybe if I had protected that which Wanda had given me and the money I was hustling myself, things would have no doubt been better, but I was gambling. I needed so much and I wanted it so fast.

I went to the Fat Man with the gambling joint on Fifty-First Street. I asked him to put me in contact with Dino, the dapper white man whom I used to sell the gas stamps to. The meeting was arranged and I was given the job running errands over the country for a group of white boys on the north side.

This job proved risky but lucrative. I had stopped my financial decline and was on the rise again. Sometimes the job meant taking money to another city and sometimes it meant bringing some back. There were times I had to accompany other fellas on trips, all of these were with black men. What their part in the trip was, I did not ask.

The summer of 1949, in Judge Miner's court, I was called to trial. Judge Miner, an amiable-faced short man, credited with being astute, sat his paunchy body atop his podium in the Criminal Court Building on 26th and California Avenue.

Clearly, the building of pale white stone gives the appearance of excellence, unlike its neighboring structure, the House of Correction, with its ancient red bricks which concealed living conditions so unbelievable that its south cellhouse was condemned shortly after Ben and I were released.

The courtroom, when I entered, was only sparsely filled. Black Willie was sitting on one of the well-shellaced benches and the thin-faced white man, who sat beside him—though nothing he did created it—caused my stomach a slight seizure of nervousness. A lawyer Black Willie did not need, for had I not paid his hospital bills plus sent him an agreed upon financial sum, and talked to him over the phone? Knowledge of frequent crosses in the ghetto alarmed me, that maybe now I had fallen into one.

It was only moments before my attorney joined me. I began to inform him of my fears as the bailiff called my case. I had explained my clandestine actions to my lawyer, who had failed to inform me that there was nothing illegal in what I had done. Most elegantly, he explained to the judge the financial atonement I had made; wherein the judge asked Willie if he was satisfied. Willie's response was positive. My attorney's exposure of my actions shook me.

We were sent into Judge Miner's chambers, followed by my attorney and another appointed court official. Thus some legal papers were placed on the desk before us and, if memory serves me right, these I signed. Everything was legal and above reproach—to my surprise.

We were brought before the judge again and given a long reprimand concerning what the results might have been. After again asking Black Willie if he was satisfied, the judge placed me on one year's probation and I was released.

As my lawyer and I left the courtroom, the bailiff was calling a robbery case. The sharp-faced white man whom I'd mistaken to be Willie's lawyer, was the culprit in the case.

I had previously informed Dino and his friends that my errand-running days would cease at the conclusion of my trial. I worked for them another month, or it might have been two, and I parted from them in good standing.

## Chapter Fourteen

IT WAS 1950. My green coupe Cadillac had been traded. I now owned a black '50 Cadillac sedan, and pimping had become a full-time job for me. Wanda had matured and so had I. The bond between the two of us really appeared unbreakable.

In the last six months I had copped Sarah, another girl I'd met while doing my thing. She was not as attractive as Wanda, though her voluptuously built body displayed hefty hips, large busts, a semi-small waist and very sturdy legs. Her face was large and slightly round with over-sized eyes, whereas her nose was faintly large above her negroid lips. It blended nicely or maybe it was her ebony complexion which blended so well.

It was a week after I had copped Sarah; and the news had spread that our newest state, Alaska, was jumping. And, of course, being the possessor of two choice ladies, Alaska was my next endeavor.

The trip was planned, and in a moderately span of time we were on our way. Sarah wanted to stop in Kansas City, Missouri. A barmaid friend of hers worked there in the El Capitan Bar. We stopped and had a few drinks and from there we went to an after-hours joint.

Helen, the barmaid, called me to her side and then ran down to me how friendly she and Sarah had been since their childhood days; then she ended her confidential and theatrical speech with, "I wish you all the success, but, Trick, please treat Sarah nice."

I told Helen that I could understand her concern, but not to worry. Sarah was in good hands.

Full of the watered-down whiskey from the after-hour joint, I figured it best not to hit the road until later on in the day. We went to the Street Hotel and there I rented a suite with two bedrooms. The suite was decorated in colors of brown and gold. There was no door leading to the second bedroom, merely a large oval-shaped portal which had brown and gold drapes shrouding it.

"I think I'll sleep with Sarah," Wanda said. "You know how loud you snore when you drink that whiskey."

"Crazy," I answered. I wanted to stretch my six foot, three inch frame anyway, and the standard size hotel bed was barely large enough.

I don't recall what time it was because it mattered least. My bladder had urged me to the toilet and on my return to bed, I heard a sound that assured me one of the girls was having a nightmare. I wondered why the throaty sounds hadn't awakened the other sleeping companion, and I was only mildly surprised to find that they both were very wide awake. Yes, they were making love in a very torrid fashion. Wanda was on her back, eyes closed, and a grotesque expression on her face as her fingers clawed at the sheets on the bed.

Sarah, I did not see, but the rhythmic bulge midway the bed gave evidence of her presence.

I was fully aware of Wanda's sexual deviations; however, in view of Sarah's present position, I was forced to recollect my thoughts. I left the girls to their fun and returned to my bed and it goes without saying that I did not sleep. Not that the present bed scene had shocked me out of my slumber. On the contrary, it had been an open fact to me that the majority of girls in the fast life had at some time or another enjoyed these bedroom pleasures with other females. However, the scene did drag my thoughts back to Helen and the devoted interest she had shown in Sarah's well-being. Could it be that they had been lovers?

I recalled Helen's reluctance to speak of her man. With all these recollections joined together, it was now ostensibly clear that Helen, no doubt, was a stud.

Once again we were on the road and, as usual, I was enjoying the passing scenes. When we reached Tulsa, Oklahoma, I stopped at a small restaurant called Spinners. It was owned by a fellow I had met during my first trip out west, which had been a few years past, and if my memory serves me right, the hotel next door had the same name as the one in Kansas City, Missouri. It was called the Street Hotel or maybe it was Smalls Hotel.

There was a black-owned garage across the street facing the hotel in which I parked my car. There was no bellhop at the hotel and I was forced to carry up the luggage myself, some of which I started to leave in the car trunk. But, being aware of the ghetto rip-offs, I was inclined to change my mind. After a good night's rest, I reloaded the car and we were on our way again. Yet, there was one thing which I noticed particularly. Unlike Oklahoma City, I didn't see as many oil pumps going up-down, up-down.

I had been wised up through the grapevine that my ole buddy Mooky D. had moved to San Francisco, California. Therefore, I made two more stops for sleep and rest, then finally pulled up in the Fillmore District of San Francisco.

This was San Francisco's "Harlem." Here you would find the prostitutes, the pimps, the fakes, the people on the wild side, the people of the night, and, of course, there was multiple daytime action, too.

I checked into the Booker T. Washington Hotel on Ellis

Street and began to seek out Mooky D. I had never visited this city, which stuck out into the waters of the great Pacific Ocean. Its blatant reputation stemmed back past the tragic 1906 fire which left 500 hundred dead or missing and property damage about two to three million. To be sure, it was a much changed city now.

Up till then, my hustling activities had been limited to eastern territories. Had I been in Detroit, Cleveland, or even New York, my task of finding Mooky D. would have been many times feasible. Clearly, I had no time to waste. With two ladies to feed and maintain, I would have to secure the rubber band around my bankroll.

After completing Wanda and Sarah in adjoining hotel rooms, I walked down the street a short distance until I came to the crossing at Fillmore Avenue. There, the merchants' shops of all designs greeted me. There were restaurants aplenty, owing to the substantial influx of Orientals who were the major owners of these establishments. Assuredly, there also were other shops hungering to fleece the post-war migrators. There were tailor shops, bars, meat-markets, laundries, liquor stores, barber shops and shops with "for sale" signs in the windows. Of the latter, only male adults went in and out; and in the daylight it was most obvious.

I strolled down Fillmore Avenue until I spotted a bar which I figured would suit Mooky D.'s taste. I say "down" because, when in San Francisco, you're always going "up" or "down," beyond a doubt.

As I correctly had figured, it wasn't too long before I got a wire from one of the locals that Mooky D. had leased an establishment and now called it the "Chicago Hotel."

The building wasn't hard to find, as it was only a few blocks away near Spring Street, and the structure was made up of wood and bricks. Oh, yeah, it was a three-story building, the same as its surroundings.

As I made my way up the four or five steps of concrete, I recalled the Japanese temple which Mooky D. had leased back in Los Angeles a few years past. I would remember to ask, did he ever see the two tall detectives again? I received a hearty welcome at the door.

"Trickshot! Well, what do you know, ole buddy?" Mooky D. raised his hand real high and greeted mine with a thrusty slap. The few years I didn't see him hadn't changed his appearance too much, if any, and his humor was ostensibly the same. "Come on in here, man," Mooky D. said, "and tell me about back home." A little white poodle pranced up to the door as Mooky D. let me inside.

"I thought I heard a dog barking as I rang the bell," I said. "What happened to the other black one?"

"I lost him," Mooky D. answered. "Either he ran off or somebody stole him."

"Too bad," I said, "he was cute. How long have you had this one?"

"Oh, about two years," Mooky D. answered again. "I bought him for Evelyn. She's crazy about dogs." The little white pooch was bouncing as though there were wire springs in his legs.

"How is she, Mooky?" I asked. "You know, I didn't get a chance to see her when we were in Los Angeles before."

"Come on in the office a minute. I've got to make a call. Aw, Evelyn, she's all right," Mooky D. said as he dialed the phone.

While Mooky D. was talking, I busied myself scanning the place. It appeared to have been an old apartment building, which had been cut up to make an apartment hotel.

Mooky D. cradled the phone, then turned to me. "Now, sit down, man, and tell me about things back East," he said.

"Oh, things have changed," I said, "but I think it's because the war is over. That made a big difference, you know."

"But tell me," Mooky D. said, "why do you have to go to Alaska when there's plenty of bread right here?"

"Yeah," I answered, "I can see that there's plenty of action going on here, but from what I hear, they're just throwing money away up in Alaska."

"You really should check on things down in the valley," Mooky D. said. "Some of the fellows from here take their girls down there during the season, and boy, do they come back rich."

"The valley?" I asked.

"Yeah. There's quite a few small towns in the San Joaquin Valley that will put Alaska to shame. That is, when the season opens," Mooky D. said.

"Well, what kind of vacancy do you have?" I asked. "You know, I'm getting out of that bankroll-eating hotel."

"I've got a nice place for you upstairs," Mooky D. said. "Don't worry. Just bring the luggage and the girls. Things will be ready when you return."

I looked at my watch. "I've got a few hours before check-out time," I said, "so there's really no hurry. On the other hand, maybe I should get some rest."

The next day, the sky was shining brightly and Mooky D. took us sightseeing.

He took us to Nob Hill after winding through streets which consisted of trees and knolls. There were large, palatial homes, some of which had spacious concrete porches with large pillars supporting the higher verandas. Others had tall dome-shaped rooftops which boasted of another era, but still maintained the elegance to be a showplace even then.

Intending to satisfy everyone present, Mooky D. guided us to a spot along the bay. There were long binoculars situated along the area the same as parking meters, and with the drop of a dime, one could actually see the prisoners moving around in the yard of Alcatraz.

The sightseeing tour extended across the bay into Oakland, California, which was then a thriving, serene community, and it was not thought of as the "Black Panther's National Headquarters," a name which yet had not come into being. As we were returning over the Bay Bridge, I caught a faraway view of the Golden Gate Race Track, which was situated in nearby Albany. I knew then that a lot of coming days would find me hanging over the fence with the rest of the railbirds.

The following day, Mooky D. and I took a trip through the San Joaquin Valley. Mooky D. knew a fellow who was in Stockton at the time, though in reality the guy was out of New York City. We arrived in Stockton about noon.

Mooky D. introduced me to W.C. and the three of us sat on the porch smoking the delicious pot which W.C. shared with us. W.C., a small built man with a brown complexion, had the facial features of a pygmy. You know, a small face and a large head, though when it came to dressing, he was most immaculate. I glanced at his imported leather brown loafers, his expensive slacks, and his dark brown suede jacket which showed the cut of master tailoring.

"I hear things are rather hot back in Chicago. How many girls have you brought with you, Trickshot?" W.C. asked, as he dragged deeply from the skinny stick of pot.

"Yeah, I had to leave the ole town," I answered. "Oh, I've got two broads who are raring to get 'down'—that is, if they can get down right. Mooky tells me I should stash right here in Stockton."

"Well, he's telling you right," W.C. said. "That is, if you can afford to lay dead for a while." W.C. was carefully placing the short roach into the end of his cigarette.

"How long," I asked, "would I have to lay before the season starts?"

"Oh," W.C. answered, "they should be coming in about

a month from now."

I looked at Mooky D. who also was listening attentively.

"Explain to me just what happens that I should postpone my trip to Alaska?" I asked.

"Well, Trickshot, it works like this. A month from now, you'll see thousands of Mexicans from across the border migrate into this town. Some of them, of course, will be so-called 'wet-backs.' "

I interrupted W.C. "Wet-backs?"

"Yeah," W.C. said, "that's what they call the Mexicans who are here illegally. At certain points, some of them swim across the Rio Grande River."

"How many Mexicans come into the States during the harvesting season?" I asked.

"Oh, I'd say twenty or thirty thousand," W.C. answered.

"That many easily," Mooky D. said. "You see, they pick lettuce, tomatoes, asparagus, and many other farm products that are grown out here."

"And just where do all of these new farmhands stay?" I again asked.

"Some of them stay right here in town, while others stay on the farms where they work. You know, they've got camps for these farm workers, too," W.C. said.

"Yeah," said Mooky D. "I know some guys who take their girls to the camps every payday."

"Is that right?" I queried. "Where do the girls turn their tricks while in these camps, and is it all right with the bosses or whoever it is who runs the camps?"

"Oh, the camp bosses very seldom say anything. They want to keep the workers happy," Mooky D. interjected.

"That's why we get a nice break here in town. Imagine having thousands of workers away from home and no place for them to go." W.C. was gesturing with his hands as he explained to me.

"You're guaranteed two hundred a day," Mooky D. said.

"That's a hundred a day for each girl, and some days it's going to be more. Boy! I wish Evelyn was a few years younger. I'd have her right down here."

One glance at Mooky D.'s eyelids told me that the soothing pot definitely had taken effect.

"I come here every year," W.C. said. "And when I go back to New York, I lease the house out until the next year. Now, if you want the two vacant bedrooms, I'll keep them for you. I've got two girls myself, but one of them lives in the house that she hustles out of which is just up the street apiece." W.C. pointed his finger.

To be concise, I wasn't going to Alaska. I suddenly had made up my mind to stay in Stockton, California.

That night we arrived back in San Francisco and I explained my plans to Wanda and Sarah, who were only mildly disappointed. Stockton was forty-eight miles from Frisco, and two days later, we were on our way back there. At first sight of the house the girls showed mild surprise.

"It isn't as bad as I had pictured it to be," Wanda said. "With a little fixing up, it could be real cozy."

"I dig this front porch," Sarah said. "It sort of reminds me of Uncle Rufus' place."

I introduced them to W.C., then the girls went about familiarizing themselves with the house. Wanda suggested placing the dresser on the other side of her room. Sarah didn't like the direction in which her bed was facing and while they satisfied their womanly whims, W.C. and I decided to take a ride.

As we cruised down Capital Street, W.C. had an idea. "Say, man, why don't you rent that vacant house down the street from us?"

"I don't know, really. I've never given it a thought. How would I go about making contact with the police?"

"Oh, I'll take care of that part, as long as you're sure you want the house. At least there'll be no madam to contend with," W.C. answered.

"Of course I'm sure. I'd rather have my own whore house any day, than split my bread with some veteran broad."

"Then it's all set. I'll see my police connect tomorrow. I'll also ask if he's willing to meet you."

After returning from the ride with W.C., I sat out on the front porch alone and put my thoughts together. I had viewed the smallness of the town. There really was only one place in the black community serving mixed drinks, which was the Elk's Lodge, located a half block from the rundown pool hall. Oh, there were other places up in the heart of town; however, these were dominated by the whites and Mexicans; and of course, blacks also would be served.

It was most rare to see the town fellows dressed clean and neat unless it was a special affair or maybe on Sunday. At other times, the majority of them would wear blue jeans. For me, it would have been ostensibly inept to settle in a town such as this and flaunt a lurid Cadillac car, two attractive girls, open up a whore house and maintain a dashing attire.

I rented a small garage from our next door neighbor and that was where I kept my car. I could not picture myself wearing blue jeans or coveralls. Thus, I merely toned my style of dressing down. You know, dark slacks, conservatively colored shirts and quite often my hair would be in disarray because there were no process barbers in the town. Whenever this problem would become pronounced, I'd back my car out of my neighbor's garage and head to San Francisco, and I would sometimes take a forty mile jaunt to Sacramento. However, I preferred Frisco which had a better selection of barbers and I would enjoy the chance to see Mooky D. These trips would be timed with the girl's monthly period which was the only time she could take off.

## Chapter Fifteen

THINGS IN THE MONTHS to come worked out fine for all concerned. I made friends with the local home-guards, although, as would happen anywhere, I found a few pockets of resentment. But with my new-found connection, the vice detective, I didn't allow anyone to disturb me.

Wanda and Sarah were getting along most graciously. And why not? To be sure, they quite blatantly were lovers.

Though I had progressed steadily in my knowledge of the pimp game, I would frequently reach back for the "tricks of the trade" in which I labored. I would make it a point to be more attentive to the one which made the most money, thereby each worked harder while vying for my affection.

I never really found out the reason, but my vice connection told me to close down along with the other whore houses, of which there were two more. As bad luck would have it be, there was a big payday due in a few days.

I talked to W.C. that morning. "Say, man, since we've got to close shop, why not take off some of those farm workers' camps which I've heard so much about?"

"Well, I was going to lay dead until we got the word to open again," W.C. answered, "but I don't see why we can't pick up that extra bread since it's just lying in the streets. Ordinarily, I avoid those work camps, especially if my bankroll's in good shape."

"Avoid them, why? I thought you said out there the girls would make a lot of money."

"Oh, yeah, the girls make money all right, but it's the conditions they work under that's such a drag."

"A drag?"

"Yeah. They have to—well, just wait and see for yourself."

That night, we loaded the girls into the back seat of the car, including W.C.'s girl Ruth, who was a tall, light-skinned shapely girl, and she seemed to wiggle when she walked. We drove out El Dorado Avenue, then turned left at Route 99.

"How far is this camp?" I asked.

"Aw, it's only ten or fifteen miles," W.C. said. "In fact, it's right near Modesto."

"Modesto? Where is that?" Wanda spoke up.

"Why that's a small town about fifteen miles from Stockton. I keep forgetting that none of you know where you're at."

The girls were dressed in their "come-hither" clothes. Wanda was in a white blouse and very short blue skirt. The short skirt had pleats and it stopped midway her thigh, but when she did her jazzy walk, the pleated material would flutter. Voluptuous Sarah wore a white, see-through blouse and blue pants which were called shorts, but looking at Sarah from the rear, one would have sworn they were called tights. W.C.'s girl Ruth, the tallest of the three, wore a knitted bra which showed the nipples of her tits and the short skirt she wore had slits on each side that extended to her hips.

"Tell me, man. How does a person communicate with these Mexicans?" It was really a question I should have asked long ago, I mused.

"They always bring one or two fellows with them," W.C. said, "whenever they come to town, right?"

"Right," Wanda answered.

"Yes, they do," Sarah commented.

"Well," W.C. said, "that's the same way things are done out at the camps. They always carry their interpreter along with them."

"Every now and then," Ruth said, "you'll get one that doesn't know this from that—and he'll have the nerve to come alone, but it's usually one who's full of tequilla."

"Honey," Wanda said, "that certainly is the truth, because we had one like that just the other night."

"Yes, we did," Sarah said.

"Oh, the occasional drunks will give you a little trouble," W.C. said, "but as a whole, they're not so bad."

"Isn't this the turn, Daddy?" Ruth said, as she leaned forward and pointed.

"Yeah, damn," W.C. said. "I almost passed it by."

It was a small dirt road which led from the pavement of the highway. It was only wide enough for one car. In fact, you could stick out your hand and touch the tall weeds as the car slightly bounced and jogged along over the bumpy dirt road. We were in complete blackness; only the headlights provided vision straight ahead.

W.C. made a sharp right turn and, as if from nowhere, there were lights—big lights, small lights, colored lights. To be sure, there were lights all over the place. The scene was that of a carnival, though a lot less quieter. Mexicans in work clothes saturated the large area and there were three long rows of barracks and a few weather-beaten shanties scattered throughout.

W.C. concealed the car at the edge of the clearing. There were other vehicles standing about. These were old trucks and much older cars which were parked up on the greenery.

There were canvas covered tables with all sorts of wares—lunch buckets, overalls, pants, shirts, shoes, belts, hats, handkerchiefs and other useful commodities for the average male. As W.C. had earlier warned me, there were two or three other cars parked within the area, too, but they were concealed beneath the bevy of foliage the same as ours.

"There's Pimping Jimmy's car," W.C. said, nodding his head toward a black Cadillac sedan that was backing into the overhanging shrubbery.

"Yeah," Ruth said. "His girls work the streets when they're in Frisco, but they work the farmers' camps when the season starts."

I cast a glance toward the black Cadillac sedan and saw an ebony, statuesque lady get out of the car. She was followed by another whose complexion was much lighter, though her physical measurements were apparently less obvious. The two newly-arrived ladies strolled toward the soft drink counter which was situated in front of a large tent. It had a canopy protruding which was supported by two long poles. When the scantily clad ladies reached the pop counter, as though responding to some signal, the leisurely walking farm workers drifted in the same direction.

W.C. got out of his car and told me to follow. The girls got out behind me, only they, like the other girls, headed toward the soft drink counter. W.C. and I treaded over to the make-shift counters and like the other men who were drabbed in farmer's garb, we casually began to inspect the wares.

I looked at a finger-thin belt which was what they were featuring at that time, and then I caught sight of Wanda and Sarah returning to the partially hidden car and they were followed by two overall-clad men.

Varied lights from the tops of the merchandise structures silhouetted the strolling figures until their forms were engulfed into nothingness by shadows.

I responded to the nudge that W.C. put to my arm. "Now do you see what I meant when I said bad working conditions?" W.C. gestured with his hand out into the night, and of course, he was pointing toward the car.

"Yeah," I answered. "I see what you mean."

There was nothing for us to do but kill time while the girls went about their profitable business.

"Come on, let's take a stroll," remarked W.C.

I traced his footsteps out into the blackness and from a seemingly short distance I could hear the sound of South American music. It was coming from one of the wooden shacks which stood off in the distance a few hundred yards.

W.C. and I walked past the edge of the clearing. "Here," he said, "light this." I took the thin stick of pot and began to thump at its ends.

"How long do you think we'll be out here?" I asked as I lit the smelly reefer.

"It all depends on the action the girls get. There have been times I stayed out here until daylight—careful with that joint, here comes two dudes."

Heeding W.C.'s warning, I cupped the reefer in my hand and continued our stroll. The two Mexicans who walked past us never bothered to look up. Looking back toward the lighted area, I could distinguish figures going back and forth into the shrubbery, and every now and then, I would hear a car door slam. These scenes went on far into the night. In fact, the palor of dawn infringed upon the blackness in what appeared to be a rather short time.

It probably was due to the tutoring conversations W.C. was giving me. Indeed, I was learning quite a bit about life in the farm workers' camp.

It goes without saying that a blind man would have confused the car with a fish market. Otherwise, the ride home was uneventful.

As time passed, I became bored. I had trouble finding things to occupy my time and I actually don't think I ever went to a movie the whole time I was in Stockton. One reason was, the movies were predominately Mexican and quite certainly they were outdated.

I began to spend more time in Frisco. I would leave Stockton and sometimes stay in Frisco two or three days. One day, someone mentioned the races. Immediately my interest was inspired.

Golden Gate Race Track, situated in Albany, California, just across the bay from San Francisco, presents a beautiful scene. It is built on the flowing waters of the bay. Clearly, the seasonal opening of the race track was going to be my means of breaking the ever-mounting monotony.

I gave myself with the daily task of arriving at the race track before the first race was off. The distance between Stockton and Golden Gate Race Track was forty or fifty miles one way; however it was a pleasure that I looked forward to each day.

The weather had become extremely hot and I had traded the sedan for a brand new Fleetwood Cadillac. It was a ride which I had never experienced before. Quite often, I would cruise along the highway going to or coming from the races, and I would see the farm workers from a distance at their daily toil, some picking tomatoes, some picking lettuce, and others gathering asparagus, which I later found was the favorite produce in this particular area.

It happened one day when I decided to visit the race

track clubhouse. I had been buddying around with some of the local railbirds, but their jargon swayed my mind from a horse whom I thought should win. It goes without saying, that the horse won his race easily. Unlike at the race tracks back east, the Golden Gate clubhouse was located at the top of the grandstand and that was where I headed to avoid further mistakes.

I had my wrist stamped, which also was a new experience for me. Back east, they would give you a ticket in order to pass you into the clubhouse area. Later all tracks adopted the hand-stamping method. I proceeded to rent a box. This way, I knew I would be alone and if I made a mistake, I had no one to blame but myself. I was profoundly surprised when I realized I was in a box seat next to one of the most popular actresses of that era, the fabulous Betty Grable!

The surroundings were so different from the grandstand area of which I was accustomed to. From that day on, I continued to rent a box seat every day. I wasn't able to purchase the same box; however, Miss Grable and the attractive, brunette lady who accompanied her each day maintained their standard box and I later found out that the brunette lady was Miss Grable's sister. Of course, it was common knowledge at that time that Miss Grable who was then married to the famous band leader Harry James owned race horses.

One day I was rushing to place a bet before the off-bell rang. I bumped into an immaculately dressed gentleman and turned, intending to apologize. It was Hoagy Carmichael, the great composer and actor in the flesh. The shock of seeing this popular celebrity, who had written the immortal song "Stardust," delayed my speech, but I finally spit the apology out.

It was little oddities such as this that helped me to recall the vow I had made to myself that day back in New York. I did not disillusion myself that my presence among these affluent persons would make me a part of them, although it was elating and educational for me to see how they dressed and functioned when away from the lights of the cameras.

My theory of association was practically proven out one day. I was asked a question about a certain horse who was running in the upcoming race. The questioner was an attractive red-headed lady who appeared to be in her late twenties. The continued conversation enabled me to learn that she was from Sacramento, California, and had stopped at the race track to bet on a few races. I told her that I was from Stockton, which was in the same area. She said she would stop in Stockton and have a drink on the way home to Sacramento.

All this was fine except for the problematic side effects. It would be unquestionably improper for me to be seen anywhere in this small and tranquil town with a white lady. I told her to meet me at the hamburger drive-in which was located on the perimeter of the town. Needless to say, I did not tarry very long. I walked over to her car and a car waitress dressed in a blue and white uniform was approaching with a colorful menu, and if memory serves me right, my new acquaintance's name was Bess.

Bess waved the waitress away as I seated myself in her car. The drive-in was designed in a circular form. It had lines drawn for the cars to park, and from Bess' parked position, I noticed several customers' heads turn as I situated myself in her car. However, this was not an unexpected reaction since at the time it was rare to see mixed couples in Stockton.

We exchanged telephone numbers and made a date for later on. It actually was three days later when I received a call from Bess. Now, this was the first experience I had ever had with a white woman, and the thought of it was merely something I intended to brag about. Bess was not one of those raving beauties one could exclaim about. She, of course, had a pleasant and mildly attractive face, though she was slightly on the obese side. I had, of course, made arrangements where we could meet and yet be discreet.

There was a fellow whom I had met around the pool hall who sold pot. In a town as small as this, he had to be extra careful of the persons who knew his address. He had chosen a small shack on the outskirts of the city. It sat alone in the center of a large lot and it brought to mind the illusion of an overseer's dwelling or a watchman's quarters.

Like the rundown shack, the furniture also was deteriorated and the bed was no exception. However, the latter was capable of serving our desired intentions.

Bess had her hair rolled up in a fashion which gave it the appearance of being bobbed. Nevertheless, when she removed the bobs and pins, it hung almost to the middle of her back. I made it my business to get into bed first and from there, I watched her disrobe.

There were outlines on her body which showed she had been sunbathing, and though it seemed odd, she did not appear quite as corpulent. Bess' waist was comparatively small and her breasts were youthfully hung. You know, just a mild sag.

She crawled into the bed beside me and the radiation from her voluptuous body immediately aroused me. I stroked her firm breasts and orally massaged her nipples. I moved my hand to her waist and then to her protruding hips as I felt the infant hairs along her thighs tingle beneath my fingers. My hand engulfed her crotch as my index finger became lost. She gave out with passionate whines as her hand massaged my dripping joint. I could resist the folly of stimulation no longer as I mounted her and slowly but assuredly punctured the privacy of her vagina. The eagerness of her sex-filled body gave out with expected satisfaction and in return I presented her with my all.

She let out with screams of passion and lust which inspired my drilling and made me conscious of the popping from the rhythmic motions of our sweat-soaked bodies. It was when she raised her hefty legs in order to accept every satisfying plunge that I exploded in her a stream of life-giving fluid which left my body in a helpless tremor.

I only saw Bess once after our first and only sexual encounter. She and another white girl drove by the pool hall one evening and invited me to a ride and smoke some pot. However, I declined. It simply wasn't profitable and I would be asking for trouble by associating with a white married woman who was living a square life.

## Chapter Sixteen

IT WAS 1952, the year General Dwight D. Eisenhower restored the White House to the Republicans, easily defeating his popular Democratic opponent, Adlai E. Stevenson, the former Governor of Illinois.

It was also the year a new Senator, John F. Kennedy from Massachusetts, arrived in Washington. Few persons realized—if so, they dared not predict—that he would be the first Catholic and thirty-fifth President of these United States.

Clearly, Chicago to me was like an angel's return to heaven, because, truly, it was a place which I have always loved. Its reckless flamboyance will force one's blood to tingle—that is, anyone who loves to live life to its fullest.

Yes, Chicago had returned to normal. That is, as far as the police were concerned. As we all know, there had always been and there might always be harrassment in the ghettos regardless of color or creed. It is just something which the underprivileged have to live with. Outside of that, the ole town was still swinging. It did not take long for the news to spread that Trickshot was back in town, and as the age-old stigma says it, "Nigger rich."

I rented two suites in the Pershing Hotel at Sixty-Fourth and Cottage Grove. At the time, it was managed by Sonny Boswell, best known for his outstanding skills while performing with the famous Harlem Globetrotters Basketball team. We had become friends when he had previously owned the "It Club" at Fifty-Fifth and Michigan Boulevard. As I looked from the lobby into the Pershing barroom, I reminisced of the past scene I had had with Wanda and Black Willie.

I had been situated in the hotel a week and one night the telephone rang. It was a long distance call from New York.

"Hi, Trick, this is Penny. I heard you were back in Chicago, living at the Pershing Hotel."

My thoughts did some fast recollecting and I recalled the cute little redhead, whom I had met at Red's party in New York.

"Oh, hi, Penny. What's been happening with you?"

"I've been fine, except for a thirty-day bit I did in California. It was an old charge of prostitution and I had jumped the bond when I ran away from Henry who was my man at the time. Oh, yeah, I heard you were out in California for a while. How did things go?"

"Aw, things were okay. What happened to bring you back to New York?" I inquired.

"I came here for the Businessmen's Convention. I always make nice money when they're in town. Say, do you still have that jealous wife? Boy! She really couldn't stand me!"

"Naw, I cut her loose a long time ago. The strain was a little too great. Tell me, Penny, what's on your mind?" It was a question which I had been itching to ask. A broad doesn't meet a man one time and then wait a few years to call him unless something is on her mind.

"Oh, I've always thought of you, ever since the first time we met, but you move around so much, it's really hard to keep track of you."

"Aw, I'm not too hard to find. Who told you I was stopping here at the Pershing?"

"Rabbit and his two dip broads arrived in town a few days ago. He said that he had talked to you before they left Chicago and then he gave me your phone number."

I did recall talking to Rabbit in the lobby of the hotel, though I did not know that he and his team had left town. I imagined the girls must have taken off a big piece of bread and had to quit the scene in a hurry.

"Yeah, I did see Rabbit a few days ago. How's he doing in New York?"

"Well, Trick, you know how that goes. You see a dude with his jewelry on and he's buying everybody drinks. You just take it for granted that things are all right for him. Then on the other hand, there are so many fakes out here."

"Yeah, I know what you mean, but you still haven't told me what I want to hear."

I received a feminine giggle through the phone receiver. "Well, it's like I said before, Trickshot, I've always thought about you. I think I might like being with you."

It seems unnecessary to explain that with the potential of a new woman and fresh money, I arrived in New York City the next day. On the way from the airport, Penny explained a situation she had neglected to tell me over the telephone.

It shortly became quite clear that she didn't have her business straight. On the way to her residence, the Taft Hotel, she ran down to me a precarious situation that I was, unknowingly to her, soon to be confronted with.

The cab was coming out of Central Park as I mused over the intricate situation. "What kind of a dude is he?" I asked, as the cab maneuvered through the heavy traffic.

"Oh, he's a young dude, like yourself, only he's much lighter than you, but his height is about the same as yours. You know, I like tall men." Penny forced a smile, then her face was serious again. "He was all right when we first got together, but then, he started running with a gang out on the coast, and that's when he began to fight. You see, I just can't stand a man who wants to fight all the time." Penny turned her head and looked at me. She was making sure I had gotten the message.

"Yeah, I know what you mean." My answer was to Penny, but I was looking at the cab driver who was just pulling up in front of the Taft Hotel.

I paid the fare and we headed into the lobby. As we approached the elevator, I heard a voice call out, "Penny!"

We both turned around. The owner of the voice was striding toward us. Penny's description of Bob was confirmed. He was tall, very nice looking, and his process was immaculately in place as was his attire.

"Why did you take the key?" he coolly asked, ignoring my presence altogether.

"Trickshot, this is Bob. Bob, meet Trickshot."

I extended my hand as I turned to face him.

"Hi," uttered Bob, disregarding my hand and focusing on Penny. I could see perplexity had engulfed Penny.

"I told you to move your clothes, so why should I leave my key as if you live there, too?" Penny was standing between Bob and me. I stepped around her and started to speak, but I was thwarted.

"You shut up," he said. "You have nothing to do with this."

I now was standing in front of him. "I might have more to do with it than you realize," I answered, and his light-complexioned face became flush as he remarked, "So this is your new man?"

Bob had turned to look at Penny, who wasn't hesitant with a most proper "yes."

Bob looked at me and saw that my black features were unflinching, my youthful frame was unwavering, and my dark brown eyes were unblinking. Though, I imagine, he didn't attempt what he plainly would have loved to have accomplished. Instead he turned and cast a threat. "I'll see both of you later on." Bob had made only a few steps away from us when Penny called after him.

"You'd better get your things before you go."

He turned and said, "Don't worry, I'll get them later."

Putting myself in the driver's seat, I interjected, "I think you should get them now. You see, Penny's checking out of her room and moving in with me—now!"

The first flush on his face was simply nothing compared to the present. His tall handsome frame appeared to be steadfast. I knew he was musing over his embarrassing position. With no luggage present, he would be forced to travel the lobby in humiliation—clothes nakedly in his arms. Bob moved toward the elevator as other persons emptied from it, and there was torrid tension as the enclosure carried us upward to the preferred floor.

To underestimate an adversary is past the foolhardy—it is stupid! I had rented a room just a few doors from Penny's and after Bob had removed the few clothes he owned, I remarked to her, "Come on, we'll move your things later. I told you those beans were too filling. I think I'll lie down for a while."

Bob was standing in the spacious hall awaiting the coming elevator as I unlocked my room door.

After the task of moving Penny's things to my room, later that night, I was enjoying the television while Penny went out to take care of her business. If memory serves me right, I was thinking about calling Wanda. It was then that a knock came at the door. Surprised, I sat up in the bed and yelled, "Who is it?"

"House security," was the gruffly spoken answer.

I was slightly puzzled. "Who?" I repeated.

"House security," the same gruff voice chimed again.

I instinctively glanced at the smattering of cocaine which Penny had left resting on the corner of the dresser. With one swipe of the man-sized Kleenex, the flakey white crystals polluted the air and the knock was heard again.

"Okay, I'm coming."

I was in my pajama bottom and didn't bother to get the top. I released the safety lock and opened the door. Wham! The force of the door propelled me against the wall. I did get a perfectly good view of Bob's light-complexioned face. However, it was no longer handsome. It was twisted into a grotesque mask as it spoke. "You motherfucker."

Large pale knuckles were coming swiftly toward my face and I knew I had to avoid the impact, but my attention was distracted by two more large individuals whom I could only see through a painful blur of flying fists. It would simply be the lie of the century if I said that I had tried to fight back.

Honestly, I was trying to cover up my head, my ribs, my stomach, my shins. I found energy enough, though I did not think I had any left, to try and call out for help. I say try because the words obviously never came out. A large hand was clasped over my mouth, but it was the tremendous blow I felt in my stomach which almost caused me to whoosh the hand away. If praying would have been beneficial, I am sure I would have tried. However, I profoundly had no time to pray—like seriously—I was in big trouble. Grabbing your opponent's crotch, biting your adversary's finger or even sticking your fingers in the eye of your enemy were some of the tactics of the ghetto. However, none of these maneuvers could I try or recall. I felt an excruciating pain in my side and instantly a terrific blow entered my back. I could tell the taste of the salty sweat, and I knew it to be blood. I simply had no time to see or get myself together. Indeed, I was in a whipping machine. The last thing I recalled, which was highly appreciated, was the falling of the room when someone had mercifully switched out the lights.

Penny was dabbing my face with a cold towel. At first I thought she was also whipping me because every time the towel touched my face, honestly, it would hurt. The room finally stopped its turbulent rocking and Penny's face, which had been grotesquely disfigured, was once more back into a lovely focus. She was looking down at me and I was still on the floor. I moved my arm, attempting to raise myself, but the pain in my back was the only thing that responded, or maybe it was my side. I changed my mind and whispered out the first words I could recall since I had first opened that door.

"Just let me lie here for a while."

Two days later, Penny and I were lying in bed talking; I wasn't up to it.

The telephone interrupted; though I was unaware of who the caller was, I was glad to get off the hook. I uncradled the phone. "Hello! . . . This is a hell of a way to tell me. . . . You and Sarah, huh? . . . What do you mean take them to my mother's house? Just leave them there. I'll be home in the morning."

"Hello! Hello!" Frantically, I juggled the telephone until I noticed Penny curiously staring at me. Those damn pains were giving my stomach hell—like having guts made of gum that were entangled in fish hooks.

"The bitch hung up on me."

"What happened?" Penny asked. "It did not sound as though you two were arguing."

"Wanda," I answered. "She is leaving and taking Sarah with her."

"Leaving?" remarked Penny.

"Yes, dammit, leaving. Can't you understand English?"

Penny's bewildered stare made me morally conscious of what was happening to me. I had to get out of that hotel room—out of Penny's sight. It was obviously apparent that I had to think. Therefore, I had to get by myself—alone.

The morning air was more than just stimulating as I discovered myself sauntering along Fifth Avenue. The tank-like trucks were actively collecting the garbage and the cabbies who had spent the night with their floosies were now busy picking up in order to make up.

I paused to view a female mannequin in a fashionable boutique window; the beautifully designed dress instantly reminded me of Wanda. How could this have happened to me and it had happened so fast? Primarily, I had visualized losing Sarah some day, but the vision of losing Wanda had never entered my mind.

Well, one thing, I had copped another woman and I still had some money. The thought of the money resting safely in a deposit box at the Drexel Bank at Oakwood and Cottage Grove Avenue was a tranquil sedative. However, the men in blue, namely "New York's finest" did not allow the thought to linger. I imagined they had pictured me fleeing with yon fair mannequin under my arms, flowing dress and all. At the sound of their purring motor, as their numbered chariot brushed the curb, I made tracks under their watchful eyes, and continued down the fashionable avenue.

This game of pimping had me all turned around. Was I wrong in allowing Wanda and Sarah to become so tight?

My mind went into retrospect as I visualized Lock schooling me, and I recalled him saying, "When one woman leaves, they all might go." I had wandered aimlessly through the concrete corridors and massive colossals and found myself on the corner of Times Square. The gigantic replica blew smoke from his cigarette, then I walked over to the all-night automat.

I don't really recall what I purchased, but the memory of not eating it is quite vivid. It wouldn't have appeared quite so bad, I thought, if I had explained to Wanda and Sarah of my intended mission. But as things turned out, it now appears as though I was attempting to deceive them. I thought of all those retrospective mistakes as I left the morsels of food on the eating counter.

As I slowly pulled myself together, my present dilemma had helped me to ascertain that the asphalt jungle wasn't so easily conquered. The last and final lesson, I vowed to remember as I hailed one of the orange-hued speeding cabs, was that a thirty-two-year-old man could not possibly know it all. I conceded to the fact that I just had been plain lucky. I slammed the car door and told the driver to take me to the Taft Hotel.

## Chapter Seventeen

PENNY AND I, now airborne, were gazing out into the clouds. We would arrive in Chicago on the present flight from New York in three hours.

Back in Chicago at the apartment, which, due to constant travel throughout the country, had been my first in quite a number of years, I should have been able to draw "old age compensation" from the Hotel Association. As it was, and still is, when allowed by whomever the controlling establishment might happen to be, blacks had extended farther southward in their effort to find better and more spacious homes for themselves, thus occupying the more liveable homes from which the obviously uncertain whites had been commercially conned into fleeing. I leased an apartment far south, but it most assuredly would have been called east. It was two blocks from Lake Shore, which earlier had been called the outer drive.

It was on the top floor of a real estate-owned apartment building, with the largest living room I ever had been able to call my own.

Before I took to the illicit jungle, there only had been my mother and me. Thus, she had no cause for a large place which she could ill afford. My apartment had an L-shaped hall with a bedroom situated up front next to the large living room. A bathroom was across the hall. Around the corner and down the hall was another bedroom and there was another large room which might have been used for a dining room because it was right off the kitchen.

I would have enjoyed furnishing the floors with different hues of carpet in each room to match each individual decor, but I ran into a deal on some carpet and had to buy the whole bulk. It was deep shag, colored beige. The building's two entrances were set back in alcoves, thus all of the living room windows, of which there were eight, were protruding. Over these were spread dark green drapes. All of the furniture was Mediterranean. The couch and lounge chairs were upholstered with a light brown fabric. The light was created by lamps. An oddly-shaped one stood from the floor up. Penny thought it was unique, but I thought it grotesque. Only one large painting of accentuated the room, and near it sat a small plant.

The front bedroom carried furnishings that complied with my king-sized bed, and the other bedroom was fixed up for a queen—not just meaning the bed.

I wasn't very long making Sheila forget about my ungrateful flight. Sheila was not light-skinned, but neither was she dark; unlike Penny who was brown, Sheila was what I would call tan. Yes, her complexion had a reddish background, which left me to conclude that like the white man, the Indian also had sometimes stepped across the line.

Sheila, like me, was in her early thirties. She was married to a doctor and had been for ten long years and it did seem rather strange that there were no kids. Tall, high-cheeked and shapely, Sheila had run down to me what was a unique story of the doctor's accident during his earlier stages of life, bringing on an intricate surgical operation which had left him completely sterile.

I had met her at a prominent and rather dignified affair, while pursuing more classy and affluent prospects. Sheila was most clearly a lady of leisure with no one excepting her dog and the bottle. That is, before I came along to keep her company. I began to introduce Sheila to things and ways of life that, to be sure, she would have never dared sample.

During office hours, the racetracks became frequent meeting places while they were open, and during the winter months, what was said to be card parties turned out to be cocaine parties and games of sex. Meantime, Penny had found it more difficult to relieve the gentlemen in Chicago of their wallets than she had found it to be in New York or California.

I was in the living room, lying on the couch, when Penny appeared from down the long hall.

"Say, Daddy, I saw Flo last night on my way home and guess what? She wants to teach me the drag."

Snatched from some far away thought I responded. "Flo, what Flo?"

"Ah, baby, you know Flo, that big white girl who is with J.C. J.C. is out of New York and they've been in town about a week. Flo said that she fell out with her working partner last week."

Frankly, I had recalled the name, even before Penny had finished. "Yeah, I know now who you are talking about. What was that part about her partner?"

"Her and her partner have broken up. You know. she always works with a black girl. She says a salt and pepper team does real good out on the stroll. That's why she would like to teach me. She claims it will only take a day or two."

Penny really appeared elated.

"I don't know about that drag game, baby. I hear girls sometimes go a while before they catch a real good sucker." I remained phlegmatic.

"Well, I want to try it because this chicken-feed I'm getting around this town is not worth the trouble."

Penny had asked me, but she appeared adamant about her intentions. The added years since I had made that inexcusable mistake with Wanda and Sarah had taught me flexibility. I sensed that Penny's desire for the drag game was strong—so strong, in fact, she probably would venture into the game anyway, with or without me.

"Come to think of it, if you could take off a good sting, I would take Flookie up on that proposition he's been offering me." I was bending with the tide—a pragmatic one.

"Oh, Daddy! You, a tavern owner. I would just love that."

Penny moved to the couch, bent over and kissed me and then reached for the telephone. I heard her speak into the gab-piece. "Hello—yeah, honey, everything is mellow."

I went back to my personal thoughts. I had been serious about the plan which I had just divulged to Penny. Edward Cain, of course everyone knew him as Flookie, had opened the old landmark of the female impersonators. It had formerly been called Joe Hughes', but then Flookie had changed the name to the Surf Club. It was located at 63rd and South Park, later called Martin Luther King Drive. Unknowing to Penny, I had already asked Sheila for the bread to finance my latest venture, and she had answered most favorably.

It was the following day when I asked Sheila to meet me at the Surf Club. I wanted her to see the place which I intended buying into. The bar was long enough to seat thirty or forty people. A platform which held a piano was built behind the bar, and on this there would be live entertainment. There were three booths on the wall opposite the bar; farther back a small kitchen could be found.

I walked Sheila from the front bar, with its multicolored lights, and strolled her to the rear of the lounge. Here, I showed her the large club room and stage. The room would hold three hundred or more people and there was room for a twelve-piece band, also room for persons to dance on the revolving stage.

Sheila was quite pleased with my future venture, and to prove her point, she said, "You meet me here tomorrow. I'll bring you the money."

"What time tomorrow?"

"I've got to go by his office at one o'clock, so you had better make it two. Yes, two o'clock would be fine."

I knew Sheila was speaking of her husband when she had mentioned the office. I had often heard of him from persons in the street; however, Sheila, though our little intimacies would bring about discussions of many things, would never allow his name to enter them.

After telling Flookie I would see him later, possibly tomorrow, we left.

"He," Sheila pointed out, "seems like a very nice person. He should make a real good partner."

"I have been knowing him," I stated, "since we were kids, and he has always been a swell guy." I wasn't just giving Sheila a line of con in order to make sure of the money. The words I had said were true.

Flookie, a tall brown-skinned man with a slightly ruddy and amicable face, had, without doubt, been a nice boy, even when we were in the playground at Forty-Ninth and Calumet. Flookie was living on Forty-Eighth and Prairie, while I, with my mother, was living on Forty-Ninth and Calumet. To be sure, our house faced the playground.

"Oh!" Sheila remarked, showing surprise. "I had no idea that the two of you had been friends that long."

(At this writing, Edward "Flookie" Cain, owns the most fashionable lounge on Chicago's south side.)

It was an established fact, that in the categorical groups, as bartenders are mentioned, Flookie was amongst the best. However, as a businessman, his expertise was nil. Thus brought on the popular assumption that Trickshot's popularity would spark the lounge with new life. This theory, for a while anyway, proved most accurate, and the crowds continued to shuffle in. Wherever the place, though uncommercially situated, if the females are in abundance, there will be crowds. Within the eyes of the ladies at that given time, my prestige had reached the apex, and the stools were constantly topped by a composite of giggling belles.

Preparations were being made for a gala two day "Grand Opening Party." Penny came through the side door and surprised me as I was making out the announcements. The door was used for our beer deliveries.

"Oh, hi, baby. I didn't see you come in. Why the side door?" I gave Penny a "hello" kiss.

"What are you doing?" She continued. "And why didn't you come home last night?"

She ignored my question. I noticed her eyes scan my suitcoat lying on the bar. My shirt collar was open and my necktie was dangling, obviously untied. Before I could look up from the announcements that I was busily addressing, Penny continued. "And just look," she said, leaning over and lightly stroking my overnight beard. "Your face looks a mess. Well?"

"Well, what?" I had abruptly stopped writing and was looking at her.

"Well, don't snap my head off," Penny said surprised.

"Aw, you sort of surprised me when you came through the side door. Plus, I am busy trying to get these announcements out in due time." I turned back to the announcements because I had heard every word, including her request as to my whereabouts last night. I could see her anger was about to become quite prominent.

"Are you so busy," she asked, "that you can't turn around and talk to me?"

Immediately I spun around on the stool. "Now, what is it? Just what is it, baby?"

The latter part of my phrase did nothing to quench Penny's rancor. In fact, it appeared to cause more umbrage.

"Don't baby me." Her jaws were filled with chafe.

I looked at her standing before me. She was equally as tall as me as I sat there on the stool. Penny's hair, as usual, was in a fluff. Her breasts, which were over-sized for her proportions, were beginning to give a slight heave. Her petite frame was accentuated by her hips, which were so tightly grasped by her brown pants.

"I like that brown outfit. Is that the knit suit that I bought you while we were in New York?"

"Yes, this is the brown suit that you bought. You also bought these boots." Penny raised her leg, pulled up the pants and disclosed the light tan boots. "Now will you tell me where you were last night?"

"I was just out snorting cocaine, why?"

Hand on her hip, pocketbook dangling in the crook of her elbow, Penny raised one foot on a stool and tapped the bar with her free hand. "Bring me a drink, Butterball, and make it heavy on the scotch."

Butterball had been busy, supposedly washing and polishing glasses, but I knew her ears were getting charged—actually growing in size.

"Look, baby, if you're angry about something, let's go in the office, or better yet, let's walk back into the clubroom."

"I don't need no office and no damn clubroom to say what's on my mind."

I looked at Butterball, the barmaid, who could hardly

refrain from laughing.

"Now look, Penny, if you want to make an ass of yourself, I can't stop you, but I don't have to stand here and let you browbeat me." I reached to the bar and picked up my coat.

"Just look at you. You've got 'motel' written all over you."

Butterball, who was bending over soaking a glass, dipped her head farther. I knew she was having a good laugh.

"What do you mean motel?"

"I might as well tell you that your rich lady friend was looking for you, too. She called the house this morning asking for you."

I mused to myself. Boy! It's good that I did not say I was with Sheila. That's why Penny was so dogmatic about my whereabouts. I had to play it cool. Penny had pegged me right. I had been off "chipping."

"What did she say? Was it anything important?"

"No, she just left her name, but you know it must have been something, because she doesn't call the house too often, especially early in the morning."

The words were quite true and caused me some inward disturbances, but to Penny, they were easily camouflaged. "I will take care of it, thanks. I've got to get these announcements out. Where are you going?"

Penny gulped her drink down and asked Butterball for another one. I knew then I was not out of the woods—not really.

"I hear you have been getting plenty of action from all the girls, including some of the chippies."

"I run a bar. So what do you expect?"

"Oh, I know, you have got to treat all your customers as if they were 'Miss Ann.' " Penny was straining to emphasize sarcasm.

I had my coat on. "Here, Butterball, put those behind

the bar. I will finish them later. These, I will mail when I leave."

"Don't you remember? I was suppose to go on a trip with Flo this morning."

Shit, I had forgotten. It all came back to me. I had promised Penny I would be home and bring her some expense money. What could I say? That I really disliked the drag game. That it, which is nothing but the old "Pigeon Drop" which had been acted out on TV so many times, which has been shown and explained in magazines so much, is something that I really was not interested in. Imagine someone finding some money in front of you, then offering to share it with you, but first you must put up some money or something of value in order to show good faith. Bah!

"I am sorry, baby. You know how that ole blow keeps me tied up sometimes."

"Oh, yeah, and I also know how those freak bitches keep you tied up, too."

"Come on, woman, let's get out of here." I knew Butterball's sides would get a rest once we had gone.

"My car is out this way, remember?"

I had headed for the front door.

"You go ahead. I will meet you at the house. I'm parked out front."

I dropped the announcements in the mail box and walked into the phone booth at Walgreen's on the corner of 63rd Street. I knew ole Doc was at the office at this hour of day. "Hello."

"Ah, ah, ah, let me speak to Mr. Davis."

"No damn Davis lives here," the gruff voice informed me. "Now, who do you really want to speak to?"

I hung up, then looked at my watch. My God! What is he doing home? What about his patients?

I turned the car from 63rd Street and went along Stoney Island Avenue. What could make old Doc leave the office so soon? And what did he mean by that last remark? Had someone told him about Sheila and me? Oops! Damn, I almost ran over that dog. I have got to pay more attention, but why would Sheila call the house. It is just as Penny had said. Sheila would not call unless it was important.

I turned the car from Stoney Island Avenue and parked in front of the house. Something must be wrong. Excruciatingly, those damn pains suddenly had gone to work. It was now within me, an established fact that though my pains lacked verbal power, their messages up to now had never been wrong. Uneasily, I walked to my fourth floor apartment.

"Your mother," Penny herself, said, "wants you to call her as soon as you get home."

"How long ago?"

"Well, my God! It couldn't have been too long. I just left you, remember?"

I hurriedly dialed my mother's number and it was mildly suspenseful waiting.

My mother finally uncradled the phone. "Hello."

"It's me, Mother. What is it that is so important?"

"Did you know," mother herself said, "that Sheila was held up and robbed this morning?"

"Held up and robbed! Where was she . . . ?"

"She was right there in her home," mother answered, still excited.

"What about her husband? Was he there when it happened?" I asked, still quite puzzled.

"No, he was at his weekly poker game, but wait, here is the bad part. A woman patient of his told him about you and Sheila, and he thinks the hold-up was a fake. He really thinks she has given her jewelry to you."

"Okay, Mother, I'll call you back."

I walked to the window and stared out. My eyes were attracted by two little girls down below, busy at their play.

One of them had a hoola-hoop while the other held a dangling rope. I wondered if they realized how fortunate they really were. Of course not. Their world was problem free. The only crisis the tall one feared was a miscalculation of her gyrating motions, while the other child pondered a much deeper problem—mainly, when would it be her turn?

"What was all the fuss about?" Penny had returned to the room.

"Sheila got robbed."

"What? Where?"

"At her home, so my mother tells me. But I just can't dig this happening."

"Well, it's really not too hard to imagine, if you want to get right down to it."

Quite surprised, I turned. "What do you mean? Why do you say that?"

"Aw, baby, don't act so dense." Penny went on. "Now, everybody knows her husband is rich. I don't really know, because I've only seen her once, but they tell me she's always draped in expensive jewels. That alone is enough."

Penny was right about the jewelry. I, myself, had frequently reminded Sheila about wearing them so casually.

"Yeah, I guess you're right."

"What about her husband? Did they hurt him?"

"Naw, he wasn't home at the time."

"Really?"

I happened to glance downward again. The little thin girl had her Daddy, who undoubtedly was getting home from work, by the hand while possessively clutching her hoola-hoop. Her little friend watched them enter the house, as she still grasped her skipping rope. I wondered if she had ever received her turn at the hoola-hoop.

It was on the first night of the Grand Opening parties. Flowers had been sent, ribbons of varying colors decorated the ceiling and persons saturated the place in noisy abundance. Sheila had, though quite anonymously, sent a lovely batch of assorted roses after notifying me, for reasons known to both of us, that she would not be able to attend.

At that time, in order to remain open past the standard closing hour, which was two o'clock, a lounge was required to serve food. Therefore, the small kitchen, whose stove was disconnected, enabled us to purchase a four o'clock license.

We had booked the services of the popular John Young Trio.

Penny wore a flaming pink gown, with a semi-plunging neckline. Her bulging breasts actually distracted the beauty from the gown. I had presented her with an orchid, which I tried to make match the dress.

It is an outspoken fact when I say practically everybody was there. Butterball's brother, Gilbert Marshman (a referee for the Basketball Association at this writing) was on the scene. Della Reese, who was making her singing debut at one of the larger local theatres, also was there, displaying her toast-brown complexion under the lights.

Billy Eckstein, a long time friend who was appearing at the old Mr. Kelly's before it burned, was handsome on the hilarious scene. If memory serves me right, he was seated talking to Sassy, the lady of song herself, Miss Sarah Vaughn, also a friend, who was entertaining at the old Blue Note downtown.

It was indeed a gala first night affair.

As is with most two or three day affairs, none quite ever total the atmosphere of the first night. However, the second night was commercially satisfying. It was during the second night that I met Ginger, a booster out of St. Louis, Missouri, originally my hometown. A very buxom hefty woman, Ginger, a non-drinker, had come to the party with some friends.

*by Randolph Harris*

After noticing my devoted attention to the obese lady, Penny remarked, "You must be trying to get into the boosting business now."

Penny kept right on walking after dropping this bit of sarcasm, rolling her eyes as she passed.

I had received word through the grapevine that when it came to boosting, Ginger was one of the elite. She, Ginger explained, was thinking of making Chicago her home, and the possibility was very strong that we would get together. And of course, this possibility materialized a month later.

I leased Ginger an apartment on East 68th Street, and she had her own furniture shipped from St. Louis, Missouri.

Meanwhile, the lounge was holding its own, even though I was not. Do not begin to understand the reason why I could not adjust. For causes beyond my control, the lounge became a bore. I would find myself in deep conversations with chippies who could not pay their own rent. And to be most frank, that is what had happened the night when Sheila was busy calling to tell me she had gotten robbed. I had become involved on the bar with a girl from the north side, and ended up as Penny had earlier suspected, in a hide-away motel.

Even so, it was not the basic thing, and quite naturally it added a tingle in the till. However, for me, it became displeasurable to sustain the nightly alcoholic chatter. Actually, it had become more of a job—a word I had learned to disdain.

## Chapter Eighteen

PENNY HAD GONE on the road playing the drag game. I spent my time between the place and counting Ginger's pieces. And, of course, there was Sheila occasionally.

It occurred during one of those distasteful rainy nights. The few customers who sauntered in were hurling spasmodic rhetoric at the weather. John, the bartender, coincidentally, employed at Flookie's at this writing, was working that particular night.

"Telephone, Trickshot," John passed the bar phone to me. It was Partner, an associate of many years, and he owned a bar near Sheila's home.

"Good Lord!"

John looked at me. I cannot imagine the materialization of the impossible; however, John claimed I turned pale.

Sheila was dead!

Those little guys inside my stomach began their sport of boxing. I put the phone down on the bar and I recall John asking me, "What's wrong, man?" though, again, he claimed he was forced to ask me twice.

"They've just found Sheila dead." I remember stating, and at once I thought of her husband.

The calls began to come in fast. First it was my mother, and Ginger did not give the phone a second to rest; the following call, which I later credited to a police friend of mine, was warning me to make a fast exit, and to be sure, this I did.

After stashing at the home of one of my more promiscuous female customers, quite naturally I called Ginger.

"Hi, Gin, what's the news?"

"As you can imagine, the police have been here, and guess what? They had an FBI man with them."

"How did you know he was from the FBI?"

"Why he showed me the folder. You know, the kind that looks like a wallet and it identifies them. But that isn't all. He also showed me a picture of you and Sheila. She was a nice-looking woman, wasn't she?"

"Go on, what else did they say?"

"Well, the other police did most of the talking. They wanted to know where you were, what time did you leave the house, how long had you and I been together, did I know Sheila and finally, of all things, those bastards asked me if I had any idea who might have killed her? Isn't that a bitch?"

"How did they say she died?"

Partner had already told me over the phone that Sheila had been found in her home, shot in the head. But I had earlier learned how things become drastically distorted as it travels the grapevines.

"Well, all I learned from their conversation was, the lady was found at home shot through the head."

"I am going to lay dead until tomorrow morning, and then I'll contact my lawyer."

"Yeah, Daddy, I think you had better stay off the scene until you get straight. They don't know if you offed the broad or not, but I can tell they want you real bad. Oh, yeah, I remember that FBI man said to one of the other police, 'We have been checking him out. We may not get him for this, but we are definitely going to nail him.'"

"Dammit, woman, you almost forgot to tell me that? Don't you realize how serious this is? Dammit, bitch, this is murder they're talking about. What did this Fed look like?"

"Now, let me see. He was tall, about six feet, maybe a little taller, and his hair was kinda red, not too red, but still it was red. Oh, yeah, he had a lot of freckles. Yeah, he even had them on his hands. I noticed them when he showed me the picture of you and Sheila. He was neatly and conservatively dressed with one of those light canvas-colored coats on. It wasn't a trenchcoat, just an ordinary raincoat."

If nothing else Ginger had said was correct, the heavy patter of the rain against the window made me believe the latter was.

"Okay, Gin, tell my mother not to worry."

I hung up the phone, resting atop the free-lance young lady's bed. It was quite frustrating indeed, as I blew cigarette smoke toward the brightly painted ceiling. To be a chippie, the little dark-skinned broad must have had some secret sponsors somewhere. The apartment was laid out in a decor of gold and brown. The brown ten foot long dresser was made of mahogany and the headpost of the king-sized bed looked the same. The carpet was of golden shag with a couple of brown throw rugs placed discriminately about. The heavy embroidered beige drapes were well-hung, and the nude portrait on the wall was discreet.

Indeed, the scene could have been most fitting for a time of sex. Recalling the suggestive attempts the dark wonder made, for me it just was not the time or place. However, I felt rather safe, realizing no one would think to look for me at her apartment.

The following morning, I was joined by my attorney and together we traveled to Wabash Avenue station, located then at 48th and Wabash Avenue. We were told to wait in a nearby office which was practically bare, except for a desk and two round-backed wooden chairs. One chair was behind the desk and the other was on the side.

As soon as we entered the office, we were joined by two plainclothes detectives, one of whom was tall, husky, sharp-faced and white. The other was tall, not too heavy, with a friendly face, a mustache and he was black. I was told to take the seat beside the desk, and the white detective sat in the one behind the desk, while my lawyer and the black detective stood.

I answered two or three standard questions and then quite abruptly, my lawyer interjected, "Don't answer that."

I was asked another question, and my lawyer made another interruption, only the phrasing was the same. "Don't answer that."

It was really amazing. How differently they, the police, were in the presence of an attorney. Had I walked in alone or they had picked me up, my cranium would have resembled a bunch of grapes from the knots the detectives would have administered.

My attorney, though the two of us had pondered it earlier, presented them a reasonable question. "And just how much does the deceased's husband figure in this?"

The seasoned officer looked up from the desk and sternly remarked, "The doctor was busy in his office at the alleged time of death. The immediate patient and three more who were in his office waiting substantiated his alibi."

Well, this answered my biggest question and solved my

toughest puzzle. I was, as everyone else, at a loss for an explanation to Sheila's murder. Oh, but definitely, suicide had been ruled out.

As far as the police, themselves, were concerned, no one had indicated that I had committed the crime. It was merely common knowledge that Sheila and I were friends. Considering the presence of my attorney's professional wit, the detectives found no cause to waste their valued time.

I was excused without the usual cliche—"Don't leave town."

When my attorney and I departed, he handed me a paper which he declared to be some type of writ. "If they or any other policeman picks you up, present them with this."

I graciously took the legal document. "Thanks, counsellor. I will stay in touch."

I thought over my present situation and was forced to conclude that it was far from good. By me not frequenting the lounge the same way I had in the past, I didn't need an intelligent person to tell that I was putting money in and not getting any out. And, anyway, this tavern business was not my thing. I was used to being on the go.

Primarily, persons would have to catch me by chance, but with the lounge, everyone knew where to find me, and now the police had been to one of my apartments. Yes, that would be the first thing. I had to move.

Being in the limelight, which is where the lounge had placed me, was simply and profoundly too much exposure. Oh, it had been great when I was young. But just recently, I had noticed some freshly sprouted gray hairs and I would not contribute them all to my clandestine way of living. It would be inane not to consider age.

When I left my lawyer at the police station, I drove down Fifty-Fifth Street and reminisced about the past. The car cruised past some of my old haunts. The pool hall years ago had been moved farther up the street. The 315 Club was still there and so were some of the old crowd standing out in front of it. I had no time or thought for any of the gang at this particular time. I drove on and the car spilled into Washington Park.

How fast the years had flown. Here I was a man in my thirties, and I have never thought of raising children. And my mother, what did she think of me? And, indeed, it was a fact, as I was obviously getting old, my mother had apparently gotten older. I recalled a day in the past when I had sincerely promised that I would come by and see her. How could I, in good faith, predict that I would be in Lawton, Oklahoma, that following morning?

What if my mother suddenly had become ill? There were no brothers or sisters to inform me, and in fact, if there had been, none would have known where to find me. I had selfishly sought out a life of ease and pseudo-comfort. In retrospect, my accomplishments in life were completely nil.

My car drove out of Washington Park and poured into Cottage Grove Drive. I was at once engulfed with a feeling of guilt, brought on by years of selfish scheming. I made a decision that would change my entire life. I would cease to travel. I would find some sort of business and attempt to accomplish something constructive. Policy, race horses, the numbers game, all of these illicit operations which were looked down upon by the white establishment were gazed upon by the persons in the ghetto as amazing signs of success.

In the years gone by, I had adjusted myself to the taste of affluent living. Therefore, my choice of venture would be expected to bring me fabulous returns.

When I reached the apartment, I was still deep in thought.

"What," Ginger asked, "did they do to you down at that jail? Ever since you have been home, you appear to be in a trance. Why, you have barely touched your food."

"Oh, I have been seriously thinking of getting rid of my interest in the lounge."

"Well, I am glad of that, anyway. You have never gotten anything out of it but a lot of unwanted notoriety. Who are you going to try and sell it to?"

"Aw, I don't know. I'll ask around and see who has got some bread to invest. If not, I will give it away."

"Give it away. Are you—"

"Dammit, that's better than continuing to put money in it and getting nothing out, isn't it?"

"Yeah, I guess you're right. But just to give it away. Oh well."

Ginger shrugged her hefty shoulders and left me alone with my food. Moments later, I heard her dialing the phone. I knew when she was through gossiping, the news would be spread over the entire ghetto.

I hit upon, what I imagined, was a unique idea. I would find a nice storefront in a busy locale and open up a cleaners. It would be an ideal place to sell the hot clothes that Ginger was stealing.

Later that night, Buddy Walls called the house.

"What d'you know, man?"

"Hi, Buddy, what's new?"

"I just left your place and Flookie tells me that you want out."

"Yeah, man, the joint is interfering with my other business. Plus I am getting no bread out of it."

"Well, why not give me a shot at it, man? Of course you know, my bread is funny."

Well, there it was. Buddy had asked me to give the place to him. I knew he did not have any money, but we were very close friends. Neither one of us was doing too good, but I was doing better.

"I will talk to Flookie and hear what he has to say about

it."

"That will be crazy, Trick. If I cop a decent broad, I'll take care of you."

Buddy knew that a place of business is always good copping territory. For obvious reasons, women always go after the bosses.

"If things work out all right, I will talk to Dan Burley and maybe he will give you a boost," I said.

Buddy thanked me again and then hung up.

The late Dan Burley had a weekly column in *Jet* magazine and had given me a tremendous write-up when I bought into the lounge. The black peoples' pocket-sized magazine has a fantastic national circulation, and as far as I know, it might be international. On second thought I am sure of it.

It was a few weeks later when I turned my keys to the lounge over to Buddy. I was free of the white elephant. During this time I had found a little two-level home farther out south. It was ideal in price and size. I moved Penny's things which she had left and began to set up the first actual home I had ever owned. The house had three bedrooms upstairs, living room and kitchen downstairs with a comfortable-sized basement and a very large yard. And, of course, it was red brick.

The investigation into Sheila's murder went on, and as it often had been in the past, it was listed as just another black person killed in the virulence of the ghetto by a person or persons unknown.

I was not long finding a spot in which to open my new cleaners. The owners of the Mansfield Hotel had a vacancy next door to the hotel at Sixty-Fourth and Cottage Grove. I rented this place and called it the Mansfield Cleaners.

I have always been a believer that beauty attracts crowds. Therefore, my presence would be quite scarce. I needed an attractive manager. Thus I hired the services of the beautiful Miss Sonji Roi, though neither of us realized at the time that in only a few years, she would become Miss Sonji Clay, wife of the colorful heavyweight champion Cassius Clay.

It was the beginning of the blatant sign era. A five-cent hamburger stand might display a hundred thousand dollar electrical bulb sign. It was just the fashionable way to advertise. For the cleaners, I purchased a lurid sign with the words "Mansfield Cleaners" in running lights. This was done on an installment plan. As time fled, the cleaners began to show a profit—not a large one, just enough to pay the utility bills. I paid Sonji's salary out of my own pocket.

However, without the knowledge of Miss Roi, the hot pieces in the back room were selling at a steady pace.

Penny had made one trip home and told me how much she liked the new house and then she had hit the road again. It had been two months and she had not taken off a sting. As if it was not bad enough, Ginger came down with an illness and had to be hospitalized. I needed money in the worst way. And there was no one I could think of at the time but my boyhood chum Ted.

But, of course, I remembered the last time I had needed a favor most desperately and was lucidly refused. But since then, I had befriended him to the sum of a thousand dollars, and as one would easily guess, I was paid like a bitch dog having her monthly droppings. However, this did not alter the undeniable fact that I was going to ask Ted for the favor which I presently needed.

I can recall the night as though it was now. I had called the Provident Hospital at 51st and South Park and promised Ginger I would be there that night. Night visiting hours began at eight o'clock p.m.

Rain was coming down so thick that fish could have used the streets for a playground. I drove along Sixty-First Street and the neon signs glowed mystically through the down-pouring rain. I glanced at the Archway Lounge, then owned by the late Harold "Killer" Johnson, once manager for Sugar Ray Robinson, and saw Chink's car parked out front.

My car slushed across Calumet Avenue and turned at Prairie. Lightning flashed its jagged teeth and illuminated the turbulent night as the car splashed its way north.

I viewed the two men in blue as they slouched in the front seat of the luridly numbered parked car, and my car continued. I braked the car in front of Ted's place, gazed out at the downpour that now resembled a monsoon and made a dash that assured me of getting drenched.

Only two of the leathery-trimmed stools were topped by local beer tasters. The booths along the wall were empty and Ted, with one foot cocked up on a beer crate, was staring through the window into the watery night.

As tall as me and much lighter, Ted turned grinning. "I didn't think you could run that fast."

"I didn't either." I was shaking the rain from my process. "Put a double shot up here," I said, pointing, as I mounted a stool.

"How is Ginger?" Ted walked down along the bar as he looked back.

"I think she will be all right. That's what I want to talk about."

Ted placed the shot glass and poured it full, spilling a similar amount into my glass.

"I'm on my way to the hospital now. I figured I could stop by and get a couple of bills. I have a few pieces that I could possibly down, but this damn rain!" The staccato patter echoed my every word.

"You should have called. You would have saved yourself a trip. I have a little bread, but I intend to gamble after I lock up this morning."

Reluctantly, I glanced out at the downpour and avoiding

Ted's eyes, I lifted the drink, paid my bar bill and walked out into the blowing rain.

I cranked the car with the twist of my key. I would no doubt find one of the fences home on a night like this. As the car plowed through the slippery streets, I began to think of Ted, and again I became nostalgic.

I recalled Mr. George Gordon Byron's quotation, "Friendship is love without his wings."

My car continued north into the ominous night.

Need I say that it was shock, rather than relief, when the next day I learned Ted had blown two thousand in the crap game.

Ginger had been out of the hospital three weeks and was working with gusto. How was I to know that this velocity of effort was the beginning of a plan that was designed to put me out of business. A plan, no doubt, created in Ginger's mind during the lulling hours of her hospital confinement.

Sugar Ray Robinson was exercising his skill against a known fighter in Detroit. And, it was after the flamboyant Mr. Robinson had recently returned to boxing from the retirement of his short-lived stage career.

On my arrival in Detroit, I associated myself with the standard group of Motor City homeguards: Babe, Phil, Dean, J.J., Buddy, King David, Rabbit, Jimmie Trice and a few others whom I have no intention of slighting.

After Sugar Ray's hand was raised in victory, the crowds scattered to more discreet places to continue other expected fun and games.

Two days later, badly in need of a good sweating out, I was on my way home. I had been calling Ginger, but had received no answer. I called my mother who would surely have known if Ginger had gotten busted, and the answer was nil. No word had come from Ginger.

As expected, the pains were on time. My guts felt like the confines for termites who were trying to gnaw their way to freedom. For me, the concreted lanes became speedways, while frustration shrouded me. What could be wrong? Had Ginger gone on a boosting trip? But why a trip as soon as I leave town? No, something was definitely amiss.

My car sliced down the expressway exit and came out on Stony Island Avenue. I turned into South Chicago Avenue and pointed east and home. The most explosive thought, which I repeatedly pushed from my mind, was that Ginger had fled! The vision of my old adviser Lock materialized in my cogitation. "When one of them leaves, they all might go."

First Sheila, though to be most clear, it was not her personal desire. Then I was forced to reconsider, possibly, about Penny. I leaped from the car and my focus was shooting upward as I dashed into the vestibule. My hands fumbled as I selected the correct key. The four flights of stairs were no barrier, as I gazed at the crack between the door and the floor, hoping to see a tinge of light.

I unlocked the door and the void of blackness answered my most feared reasoning. The vacuum of the structure was immediately present as I felt for and switched on the hall light. My vision fell to the slim red cord. It traveled halfway the length of the room and there at its end was the bright red telephone. Nothing else was in the room. Even the drapes were gone. I sauntered from room to room and they all were similar—empty!

There was no time to ponder whether or not through the years had this ever happened before. To me, it was an undeniable fact that it was happening now. Finding no reason why I should remain at the apartment, I departed.

On the way to the house, the music from the car radio made nostalgia come easy. I was forced to smile at my own stupidity. From the first day she had left the hospital I had noticed the extra surge in her professional efforts. To be sure, she was getting her bankroll together then.

Ordinarily, when I prepared to take a trip, Ginger's bottom lip would hang like a blacksmith's apron. And this time she had been very casual, which should have warned anybody. Thus, at this late stage in the game, I quite unexpectedly had learned another lesson.

The next few days found me in the bars and frequenting the social affairs. That is, the ones I could afford, and making the gambling joints and the after hours places my hangouts.

## Chapter Nineteen

AS ONE COULD EASILY GUESS, there was the usual crop of young, inexperienced beauties, but their slights were for some younger and more dashing males than I. The older broads purred and asked where did I keep my fountain of youth, but like their words, their purse strings were carried tightly.

Indeed, prey in this asphalt jungle in which I had roamed for many years was not too accessible. Some associates had opened a gambling establishment in one of the southside hotels.

I was invited into the combine with the understanding that my name, though of fading prominence in the eyes of the young, yet carried with it the respect of seniority. When the hotel lounge would close at four o'clock in the morning, our upstairs gambling and drinking establishment would often rock around the clock.

During one of the busy nights, I had a mild rumble with a customer, one I had not seen around the hotel too often.

A week or so later, I received a wire through the grapevine that I should be careful. The word was out that the fellow with whom I had the trouble was around making drastic threats. During the ensuing weeks, I had become lax concerning the past warning.

I was at a lawn party given by another associate, this time a lady. I arrived at the party about two a.m. The early closing taverns were just unloading and persons aplenty trodded over the grassy area. As I walked into the yard, there were Oriental paper lanterns strung on wires above the yard. A scattering of tables were choicely placed. A round-shaped loudspeaker rested atop the back porch and spat forth melodious tunes as the crowd circulated.

Some were rhythmically popping their fingers while others were spaced off in clandestine groups. And a seven foot wooden fence presented the scene as being semi-private.

A friend, Lionel, tall, thin and light-complexioned, was bending over a table talking to a seated few. I smiled, waved and nodded to several gesturing greeters, then casually I made my way over to Lionel. I touched his elbow and received his immediate attention.

"Trickshot! My man!" Lionel was extending his palm. "Did you just show on the scene?"

"What do you know, dude?" I presented a sincere smile. "Yeah, I just showed."

As if on cue, Lionel's face modulated into a frown. His eyes darted towards the rear steps of the building. Then he abruptly pulled me to the side.

"Say, man, you know that dude you had the rumble with is upstairs." Lionel raised his eyes.

"What du—" Instantly the impact of his words had settled in my midriff. Yes, those telepathic predictors within my stomach were giving out with their usual message: *Something was amiss.*

"Yeah, I know who you're talking about. Where is he?"

"He's upstairs snorting cocaine with Amy. She's the broad who's giving this lawn party."

"I know. She mailed my invitation to the cleaners the other day."

My hands were damp. I could not run. That would only be delaying the inevitable. What could I do?

Nervously, I asked Lionel, "Have you got your rod on you?"

"Naw, the way that new Task Force has been stopping dudes, I figured it was best to leave it home."

"This is a bitch," I muttered as someone could be heard coming down the wooden stairs.

Lionel stopped talking. His head was turned inquisitively toward the creaking steps. If it was Mark, what would I do? Yes, that was the braggard's name who had indirectly threatened me. What if he had a rod? What would stop him from openly pistol-whipping me? My legs wanted to remove me from the scene, but the thought of humiliation made me steadfast.

The footsteps became prominent at the rounding of the stairs. It was the janitor. He was carrying a container filled with ice cubes.

"Say Lionel, you live closer than I do. Why not slide home and bring me your rod? I'm up-tight, man. I need it bad!"

"Yeah, that's crazy, but what will you do in the meantime, if Mark decides to come downstairs?"

Lionel half turned. He was waiting for an answer. I looked at the basement door and noticed it was cracked.

"I will be down there."

Lionel looked at the door and nodded, then swiftly departed.

I eased toward the basement door and glanced back at the yard full of funsters. I quickly pushed the door open and stepped inside. A dusty yellowish bulb hung from the socket of an electric cord. Someone was coming down the steps into the basement. I knew Lionel could not have returned so soon, and I doubted if Mark knew so readily that I was even at the party.

"Hi, Trickshot, I thought I saw you come down here."

With a sigh of relief, I said, "Hi, Helen, long time no see."

"What are you doing down here by yourself?" she asked.

"Aw, I just came down here to sneak myself a blow," I lied.

"Gee, your game must not be up to par. Sneaking away to keep from giving up a little ole snort of cocaine!"

I fished around in my pocket and grasped one of the few capsules. "See, I only had one cap left, and you know that's nothing to pull out in a crowd."

There was an old washing machine that looked as if it had seen its last days. Helen was leaning back on it with her hefty brown legs protruding. Her breasts were slanting upward as she held out her hand.

"Put some of that cocaine right here. That's it. Right on my thumbnail."

I gingerly spilled the powdery dust on Helen's thumb, but my eyes were constantly on the door.

"Why," Helen asked, "are you so damned nervous? You keep watching the door!"

"Oh, I am expecting a friend to bring me some more cocaine and I told him to meet me down here," I lied again.

"Trickshot, I know I don't make as much money as some of your girls, but that doesn't mean we should not have a little fun."

Helen had stepped closer to me now, and her hand was busy at my crotch. I backed up slightly.

"Look, Helen, there is no doubt you would be a load of fun. In fact, I have heard you are boss. But baby, I just can't freak off with every broad that wants me to. It would just be against my code."

I turned my head towards the door and unconsciously I must have looked at my watch.

"What in the hell is wrong with you? Every time I look up you are constantly watching that door."

"I was wondering what's taking my friend so long." To be sure, I was not lying this time.

"Come on, Trickshot, let me sprinkle a bit of this cocaine on the head of your prick. I promise to make you feel good."

"Aw, baby—" I heard footsteps. I pushed Helen away from me and made a step towards the door. The door was opening. It was Lionel!

"Damn! I was wondering what happened to you!"

I extended my hand and Lionel reached in his belt and from under his sportcoat he handed me the snub-nose .38.

"I'm getting out of here!" Helen pushed Lionel aside and disappeared through the door.

With a new feeling of self-preservation, I returned to the yard with Lionel.

We entered the yard and began to mix with the rest of the boisterous revelers. Though I must admit that my mind and my eyes were on those dreaded stairs. Whenever the door of the apartment would open, a sense of awareness would take hold on me. And finally, I could stand the waiting no longer.

I found a vacant chair and arranged its position to face the stairs, then with the pistol in my side coat pocket in readiness, I sat down.

Lionel was socializing but I knew his eyes were on those stairs too. For a while, I thought my vigil was in vain. Maybe Mark had gone out of the front entrance. I was about to call Lionel and ask him to go upstairs and check.

The door of the second floor apartment opened and through it appeared a stocky man of dark complexion, his face slightly rounded. He was dressed in a brown suit and wore a brown hat.

I was alerted and immediately recalled the night we had confronted each other. It was the crap table of our gambling establishment in that southside hotel. I looked for Lionel and spotted him talking to two fellows over by the wooden fence. His head abruptly twisted in my direction, and I knew he had seen my alleged adversary.

Mark was talking to a girl as they both descended the steps. I shifted my chair and leaned back in it. I wanted the pistol in my side coat pocket to be aimed up, without my removing it.

Mark and his lady companion reached yard level and cast hello greetings to some of the revelers. As memory rushes to my aid, I am sure that Mark also spoke to my friend Lionel. However, it was impossible with all the yard lights aglow, for this man Mark not to have seen me.

But he and his lady companion walked right past me without so much as a nod. I relaxed my chair to its upright position, then settled back in it, immensely relieved.

Good Lord! That's when I heard it. *Bang, bang, bang, bang, bang!* Five shots rang out. A sort of confused panic had blanketed the crowd. The people could tell that the shots came from the other side of the fence. Through the gate of the wooden fence Mark's lady companion appeared. She was holding a brown felt hat. I recognized it as the hat Mark had had on his head just a moment ago. The lady appeared to be in a daze, or rather, I should say shock! Then she finally said, "Someone just shot Mark. I think he is dead!"

The news of Mark's death caused more panic than the shots. Persons were scrambling for the exit gate to avoid questioning by the expected men in blue. I met Lionel halfway.

"All right, man. What are you going to do?" I asked.

"There is nothing for me to do except go home."

"Here, take your rod, I won't need it since I am also going home."

A lady said, "Oops! Pardon me," after which Lionel said, "Come on, man, let's quit this scene. Everybody is leaving."

The crowd was trying to enlarge the gate.

"Okay. Thanks for the use of the piece. I will talk to you later on."

Dogs were barking and people from the surrounding buildings were peering out of windows. Some were giving varying accounts of the tragic incident, while others were giving hand-raising oaths that they had not seen a thing. Still others were rushing around in the alley to view Mark's last remains. I was one of the horror viewers who had to quench my thirst with sight of the unknown.

Mark's body, all bloody and punctured, was in the front seat of the late model car. His head was lying back as though he was looking at the ceiling. It appeared that vicious vampires had snatched splotches of meat from parts of his neck and the blood-splattered windows could have been caused from the two large holes in what was once a head. Oh, yes, he was dead.

I had seen enough, including the police car which was coming from the opposite mouth of the alley. I split.

I had been home only shortly when my mother called me on the phone.

"The police have been here looking for you," mother excitedly stated.

"What," I asked, "did they say?"

"They wanted to talk to you about a murder. What is it all about? What have you done?"

"Oh, I have done nothing, but I was at a party where a fellow was killed."

"They wanted your address, but I told them I didn't have it. I think they knew I was lying."

"Okay, thanks, Mother. Don't worry. I will be all right. Call you later."

I cradled the telephone. I knew it would not be too long before the police discovered my address. There was really no reason to run or hide, even though I detested the inevitable inconvenience.

I threw myself across the bed. I had stripped down to my shorts and sleep came almost immediately. The door chimes aroused me from my slumber in what only seemed like five minutes later.

At first I started for the door, and then I stopped. I wiped my eyes. I was cleaning the sleep from within me. I thought of the remaining capsules of cocaine that rested on my dresser. I wheeled to the dresser and retrieved the shining pellets of gelatin and in two more huge steps I had flushed them down the commode.

The chimes sang out again and I tip-toed to the window. Yep, the police were out there. The black unmarked car with its long antenna sat silently obvious. A large conservatively dressed white man was walking over and peering inside my car. He opened the car door and I could see his hands from my perch. They were coming out of my car's glove compartment, gripping what looked like old bills. The man stepped from the car. Another man, big husky and black, walked from my building's entrance and stood talking to the white man who was indicating the papers. The big black man stepped into the police car and drove off. The white man, who still held the papers, walked back towards my vestibule.

Confusion had overwhelmed me and I knew my telephone was about to ring. From my car compartment they had discovered an old phone bill with my number on it. I was unable to peer around the corner and downstairs. But, I would have laid astronomical odds that overeager policeman were also in the rear.

*Ring-g-g-g-g.* The black cop must have used the phone booth at the corner filling station. I would not answer the phone as I sat on the couch and listened to it vibrate. Whenever it stopped ringing, I intended to call my lawyer. Finally, the sound of the telephone ceased. I uncradled it, which might have been a mistake, in case the officer decided to call back.

I dialed my lawyer's number, but I never completed the call. *Bang!* I was correct in my betting: the back door was being forced.

"Open up in there, police officers!"

"Okay, all right, I—"

Before I could finish the words, the back door flew open.

"All right! Lie down on the floor and stretch your arms straight out."

"I'm up front sitting on the couch with no clothes on," I yelled down the hallway to them. I did not care to be shot, knowing I had committed no crime.

"Who's here with you? Watch it, Bob. Careful of that door."

I heard them moving stealthily along the hallway while cautioning and talking to each other. Three men, two white and one black, had come up the hall after smashing in the rear door.

When they came even with the front door, the shortest of the white officers reached out and opened it. Standing there was the same white man I had seen enter my car. All of the officers' guns were drawn. The tallest of the white policemen was carrying a sawed-off shotgun. (In those days, it was called a riot gun.) I was immediately handcuffed, right there on the couch.

In a short period of time, the black detective entered the house, his pistol drawn.

Methodically they began to search the house. They were crude in their handling, but in all fairness, they were neat. My personal belongings were not scattered around. Eventually, the search was completed and it was then that I was told to dress.

Still firmly shackled I maneuvered the task of donning my clothes. It was shortly before we headed for the door and the stairs that the large black detective who had rang my gab piece said, "Trickshot, quite a few of your neighbors have become curious. I'm going to release you from the handcuffs. However, if you attempt to run, I'm going to kill you."

While expressing my thanks, I could not help wondering—a skepticism acquired in the ghetto—if he was releasing me in the hope that I would actually run.

The black unmarked police car headed east, then turned south. It was passing the old Harper Street police station which was near my house. I wondered why they did not take me there. Then I recalled hearing somewhere that the police usually return the suspect to the district where the murder was committed. The scene of the murder was in the vicinity of 47th Street and Lawrence. The policeman who made the telephone call was driving and the policeman who took the phone bill from my car glove compartment was sitting beside him. I was in the back seat as the black car sped through Jackson and then Washington Parks. The car came out at 51st and South Parkway, later called King Drive. When it turned west at 48th, I recollected that it was not too long ago when I was at this same Wabash Avenue police station with my lawyer, and both times it was because of murder.

I was not really overwrought. I could sense from the

detective's reactions that I was merely a suspect. However, I could not help recalling my friend Strong Jones, after visualizing the electric chair during months of illegal confinement, he was released and told, "It was all a mistake!"

I was allowed to call my lawyer and after an overnight stay which was not too adventurous, I was released on some kind of bond. It was about two weeks later at the inquest that an old lady, who surely had lived man's promised amount of years, approached me in the hall of the building which also houses the Chicago Mortuary and said, "I had to step out here and look at you. They say you might have killed my son."

There was no hate in her eyes, and her frail voice did not carry ominousness. I faced the fragile and kind-looking old lady and uttered, "I have seen your son only twice, and at neither time did I take his life, which I am sure the inquest will reveal."

She peered at me for a few seconds, then turned and walked back into the room where the inquest was to be held.

I would like to think at those given seconds, that she believed me. After the majority of the witnesses had been questioned before the Coroner's Jury, the officer in charge was asked why I, Trickshot, was picked up concerning the murder, to which the police officer answered, "When we arrived at the scene of the murder, we asked the hostess, Mrs. Amy Hall, was there anyone at the party she figured capable of such? And that's when we received the suspect's name. Shortly thereafter, we received information that there had been a misunderstanding between the suspect and the deceased. We had no other alternative than to pick him up."

The lady companion, who was with Mark when he was gunned to death, took the stand and described how a gun appeared through each of the rolled down front windows of the car and began firing. One of the guns was fired across her person.

She was under oath when she also declared that she did not see who the assailants were. Before the inquest was over, the police officer produced items which he said was taken from the deceased's home. Some of the items had been identified by victims of various robberies. Whereby the jury rendered a verdict of "killed by persons unknown."

I was released from the bond and as I left the inquest room Mrs. Amy Hall confronted me in the spacious hallway and stated, "Trickshot, I don't know why that detective should say that I gave him your name. I want you to know that he lied."

"Aw, it's all over now," I answered. "It really doesn't matter."

As I turned and walked away from Mrs. Hall, she had no idea how serious I intended my words to be. I meant that it was all over for me and the fast life. I mused as I met persons leaving the County Hospital which was just around the corner. I visualized myself coming astoundingly close to senseless murder, when I was challenged by Black Willie, and how could I delete the vision of me lying flat on my back while a youth was poised over me on a California sidewalk, holding a knife. And the thrashing I had taken in a New York hotel, would have made a world champion retire from the ring of boxing. And of course, Fat Daddy and his subordinates could have finished me long ago in a garage on Chicago's south side.

To be most sure, it really did not matter anymore. I had decided to free myself from all of my underworld vices. Through years of traveling, and associating with people who were among the affluent, I had acquired the taste of living which an ordinary job would not allow me to afford. I had never had a job. Therefore, in what legitimate way was I equipped to maintain myself?

That following weekend, the *Chicago Defender*, Chicago's leading black newspaper, carried the following headlines:

## MURDER MARS LAWN PARTY

The paper went on to explain the details which had become dead news during the week before the newspaper had come out.

How was I to know that fate had decreed a test for me, that would make those in the past seem like fairytales?

## Chapter Twenty

LENNY, ONE OF OUR GROUP who had been chosen to manage the gambling room in the hotel, called me on the phone. "Say, Trick, ole Sarge just talked to me downstairs in the lounge. He thinks we should close the place because of some heat from downtown."

"Well," I answered, "what do the other fellows think about it?"

"I talked to the Lieutenant and he said, 'Fuck 'em,'" Lenny said.

I thought to myself for a moment and realized my financial condition. Ginger was gone, and I didn't know if Penny was going to return. My conclusion was obvious. "Well look, Lenny, you know we have to go along with the Lieutenant; he's a big man in the district."

"You're damn right, he is. After him, there's only the

Captain, the big man himself," Lenny answered.

"O.K., tell the rest of the guys I'm for staying open." I hung up.

The gambling joint was my only means of income at that moment. The phone rang again. This time it was Ted. He was calling to thank me for introducing him to a rather wealthy young lady, who had just moved to the city. It was rumored that her father had passed away and left his entire fortune to her, which consisted of a dress manufacturing establishment. After we had finished talking, I hung up and pondered the question myself. (Why hadn't I copped for myself instead of cutting the broad into Ted?) The reason was really obvious. She just didn't go for me.

One night the phone rang. "Say, Trick, this is Shortie. They're raiding the joint, man!"

I knew from experience there was nothing I could do but call the bondsman and get some cigarettes. When a joint like ours pulls a raid with Lenny and one of the hotel owners present, there's nothing anyone could do.

It was only a few hours before everyone was out on the street again. Lenny came by the house to run things down to me. It seems some people downtown were angry because some were getting money, and others were not.

Lenny wanted to find another spot and open up right away! I was against it because I was tired of the joints anyway.

That was when I began to notice a few grey hairs. I had always had a few strands. But now, my head was getting grey in patches. I was still wearing a process, and noticed how it was thinning. In other words, I wasn't just tired of the joints. I was getting old, and I was just tired. Period!

There are times when one thing goes bad; they all go bad. This seemed to be one of those times. I wired Penny some more money, which had become a habit! I hadn't heard from Ginger since the day she fled so unexpectedly.

The little white girl I had copped lasted only a couple of weeks. It wasn't long before I looked up and I had no money, no girls, no nothing, plus I had begun to feel older. I knew I had to get something legitimate going, and do it in a hurry.

In a few days Tony Whitey from the north side called. We made a date to meet later that night. It seems he was having his troubles too. He had done a stretch in the government penitentiary for trafficking in narcotics. I didn't know about this because I had not been in touch with him for years.

During that era most of the whiteys had all the narcotic connections. If a black wanted to deal, he had to go through some whitey. For quite a number of years, the only one who would go to the joint was the black man. However, in later years all of that changed. The authorities began to bust the men behind the scenes. Then another problem popped up. Some of the blacks began to talk. This is what happened in Tony's case.

I asked him why didn't they get rid of the stoolies as they did in the old days. He explained how the government agents witness the dope transactions themselves, therefore they are reliable witnesses who also could take the stand. The dealers, in order to beat the rap, would have to kill the pigeon and the agent. None of them were looking for that kind of trouble.

I asked Tony what was his interest in me, knowing I wasn't going to deal with any narcotics?

"Well, Trickshot, I'll put it to you straight."

"Please do!" I cut in.

"I've been out of the joint almost a year. All of the guys over north have gone into other fields. Some have gotten into legit things, others have gotten into the juice business," he said.

"Well, can't you get a stake from some of the outfit, and

get into something?" I asked. "I've always understood you people take care of each other."

"Hell, yeah! I could get a thousand guys to bankroll me, but I'd still be working on a percentage," he said.

"Well, what can I do, Tony?" I asked again.

"Well, Trickshot, you're pretty clean when it comes to a record. You've never done a stretch and neither have the guys you associate with."

"So what?" I asked, waiting for him to lower the boom.

"I've got to make a couple of hundred gee's, and I can make it if I get a distributor out south," he said.

Well, there it was. Tony wanted me to find a distributor for his poison. I didn't let him know what I was thinking, because I had learned better through the years.

I told him I would think about it and call him the following night. That night in bed was a night of tossing and turning.

I thought of my financial condition. I thought of all the young blacks who would be getting this poison. I came to the conclusion about daylight the next morning. I didn't intend to be a part of this distribution of destruction. I thought about him emphasizing the south side. Yes, he knew wherever there is poverty, hunger, dissention, and a need for hope, you will find a lot of willing black youths ready to purchase a few minutes of joy. Not realizing they are making themselves slaves, thieves, murderers, etc. In the meantime they are fattening the whitey's pockets.

The day went by as usual for me during this bad luck crisis. Nobody called. The girls had forgotten the older guys. They were looking for newer and younger happenings. I looked on my dresser. I had a dollar in change. That was my bankroll. Penny called later that evening. I could only tell her to do the best she could, because I could be of no assistance to her, at the present time. Yes, things were just that bad for me.

I called my lifelong friend, Ted, and asked him for a loan, but I got a sad story from him too. I thought about the rich girl, who I had instructed him how to cop. Oh yes, he still had her, but I guess he figured she was for his support and not mine. However, I did receive the call from Tony. I told him I could find no one I could vouch for. Now he knew a thousand blacks who would be glad to accept his proposition, but after doing a stretch for a black talking to him, he wanted someone with better credentials this time. He knew I was lying.

We rapped for a few minutes before he said, "Look, Trickshot, remember when you were in that shooting some years ago?"

Recalling the incident, I answered, "Yeah, I remember."

"Well, we gave you a chance to make a dollar; now I need the same chance."

What could I say? I told him to give me a day or two, and I'd have somebody. There was no use telling him my views on life had changed since those earlier years. I was hooked and I couldn't get out of it. The bad part about the deal was whoever I vouched for had to be a real stand-up guy.

I had a friend called the "Professor." Now here was a real swell guy. He had been to the joint but it was years ago. He had complained to me about the big dealers charging him enormous prices for this deadly poison called heroin. His bankroll was small, so therefore he could only make small purchases at large prices.

I explained to him about the deadly people he would be dealing with. I told him he would put me in a bad way if he didn't live up to his agreement with them.

This guy, called the Professor, carried the appearance of a boxer rather than an intellectual. He was given the nickname because of the smooth, intellectual way he carried out his business. He was a six-footer with high cheekbones and his small eyes and flat nose made it appear he'd had ring experience, though I doubt if he'd ever had on a pair of boxing gloves. His dark complexion didn't change the effect.

"Did you tell this guy I didn't have any money?" he asked.

"Look, man, I know you don't have a bankroll, that's why I'm telling him to give you the stuff on consignment," I said.

"Gee, Trickshot, I'll never forget this," he said, throwing his arm around my shoulders.

I wondered how long it would really be before he forgot. You see, I've experienced this same thing with other guys. They're really sincere when they need a favor, but after a period of time they become bored with you. Never realizing it was you who made them what they are. My friend Ted was a good example.

After telling the Professor when and where to be, I left to call Tony. As I was going into the drugstore to make the phone call, I ran into Lenny.

"Whatta you know, man?"

"Hi, Trick. Why haven't you called?"

"Oh, I've been in a little bad shape, Lenny," I confessed.

"Here, man, take this C note; I've been doing pretty fair. You know Jean's been getting some nice dates out at the house." Jean was his wife, a little white girl who was rather attractive. They had been together for a few years.

Accepting the hundred dollar bill, I thanked Lenny and headed for the phone booth. I got Tony on the phone and told him where to meet me. I also told him to dress up. You see, Tony was a hoodlum. He wore nothing but jackets and sweaters. I told him how conspicuous he would appear in a black neighborhood dressed like that. On the other hand, if he dressed, he could be taken for an insurance man, a bill collector, or even a cop; though I could picture him frowning on the latter. Going to my car, I began to think, I've got to get into something legit.

Heading out the expressway, I was so deep in thought I missed my exit. As I went up the ramp, to cross over and turn around, a fellow I used to fence clothes to blew me over.

Getting out of his car, he said, "Say man, I need some pieces. What's happened to you?"

"Hi, Red. Oh, things haven't been too righteous lately. I blowed Ginger, you know."

"Yeah, I heard about that Trick, but I know you've got some other broads boosting, haven't you?"

"Naw, I had a gambling joint, and the cops raided it. Since then, things haven't picked up any."

I told him this with my motor still running. I was trying to let him know I was in a hurry, without being too rude.

"Well, here, take my card, and when you cop, don't forget I still give a third for top pieces," he said, handing me his card through the car window.

"O.K., Red, I'll give you a buzz," I said, driving off.

When I arrived at the house, the phone was ringing. It was Ginger.

"Hi, Daddy, how've you been?" Now, this is a bitch! Here's a broad who has been gone a year, and she asks me how I've been.

"You didn't give a damn how I was," I answered her.

"Oh, Trick, I got sick and then I began to think about you and that woman; I guess I just couldn't stand it anymore," she replied.

"The least you could have done was called," I said.

"Yeah, I know, but you know how women are."

"No, I don't know how a woman could stay away from a man and then come back into his life and expect him to understand."

I thought about Red, who had just stopped me on the expressway. Now this was a coincidence that could have been god-send. I changed my tone.

"Now, listen Gin, you can't expect me to shower you with love and kisses, but I would be lying if I said I didn't miss you. Where are you?"

"Now, Trickshot, I know you and I don't want no shit outta you."

"What do you mean, shit? I'd really like to see you," I said, in as convincing a voice as I could.

"You know what I mean. I can't stand no ass-kicking, and I know how you are with that bullshit code of yours," she said.

She was thinking of the code of the pimps, which implies a broad should get her ass kicked or pay a penalty if she runs off.

She said she was stopping at some hotel downtown. This I didn't believe, but I pretended to go along with it. She told me she would call the next day, after working a few stores. Then she hung up.

Late that night, the doorbell rang. Looking at my watch, I knew it was Tony.

Gee, I almost didn't know the guy. Being in his early forties at the time, Tony's hair, which had been coal black, was now greying on the sides. He was of medium height, and weighed about a hundred and sixty pounds. He looked like a successful lawyer in his dark grey suit, set off with a white on white shirt, and a maroon tie. His small mustache, which showed sprinkles of grey, looked rather distinguished.

"Are you looking for someone?" I teased him.

He laughed, and pushed past me. I took his soft felt hat, and headed for the recreation room. As I walked behind the bar, I asked him what he wanted to drink.

"I swore off that stuff years ago," he said, shaking his head.

I poured myself a small sip and sat on the stool facing him.

"You say you don't want to put this stuff in my friend's hand personally, because you don't know him well enough yet?" I asked, looking him straight in the eyes.

"That's right. You see, Trickshot, I—"

"You don't have to explain. I understand," I said, cutting him off. "Since I've agreed to pass the stuff on to him, you'll have to give him enough so that I won't have to do it again," I said, still staring him down.

"Oh, that part can be taken care of. You know the people I'm hooked up with. They can give him a ton if he can move it," he said, crossing his legs, with his keenly pressed suit pants looking like new.

"When shall I tell him you'll see him?" I asked.

"I'll say two weeks from the date of delivery," he said, lighting a cigarette. "This will give us a chance to see how fast he can move the stuff."

I didn't bother to ask who he meant when he said "us." It doesn't pay to ask too many questions.

"Now I am going to tell you how to get the stuff to me without causing any suspicion. There's a one way street going north on Indiana," I said, using the bar as an outline. "I'll be standing on the corner with an arm full of groceries when you pull up. You'll ask me for directions. While I'm leaning over pointing out the streets to you, you will slip the package into my grocery bag. In that way, if someone is tailing or watching you, they'll not see the pick-up."

"Gee, kid, you should be with us. I've always liked the way you handled things," he said, slapping me on the legs.

I stepped off the stool and called the Professor. I told him to lay around his pad the following night.

After setting a time schedule, I let Tony out and

watched him drive off. I went back to the recreation room, and poured myself another drink.

This was my favorite part of the house. It seems I could think better down here. I always got the feeling of being hidden away from everyone and everything. I thought about the plan I had given Tony. I was sure that nothing could go wrong. I knew he was an old seasoned pro. My thoughts switched to Ginger. I had to think of a way to play on her. I knew she liked me and still wanted me, but I also knew she would be on her guard. She knew I hadn't forgiven her so easily.

Whatever the situation was, I was going to handle it; I had to, because I had no money. I put out the lights in the recreation room. I also put Ginger out of my mind. I needed some sleep.

It was the phone that woke me up. My mother was calling to tell me about some relatives coming in town. After rubbing the well-earned sleep from my eyes, I promised I would see them before they left, and yes, I would go by the market and get her a watermelon.

I looked at the clock, I saw it was well into the day. There was really no need for me to hurry. I had quite a few hours before I would see Tony. I knew Ginger wouldn't call until after the stores closed. I leaned over and turned on the radio. I was just going to browse around.

It was another hour or so before the phone rang again. This time it was Kenny, a friend of mine. He was telling me about a crap game they were having on the weekend. I told him I doubted if I could make it. I did remember to ask him if he had seen Boot, who owed me some money and I could use it now that I was in bad shape. After rapping for a while, I hung up.

I must have dosed off to sleep again. When I awoke this

time, I only had two hours before the meet with Tony. I jumped out of bed, realizing the importance of all the pieces being in place. I called the Professor. Yes, he was home. I told him to lay dead until I contacted him. I took a shower and put my thoughts in motion. I knew the Professor was going to give me something for the favor I was doing him, but Tony and his cold-bloodied ass figured I owed him a favor. After dressing I looked at my watch. I had a few minutes to spare. I figured I'd have a bite to eat.

After driving to Fifty-Eighth Street, I got out of the car and went into the small grocery store near the corner. I bought a few things I needed, and asked that they be put in a shopping bag. The lady looked at me. I cut off her thoughts by telling her, "I hate to carry groceries in my arms."

"You men are funny. You only have four articles and you want a shopping bag. Tee, hee," she giggled.

I left the store carrying the bag by its handles, but I knew when Tony drove up I would have the top of it wide open.

I stood on the corner and looked at my watch. He should be coming any minute. It was dark and people were getting off from work. I chose this time because there would be a lot of activity. I kept straining my eyes for the little green Ford. To my surprise, I saw a green car coming down Indiana Avenue which was a one-way street. This little green Ford was coming the *wrong* way!

My God! Could this be Tony? As the car came closer; yes, it was Tony. Just then, a police prowl car, which was cruising, had just pulled into the intersection. Seeing this little green car coming the wrong way, they immediately put the siren on and started flashing their light. Pulling in behind Tony, they were going the wrong way too.

It all happened so fast, it's really hard to recall. Suddenly, the little green Ford stopped. Out jumped Tony, only he jumped out running. He headed for the buildings along the avenue. One of the uniformed police jumped out and gave chase while reaching for his pistol. I didn't see Tony when he fired the first shot, but I did see the first policeman duck behind a car when the first shot was heard.

I saw the other policeman, who was out of the car, running alongside the parked cars. I looked over the cars and I saw Tony, bareheaded with a gun in his hand, running towards a gangway entrance. All of a sudden, the thought hit me! The stuff! What about the stuff?

People were raising windows. Some were closing doors. I heard someone say, "He ran thatta way!" I heard two more shots. The police had chased Tony through the gangway into the alley beyond.

I looked at the little green Ford. Its door was open on the driver's side. I knew the second policeman had called for reinforcements. In a moment the avenue would be loaded with prowl cars. I had to get to that car during the excitement.

What if I was caught getting it? What if I was caught with it afterwards? All of these things ran through my mind in a flash. Whatever happened, I knew I was going to that car before it was too late. I looked around, more people were gathering. I pushed past a group of young kids who were standing near the car. I walked around the car with the expression of a curious spectator.

There it was laying on the car seat! A dark cloth bundle on the seat by the passenger side! I made a bold and daring move. As I slid the bundle in the shopping bag, two prowl cars turned the corner with sirens and lights going full blast. Without jumping away from the car, I continued to bend over; looking it over with the air of any other curiosity seeker.

"Get back—get back!" The newly arrived police were telling me and a group of young kids. There were a volley of shots and I heard someone say, "I think they've got him cornered in the basement!"

More prowl cars had arrived. The streets were blocked off in a four-block area. Everywhere you looked you could see those lights flashing. Police had flashlights going in and out the different gangways. Some police were knocking on people's doors.

I thought to myself, why did Tony panic? Maybe it was the gun he had on his person. Then I thought again. It must have been the stuff. Yeah, that was it. Fearing they couldn't miss the dark cloth bundle which was lying in the front seat in full view, he had panicked. The gun itself was enough to send him back to the penitentiary. He had everything going against him. The police would want to know where he was going, being a white man in the black ghetto. Yes, everything was against him.

"Here comes the dogs, they'll get him now!" I turned to look and a young girl was pointing. Yeah, it was the canine squad. A plainclothes detective was walking towards a squad car. In his hand he had a soft grey felt hat. I recognized it right away. It was the same hat I had taken from Tony, when he came to my house the night before. Giving it to the policeman in the car, they brought out two German Shepherd dogs. A policeman with a gold braid around his uniform cap was pointing and giving instructions. Realizing I had gotten the bundle and tucked it away in my car trunk, I started to leave—but I couldn't, not knowing what had happened to Tony.

The policemen put the dogs on a leash and headed for the gangway where Tony was last seen. Behind the two police with the dogs were two more policemen. They both had rifles.

Why doesn't he give up? I thought to myself. Prison is better than death. But some of those guys would rather die than go back. The sound of the dogs barking began to fill the night. There was the sound of running feet.

The sound of sporadic shots echoed again and again. Then I heard the loud sharp crack of a rifle! Again the rifle spoke! There was a certain tenseness. People were buzzing.

I made my way through the tremendous crowd that had gathered. As I reached the edge of the crowd, I heard a voice say, "They had to kill him, the way he was shooting at them."

I damn near froze. I turned to the old lady whom I thought had made the remark.

"Did they kill him?" I asked.

"They say they killed him in the next alley," she answered, pointing.

I went across the street and walked to the entrance of the alley. Looking up I could see a crowd of people standing around. I ran up the alley, knowing and yet hoping it wasn't true. As I pushed my way through the crowd, I saw him. There with the same grey suit, but instead of the maroon tie, he had on a dark blue tie and a light blue shirt. Tony still had his hands in a grasping curve as if the gun was still there. However, looking about a foot from his hand, a forty-five automatic was lying on the ground with a policeman standing over it. He seemed to be guarding it as much as he was guarding Tony's body.

I heard a commotion and turned to see the paddy wagon coming up the alley. Behind it was an unmarked police car. I knew this was the homicide division coming to take Tony's body away.

## Chapter Twenty-one

AS I DROVE TOWARDS THE HOUSE another thought struck me like a bolt from the blue. The stuff: nobody knows I've got the stuff, and I mean nobody! I changed my route. Turning the car, I headed south. My mind was racing, I had to go over every detail. I had never told the Professor who the whitey was. I had never introduced Tony to the Professor. Even if Tony was able to tell his people, he had never made the delivery as far as they knew. Nobody, and I mean nobody, could prove that I had the stuff.

I began to think of my condition financially. I thought about being forced to humble myself and accept Ginger back. I thought about a legitimate business. I made it final. Nobody knew I had the stuff, and I didn't intend to let anyone know it.

As I approached mother's house, there were two of my

cousins from Detroit present. Everyone was happy to see me including mother. You see, she had seen very little of me during my bad luck crisis. They were listening to jazz on the radio. After a while, there was a pause in the music for a news break. The announcer spat out the news of Antonio Sperenzo's death in a shootout with the police. It said, "he was an ex-convict with syndicate connection."

I called mother into a side room and gave her the bundle, and told her it was some essence of perfume which was very valuable. I told her I was going to sell it to a manufacturer I knew. I don't know if she believed me, but I did know it would be safe.

Returning to the living room and my cousins, I took part in the regular family conversation. Little did they dream my mind was on more important things. One was my life, which wouldn't be worth five cents if Tony's friends ever found out I had their stuff. I didn't know exactly how much stuff was there; but I knew it could be cut five times and still be good. These are the instructions Tony had told me to give the Professor.

I excused myself from the family discussion and took the phone in the bedroom. I got the Professor on the other end.

"I'm sorry I didn't call you sooner, but I was delayed a bit!"

I told him I would have to contact him later that morning. I wanted to give myself a chance to think things out. Telling mother and my cousins I would come by tomorrow, I left. As I was getting in the car, mother stuck her head out the window and yelled, "Don't forget the watermelon." I smiled and drove off.

I knew I would have some visitors from over north, but I didn't know when. I had to be very careful the way I handled things from here on out. I didn't call the Professor as I had promised. He woke me up the next morning.

"Say man, I stayed at home all night. What happened?"

I told him everything was all right. He would get the stuff later today.

"How much will it cost me?" he wanted to know.

"I'll tell you when I see you; now get off this phone with that kind of talk!"

Ginger called a few moments later. "I tried to get you for two hours last night," she said.

"I had some relatives come in town. I was down at my mother's visiting them," I said.

"It would have been all the same, if I had gotten busted and tried to find you," she answered.

"Now listen, bitch, don't wake me up with that bullshit. Are you going to bring me the pieces you got yesterday, or not?" Once more, I felt independent.

"I'm going to the beauty parlor. I'll call you when I leave," she answered.

I hung up the phone without saying another word. Isn't that a bitch! A lot of good a beauty parlor is going to do her, I thought, as I prepared to dress and go by mother's place.

I stopped at the corner newsstand. There on the second page was Tony's picture. I got in the car and drove to the park. There I stopped the car and turned to page two. It showed the two policemen who were credited with killing Tony. It also gave a detailed account of what had happened. Since no contraband was found, they figured that Tony had fled rather than be found with a pistol which was a violation of his parole. It also stated he had two more years to go before he would have been off parole.

I folded the paper and proceeded to the market to pick up a watermelon. As I left the park and headed towards the Dan Ryan expressway, my thoughts took hold again.

I really knew why Tony had panicked and so did his friends. What bothered me was, would they be satisfied not knowing what had happened to their stuff? Heading into the expressway, I saw a black sedan in my rear view mirror. I drove at a normal rate of speed, and so did the black sedan. When I turned up the ramp heading to the market, the black sedan turned too. I knew it couldn't be the police. It had to be Tony's friends. I got a lump in my throat and a slight cramp in my stomach at the same time. I pulled the car up in front of the market and got out. Looking out the side of the dark glasses I was wearing, I saw the black sedan park a half a block down the street. I had noticed it had two occupants in it.

I bought a small watermelon, got back in the car, and headed toward mother's house. For all the attention I was paying to him, the man at the market could have sold me a red-striped watermelon. I wouldn't have noticed, I was so nervous.

When I pulled off, so did the black sedan. There was no doubt about it, I was pegged. I rattled my mind. No, it was impossible for them to know for certain that I had the stuff. All I had to do was play it cool. When I arrived at mother's house I called the Professor and told him to pick the stuff up in an hour. I gave him mother's address, then told her to bring me the bundle wrapped in the dark cloth.

After taking the bundle from mother, I closed the door. I told her I would be out in a minute. I unwrapped the cloth. There was a plastic-like bag sealed at one end with Scotch tape. I juggled it in my hands, and knew from the things the jungle had taught me that this was at least two kilos. I held the bag up to my nose. Sniffing along the Scotch tape seams, I could smell its distinctive odor.

It had plenty of strength, I thought. Wrapping it back in the dark cloth, I told mother to give it to the Professor when he came. After giving her his description, I left.

Turning into the boulevard, I looked in my rear view mirror; they were still with me. Composing myself for the worst, I continued back to the house. I wanted to be there when Ginger called. As I pulled the car up in front of the house, I looked to see where the black sedan was. They had stopped across the street. They definitely were not trying to hide their presence. I unlocked the door. Before I went in I turned and let them see me looking their way. I would be a fool to pretend I hadn't noticed them. Closing and locking the door, I sat on the couch. I knew the Professor would call me after he copped the stuff and stashed it.

The phone did ring; but it was long distance collect. I knew it was Penny. I listened to her tell me her troubles. After I tired of hearing her sing the blues of bad breaks and other bullshit, I cut her off and began to sing the blues myself. After an hour of this, we decided we were both getting bad breaks and the best we could do was stay civil with each other. I told her I still loved her and hung up.

I got up to fix a sandwich and was interrupted by the phone again. This time it was Ginger. "Hi, Mr. Wonderful," she said, with her voice full of joy.

"Hi, Gin. What's happening? Are you finished at the beauty parlor?"

"Why do you sound so dry?"

"I didn't get much rest," I said, trying to hurry the conversation. "Are you coming out?"

"Yeah, I guess so," she said rather dryly.

"O.K., I'll be waiting." I hung up and walked to the window. I eased the drapes back just a tiny big. Leaning back against the wall, I peeped through the narrow slit. Yeap, they were still there, sitting motionless like two zombies. I guess they figured they could play on my nerves. They were right to a degree. But that bundle held a future for me, and I was taking a big gamble to keep it.

While I was fixing the sandwich, the telephone rang

again. This time it was the Professor.

"Well, tell me something," he said.

"Fifty thousand," I told him.

"If it stands up, that's crazy!" he remarked.

He started to talk, but I cut him off. "Listen man, I'll see you later. You rap too damn much on the phone."

With that I hung up. I knew he would stay in line, because he thought it was the whitey's merchandise. He knew I didn't have fifty thousand dollars worth of dope to give him.

It wasn't long before Ginger rang the chimes. Yes, she was as big and fat as ever, plus she seemed much darker. I guess that Florida sun had cooked her. I had heard she had hooked up with some married man in Tampa.

Opening the door and inviting her in, I took the suitcase out of her hand. It didn't seem very heavy. The bitch had started putting shit on me already. I took the bag downstairs to the recreation room. Opening it I found six inexpensive pieces. Before I could get back up the stairs, she was saying, "You know it's a bitch downtown. The stores are hotter than hell with store dicks."

I knew then she was making excuses for the amateurish pieces she had.

"Gee, you look good baby," I lied, as she went roaming through the house.

"Your mother told me you had a nice place when I called and got your number," she said, sitting her fat ass on the couch.

We rapped for a while. She then asked me if I wanted her to cook dinner.

"That would be crazy!" I answered.

That was the truth! Ginger was one of the best cooks I have ever known.

After dinner we sat around till she became sleepy. After lying in bed for a time she pulled me over on her and said,

"Daddy, I need my oil changed," which was one of her expressions when she wanted to have sex.

I acted like I didn't hear her, though she knew I did. But I guess she could read my thoughts. Here is a broad who has been gone a year. She comes back, and gives me a child's portion of pieces and then she wants to screw me to death. She didn't bring the subject up anymore.

I woke up once and looked out the window. The black sedan was gone. Oh well, it didn't matter. I went back to sleep. The next morning I went to the window. Yeap, they were back on their job.

We had breakfast. Ginger said she was going to work. She said she would see me after the stores closed.

She had been gone about an hour when I heard the chimes ring, and wondered who would come without calling. I went to the door and looked through the peep hole. It was a tall white guy with another fellow not quite as tall, but much heavier. I asked them what did they want.

"We're friends of Tony's," the tall one said. I opened the door and let them in. Once inside, the tall one said, "Get your clothes on. Someone wants to see you."

"Who the fuck are you to come in here and tell me let's go just like that?" I said, knowing I was going all the time.

"We're going to take you. It's up to you which way you go!" the tall one spoke again.

I looked at the other guy, who looked like he might be a wrestler, with his short neck and muscular body.

"O.K., make yourselves at home while I dress."

My mind was spinning. No, this wasn't a hit. At least, I didn't think it was. They wouldn't off me without first making an effort to get the stuff. As I was dressing, I heard them going through the drawers and cabinets.

"Now, look here, what the hell are you doing?" I said, coming back into the room.

The stout muscular dude upped with a thirty-eight snub-nose revolver. Without saying a word, I turned around and continued to dress. I knew I looked like a clown. I was so servous I put on mismatched socks. I told them I was ready. The house looked like they had done a pretty fair job of searching in such a short time.

When we reached the car, I noticed a third dude sitting in the back seat. When I was seated in the car, the gun in the back seat next to me spoke. "All right, put your hands behind your back."

"Now look, guys, I—"

"Shut up and put your hands behind your back!" the tall one cut me off with a growl.

After taping my hands, the guy in the back seat said, "Now kneel on the floor."

My heart did a flip-flop. "I thought you said someone wanted to see me?" I asked.

"Will you shut up, or do I shut you up?" he said, grabbing my head.

My God! Was the guy asking me to hold still while he put a bullet through my skull? He roughly tied a handkerchief around my eyes and said, "Now stay there and be quiet."

My thoughts had turned to hundreds of regrettable events. Why had I fucked with their stuff in the first place? I'll never see Mother or Penny again. Why did I treat Sheila so bad? Why? Why? Why?

The car was traveling at a normal rate of speed. I guessed they didn't want to attract undue attention before they arrived at the spot of execution. But how could they know I had the stuff? My mind was a complete jugsaw.

I knew one thing. If I told them I had the stuff, I would only live long enough for them to get it. As the car continued, I became aware that we were on a highway of some sort. My mind told me it was a highway leading to some heavy woods. I wondered how long it would be before my body would be found?

I felt the car go up a small hill. About five minutes later, it came to a stop and honked its horn. I heard something like a huge door. The care went into motion again.

"All right, you can sit up now," a voice said.

They took the tape from my hands, then the handkerchief from my eyes. Blinking my eyes I looked around. I saw a lot of cars and a couple of small trucks. It was obviously a large garage. There was a small office at the far end of it.

The tall guy, who had done the driving, got out the car and walked into the office. He talked to someone seated behind a desk, then hastily stepped out of the office and beckoned for us to come in. The ominous-looking man sitting in the back with me got out first.

"Come on," he said.

Nervously, I got out the back seat and then the muscular fellow got out the front. I was so frightened my legs damn near gave way under my weight. Stepping into the office, I saw a neatly dressed man about fifty years old with well groomed, mixed grey hair sitting in a leather swivel chair.

"You're Trickshot, right?"

"That's right," I answered him.

"Well, Trickshot, we want to know why the cops were waiting for Tony, since you and he were supposed to be the only ones who knew of the meet. You didn't tell anybody, did you?"

"No, I didn't," I answered, damn near shaking, but a bit more relieved that I was still alive.

"Then how do you account for them being at the spot you told him to be, at that particular time?"

He was tapping a large key on the glass-topped desk as he questioned me. I looked at his well-manicured nails and his expensive blue suit. His legs were crossed and his freshly shined shoes were especially obvious.

"They weren't waiting. They had just pulled into the intersection getting ready to cross," I said, looking at the other fellows who also were listening quite intently.

"The papers said they pulled him over for a traffic violation and that's when he came out shooting. Well, we don't buy that crap. We think he was set up, and you were the only one who could have. Plus, somebody has swung with seventy grand of our merchandise."

Spinning around and facing me, he slammed the key down on the desk. "Now tell us about Tony, and tell us about our stuff . . . *Damnit!*"

I'll be a dirty motherfucker! Seventy grand, he had said! Seventy whole grand! I had given the Professor seventy grand worth of heroin for only fifty gees.

"Well, I can only tell you what I saw," I said, looking as innocent as a babe in arms. My composure, by now, was coming back a little.

"All right, out with it," he said.

I did a rerun of the plan Tony and I had made. In the conclusion, I clearly said, "If Tony hadn't gone down a one-way street, they would have never noticed him."

"What! Say that again!"

The well-manicured guy behind the desk was facing me with both his arms spread out on the desk.

"Yeah, didn't you know? Tony was driving down a one-way street, going the wrong way," I repeated.

"Where's that damn paper?" he asked, frantically pulling drawers out of the desk.

"Here's one," the muscular gentleman spoke up.

Damn, I thought to myself, he can talk. That was the first time I'd heard him utter a word.

"Those lousy reporters never get things right," the fella behind the desk said, slamming the paper down. "Why wasn't somebody trailing him, anyway?" he asked, staring at the group. "Gino, you're usually with him. Where the hell were you?"

"You sent me to check on those juke boxes, remember?"

"Aw, can it!" he shouted, angrily.

His anger was interrupted by a blast from a horn outside.

"Get it, Gino," he said, pointing to the guy who had taped my hands.

Gino obediently moved to a button on the wall. Pressing it, the huge door began its mechanical upward swing. A shiny blue Cadillac pulled in and stopped. A thin, elderly man, with silver grey hair and a scarf around his neck, got out. As he drew closer to the office his face became more familiar . . . Dino! It was Dino! I had worked for him and Tony when I was involved in the shooting trouble years ago.

"Hi, fella," he said, grabbing my hand. "Looks like you're in kinda deep," looking me straight in the eyes.

"I've told them all I know, Dino," I said, looking back at him with very steady eyes.

"How well do you know this guy, Dino?" the boss spoke up.

"Well, I knew him years ago when he was on our payroll," Dino said.

"You heard about Tony, huh?"

"Yeah, I heard. But what's that got to do with him?" Dino asked, pointing at me.

"This is the guy Tony had the meet with," the boss said, eyeing me.

"Oh, I see," said Dino, sitting on the edge of the desk.

"I sent for you when Gino said Tony had told him this guy used to work for you guys," the boss spoke again.

"Yeah, he was a pretty square Joe during those days," Dino said. " 'Course, that's been years ago." Turning to me, he asked, "How many bits have you done since then,

Trick?"

"I haven't taken a fall, as yet," I answered.

"Well, now that's something. What did you do? Square up and get a family?" Dino asked.

"Naw, I took the girls for it. It seemed a little safer," I answered, looking around at the group.

"What happened with you and Tony?" Dino asked.

I went through the whole thing again.

"Let's see. That happened where?" he asked, walking to a glass-covered map on the wall. He ran his finger along part of it and stopped.

"Who's in the fifth district?" he asked, looking toward the guy behind the desk.

"I have it right here ... Mulquin and O'Malley," the boss answered, after reaching in his side pocket and bringing out a small black book. He then closed the book and returned it to his pocket.

"That shouldn't be too hard to check out," Dino said, turning towards me again. "Well, it's just possible that Tony, not being familiar with the neighborhood, did make a bad turn that brought on the heat."

Dino was talking and walking.

"But the papers still don't say anything about the stuff. Couldn't this guy have met Tony already and got the stuff before he made the wrong turn?" Gino asked.

"Naw, I don't think so. Tony wouldn't panic just for a gun beef. He knew we could square that too easily," the boss said. "But, damnit, where's our stuff?" He became angry again.

"I saw the pictures on TV. There were a lot of people around his car," the muscular guy said.

"All those cops are not honest-Johns, you know," said Dino.

I was off the hook! I knew I could beat it! I knew it! I knew it! Then suddenly I had a sinister, interrupting thought. What if they saw me on TV near his car? But that couldn't be. The other cops were just arriving. Naw, I was safe there. I returned to my elated feeling.

"Listen, fella, I haven't got this thing figured out just now, but we'll be working on it until we get it figured and when we do, somebody's going to pay for that package one way or the other. All right, Gino, get him out of here," the boss said.

"Take him in the truck this time," Gino said to the tall guy who did the driving.

They immediately placed me in the rear of a small hauling truck and then blindfolded me. They didn't bother to tape my hands this time. Gino sat in the back of the truck with me. The tall guy and the muscular fella sat up front. They dropped the heavy tarpaulin and headed out.

Retracing the ride, I could tell what I at first thought was a highway was really the Dan Ryan Expressway. When we finally arrived in front of my house, they removed the blindfold and let me out. They said nothing and neither did I.

When I got inside the house, it was really a beautiful sight. All the drawers were hanging half out, and clothes were strewn all over the floor. They had searched through the luggage, and the mattress had been turned over. Oh, what a beautiful sight! I didn't think I would ever see these things again. Quite naturally, I realized how extra careful I had to be from here out. I couldn't come up with too much money. I couldn't do anything that might cause undue attention. I would have to invent a means of going into legitimate business. It wouldn't make sense to piss this kind of money away, the way I had done in the past.

Ginger called to tell me she had to go home at once. Her mother, it seems, had suddenly taken ill. It might have been true, but truthfully, I didn't believe a damn thing Gin said. I was glad about her leaving, to say the least, because I didn't need her evil ass worrying me during the crisis I had coming up.

A few hours earlier, I had thought my day of reckoning had finally arrived. I went destitute for a week without contacting the Professor. Eventually, the phone bill, the rent, combined with other pending bills, collided with impact. I had intentionally held out as long as I could. I told the Professor that the whitey had called. We made a meet in a theatre downtown. Waiting in the second lobby gave me a chance to see if anyone was following me.

When the Professor arrived, I greeted him as if I hadn't seen him in years. Finding two seats, he passed the bundle of bills to me, which he had concealed inside his shirt that was covered by his dasing sport coat. Asking him how much was there, I wanted to jump up and leave when he remarked, "Twenty grand. Tell him I can move it a little faster once I get my pushers organized." He was giving me a message to relay to Tony. "I like doing business with those northside guys," he said.

"I don't have to tell you, if I hear my name or any of that white boy's business, you're a dead duck." I told him this to instill fear within him; also to keep him from possibly blabbing my name.

"You know me, Trickshot, I want to make some money. I don't want a lot of attention."

"O.K., that's fine. As long as you keep it that way, you'll be all right with the guys over north."

"Say, when will I meet this guy?" he asked.

"Don't worry. And don't be impatient. What do you care if you never meet him. You're getting your stuff, aren't you?" I told him, looking at him disgustingly.

I don't know if the picture was good or bad. I was sitting there trying to figure out how to spend this money without putting heat on myself. I left the theatre and made a bee-line to mother's place. I went to the bedroom and locked the door. Counting the money, I found it all there to the penny. I left the money, all except something to pay my bills. I headed for home. I hadn't heard from Penny or Ginger. I spent most of the night making plans that I was sure would reach the northside guys' ears.

The next morning I got up fresh. The sun was out, and it was a lovely day for the races. Today I was going to win. This I knew, because I had to get lucky for the next couple of weeks. It had to be the kind of luck that they could check out. This I knew they would do. For once in my life, I didn't want to be bothered with any girls. I couldn't afford the distraction.

I could just picture myself as a businessman, retired from the game. With the knowledge I had of clothes, I decided that a clothing store was to be my next legit venture. I went to the hotel. There I saw quite a few of the fellows reading their racing forms and getting ready for their daily contributions. I chose my old friend Sidney because I knew he would spread the news.

"What'ta you know, Sid? Going out today?" I asked in a casual way.

"Are you going?" he asked in return.

"Thinking about it."

"Let's ride together," he said, walking towards the car.

After saying something to a couple of dudes we were on our way. "I've got to stop by mother's house to borrow her rent money. I'll have it back to her before the first of the month," I said.

I could picture Sid telling people how much I had won to the penny. Leaving him in the car, I ran upstairs to my stash and grabbed two thousand in hundred dollar bills. Getting in the car I counted out a hundred and eighty dollars in tens and twentys which I already had.

"I hope I'm lucky. All my bills are due!" I said.

"Maybe this is your day," Sid said, still looking at his racing form.

A few moments went by and the horses were on the track for the second race. I went to the bar and had a drink. I told Sid I had liked the first horse so well, I played him with everything in the second. In other words, I had wheeled the first horse.

"Looking at the board, Sid said, "You may get a big one."

The announcer called the horses to the post. The race was off, and I gave less than a damn who won. However I pretended to be very interested. As the winner went across the wire, I asked Sid, "How much is that double?"

It was a mediocre price, but whatever answer he gave me, I claimed to have a ten dollar ticket on it. Not giving him a chance to see, I flashed the stack of tickets with the ten dollar ticket on top. I immediately walked away, and got in line with the rest of the winners. I came back ounting a few hundred dollar bills for him to see. I really wouldn't doubt that the family had some of their spotters presently watching me. If so, this would make it better still.

I invited a group of fellas to the bar; loaned a couple of guys a bet, and gave Sid a bet for himself. All of this made it authentic. We played a few more raced until the feature race came up. I had a plan that might cost me money, but it would be worth it in publicity.

The feature race consisted of eight horses. I went to the hundred dollar window and bought a ticket on all eight of them. Losing myself in the crowd, I didn't want anyone else asking me what horse I had bet. When the race was over, I threw away seven of the losing tickets, then found Sid and handed him the one winning ticket.

"Cash this while I go to the men's room," I told him.

He looked up at the board and said, "He paid twelve dollars! You'll get six hundred for this ticket, Trick. Boy, this really is your lucky day!"

Saying that, he left to cash the ticket. Little did he realize that I was still two hundred losers to the race. Figuring this was enough maneuvering for the day, I told Sid I was over two thousand winners, therefore I wasn't staying for the last race. I gave him another fifty dollar bill, and asked him to drive while I counted my winners. Seeing all these crisp hundred dollar bills, he would have sworn it was ten thousand if I had claimed such.

It was very simple for me to go to Detroit the following week and come back after hitting the numbers for five grand. These small mounts could show reason for my living in the style I had become accustomed to. I never intended to come up with any fabulous amounts.

Penny called. I don't know if she had gotten the wire about me hitting the numbers or not. However, I sent her three hundred dollars. I knew that was enough to keep her hustling. I didn't know it then, but that was the last time I was to hear from Penny. I found out three months later she had married a rich numbers backer.

## Chapter Twenty-two

I CALLED THE PROFESSOR. This time I met him in Gary, Indiana. He gave me the balance of the money due and told me to tell the whitey that he, the Professor, was low on stuff. I told him I would deliver his message. I didn't try to converse with him. You see, I had plans of my own.

I had rented a safety deposit box in Gary. When the Professor left, I made tracks for my secret box. I rented it in a bogus name, and brought the key back to my mother.

It was a pleasant feeling to relax without wondering what broad will get busted or how long will this broad stay. All of those illicit things I had thrown out of my mind. In fact, I had started looking for a store that was vacant.

It was a few weeks later when I was watching the television and the news came on. "BIG NARCOTIC RAID," the announcer began. I was sure I had heard the Professor's name.

I urgently got on the phone and called his brother. It was true! An agent had infiltrated his set-up and busted them all. I knew he would be calling when he made bond. I quickly told his brother to tell him that I would call him, not to call me. At this stage, I wasn't afraid of him talking since he couldn't prove anything. And if he couldn't prove it now, he would certainly never get another chance. You see, our brief association was over. Like final!

After looking at a suitable vacancy for a clothing store, I was able to acquire an ideal spot on Stony Island Avenue. It wasn't necessarily a fabulous location, but it would most certainly serve the necessary purpose for the present time. You see, it would have been insane for me to open up and splurge. Filling out the application and waiting for the results gave me time to buy up stock which I stacked up at the house.

It was about a month later; I had opened the store. Gino came in. "Hi, Trickshot. We heard about your place and decided to give you a little business," he said, looking at his friend, who was the muscular guy.

They proceeded, quiet casually, to look at some shirts and ties. "I see you carry a few ladies things," Gino said, fingering a blue print dress.

"Yeah, I'll get a bigger stock if I get lucky again," I said, smiling. I knew they really were there to see how much stock I had. After buying a few shirts and other articles, Gino spoke up.

"We did your house kind of bad, so we figured we'd try to make it up to you."

"Oh, I realized the way you fellas must have felt. By the way, did you ever get a line on your stuff?" I asked, with questioning eyes.

Turning around and looking me dead in the eyes, Gino said, "Well, yes and no. You know, Trickshot, sometimes these things take a long time, but we always figure them out. We can't afford not to."

Saying that, they left. He really wasn't telling me anything new. I knew they never gave up. I also knew they could never prove I had the stuff ... I thought!

Business was exceedingly good, and I would buy pieces from boosters to mix in with the legit clothes. That is, after removing the manufacturers tags from the articles. Sometimes a mink or two would come through. These I would stash in my recreation room, or down to mother's house. If a person wanted to cop a mink, they would have to make a meet away from the store. During this time, the Professor was fighting his narcotic case in court. He'd had about three continuances.

One day, while I was sitting in the back of the store reading the paper, a tall olive-complexioned woman walked in. Nancy, the woman I had working for me, began to show the customer our latest fashions. Paul, the fella who worked in the men's department, was just leaving for lunch.

After selecting an expensive print dress, the tall young lady proceeded to the dressing room. As Nancy turned to show her where it was, the attractive lady grabbed another dress and concealed it beneath the one she was going to try on. After a short time, she returned from the dressing room, holding the expensive dress in her hands.

"I don't think it does anything for me," she said, heading for the door, which I was blocking by now.

"Come her, you clumsy bitch!" I shouted, as I grabbed her by the arm, and spun her around.

"Let me go, I'll sue you," she said, attempting to put up a fight.

I pushed her towards the back room, and slapped her hard. The unexpected blow sent her reeling towards the small bed which I used for my little naps. As she fell back on the bed, I reached between her legs and got the other neatly folded dress.

"You're too slow to work by yourself," I told her. "Where's your partner?"

"I don't have one," she said, through tear-filled eyes.

"You've got to be new in town to come in this store," I told her.

"What're you going to do?" she asked, still sniffing.

Looking at her, I found her to be rather attractive. I couldn't help noticing her big pretty thighs when I snatched the dress from between her legs. I ignored her first question, and asked her one.

"Who's your old man? And what's your name?"

"Stella, and I don't have one. You were right. I just hit town two days ago." By now she had stopped crying.

"Where're you from?" I asked again.

"Detroit," she said, looking in her bag for another Kleenex.

"Who were you with before you ran off?" I asked, taking another shot in the dark.

Looking up at me with surprised eyes, she said, "Rabbit, a fella named Rabbit."

"I'll be a dirty motherfucker," I said, "You mean little Rabbit. A guy with a small mustache, about so tall?" I asked, using my hands to emphasize.

"Yes, that's him." she replied.

"You asked me a few minutes ago what I was going to do with you? Well, I'll tell you. I'm going to take you to the Greek's place on the corner. Then after you have had dinner, I'm going to take you and give you some instructions on how to boost without getting busted!"

I looked at Nancy, my salesgirl, who was laughing. You see, Nancy was an ex-booster herself. Turning to her, I said, "And you'd better get some more glasses or another job!" Nancy erased the smile from her face.

I asked Stella where she lived.

"In the Jackson Park Hotel," she said. It was just around

the corner.

The more I looked at Stella, the more she reminded me of Wanda. The only difference was her ass was wider. This might have been middle-age spread. Stella was thrity-five years old, and I was an old man who had forgotten about young girls. After having dinner, and asking about Rabbit, I walked her to the hotel and told her to call me the next day.

The next day was spent showing Stella the ins and outs of the boosting game. She said, "Rabbit was too busy with his stable to show me very much."

That was one of the reasons she had run off. I knew it to be a fact that Rabbit kept a big stable. Without a doubt, I could sympathize with her. Perhaps, it was because I wanted to.

You see, Stella became my woman, and six months later, she became my wife. It was a small wedding with a few businessmen and their wives present. As we left the church, I wasn't completely sure, but I could have sworn I saw Gino and his shadow.

The next day I picked up the paper, and read where the judge had indeed called the Professor's case. And, of course, it predicted a long trial, because of the number of people involved. A week passed and Stella called the store and told me that she was pregnant. Presently, I was on the phone telling Ted about the expected child, when in walked two neatly dressed white fellas. I figured the family must have sent some more spotters out, so I told Paul, my employee, I would wait on them.

They called my right name and my alias, then handed me some papers and placed me under arrest. I read the papers; the charge was conspiracy to violate the Narcotic Act. They must be kidding; though I knew they weren't!" I retrieved my hat, and I told Nancy to call Stella. Paul was standing there with his mouth half-open, dumbfounded. On the way out, they had handcuffed me. One of the agents, a red-headed fella with freckles on his face and hands, said, "I've been after you for a long time, Trickshot."

All sorts of ideas went through my tubulent mind. Was this a frame? I had been clean for damn near two years. Who was this clandestine stool-pigeon? The Professor's case had been pending for eighteen months or better. Why would he wait until now to open up?

During those days, the law was slightly different. Since then the Supreme Court has said you must be faced by your accuser. I couldn't figure it. No, I just couldn't figure it out. Precisely, the next morning I was taken before a federal judge and bond was set at twenty-five thousand dollars. I could have paid it off in cash, but I had Stella put up her home instead. This would keep a lot of things under the cover. I urgently got in touch with my lawyer and told him to bring the morning paper.

When he arrived, I nervously unfolded the paper and sat on the couch. There on the third page in big headlines, I read, *South Side Businessman Nabbed in Narcotic Arrest!* It went on to state in eloquent literary prose that the secret indictment had, in fact, been in effect for the last six months.

A secret indictment! I thought back and racked my brains. It had to be the Professor, or else it was a frame. My first impulse was to call in someone to off him, but then, I thought of what Tony had said. "If the agent had witnessed the transaction, it would do no good to kill the pigeon." I thought of my furtive transactions with the Professor. An agent couldn't have seen him pass me the money in the theatre. I rethought our meet in Gary. An agent could only swear that he saw us sitting in the car.

The store had been more of a success than I had figured. I had money, but I knew I couldn't buy the government.

It wasn't long before the Professor's case was over. The judge gave out sentences ranging from five years to fifteen years. The Professor drew fifteen years for being the leader of the illicit operation.

I stayed out of jail on an appeal bond for a year, during which time Stella had had a seven pound girl. Never before having an offspring that I could ascertain as my own gave me a much different view on life. It made the possibility of going to prison more unbearable, to say the least.

Stella would wake me up nights, telling me I was screaming. I soon became rude to the customers and eventually I fired Nancy, who had been with me since the day I first opened the store. However, Stella talked me into rehiring Nancy and to also put the management of the store in Nancy's hands. I wouldn't frequent the store as I had in the past. Although one day I happened to drop in by chance. After seeing that things were running smoothly, I was leaving to take Stella and Tricia—which is the name we had given our daughter—to the clinic for Tricia's regular checkup.

As we pulled up in front of the clinic, Gino and his old pal muscular Willie pulled up behind us. Getting out, Gino slyly walked up to the car.

"Hi, Trickshot. Heard you had an addition to the family?" he said, looking at Tricia, who was now a few months old. I could see the fear in Stella's eyes, as she tightened her motherly grip on Tricia's infant body.

"Yeah, we're taking her in for her regular checkup," I replied.

"You know, you can't be too careful with kids nowadays. They can get sick and die before you know it."

Saying that he walked away. Stella looked at me and asked, "Trickshot, who was that man?"

I had never told Stella where I had gotten the bankroll

for the store. All she ever knew was, I was an ex-pimp who had left the game and become a success.

"Oh, he's just one of the guys I've known from years back," I answered, but of course, Stella sensed my evasiveness. I doubted if she believed me, but Stella was not a persistent person where I was concerned.

That night after having dinner, I called my lawyer because my case was coming up quite soon. After hearing there were no new developments, I turned on the TV to get the evening news. I was just in time to hear the announcer say, "Dino Saratelli, well-known syndicate hood, was pronounced dead on arrival. From what doctors say, it was a fatal heart attack."

So my old buddy Dino was gone. I pictured him getting out of that blue Caddy the day I was in the garage. Well, one thing, he didn't wind up in a trunk, which might be my fate. Do they ever five up? I guess not.

As time drew near for my court date, I could see the strain on Stella's face. Her beautiful face had developed a few curving lines. Often, I would sit reading, and I would catch her eyes furtively watching me. Damn, I thought, I wish this thing would come to a head soon. It wasn't long before my wishes were granted.

My lawyer called and quite eloquently told me to be ready for trial. The trial began with all the flambouyance of a movie extravaganza. In those days reporters weren't barred from taking pictures. And when I entered the courtroom corridor, cameras began to pop. A few of my business friends were present. I doubted if they were there for moral support; it was, in fact, more through curiosity than anything else. As Stella later remarked, "They were there so they would have something to rap about over the poker tables."

The first professional strategy my attorney exerted was a

motion to suppress the evidence. This was immediately denied by the judge. Well-groomed in legal expertise, the government prosecutor made an opening speech to the jury, saying that he would prove beyond a reasonable doubt that I did conspire and did willfully sell narcotics in violation of the Narcotic Act, of said section blah, blah, blah.

I sat through all of this legal procedure, hoping they would get to the basic foundation of the case. The agent who first took the stand was my old freckle-faced friend. Under cross-examination by my lawyer, it was brought out that he, the agent, had been trailing me since the day I met Tony. Ah, hah! I thought to myself. I had gotten all the heat from Tony!

He stated that he was on the scene the night that Tony was killed. My God! I was waiting for him to say he saw me get the bundle. Instead he told the judge and jury that it was one of his shots that was instrumental in killing Tony. However, his bureau boss had thought it best not to mention it publicly, for rear it would notify the family-controlled narcotic ring that the government was on their trail. This being the case, they, to be sure, would go into hiding.

Later the prosecutor presented, over the objection of my attorney, a photograph of Tony entering my house, with the address plainly showing at the top of the picture. This was presented to show there was definite association between a convicted narcotic peddler and myself.

Another agent was called to the stand by the prosecutor. This time it was a black agent. Up until that time, I really didn't believe there were any black agents on the bureau. However, this agent testified that he had followed the Professor to Gary, Indiana, and saw him get into my car.

Damn! These sonofabitches were damn near sleeping with us, and I never had any dream of their presence. The judge said there would be a recess until tomorrow morning.

Stella, who was ever-present, nudged my arm as we were leaving the court room.

"Isn't that the same fella we saw at the clinic?" she said, nodding toward a tall white fella who was leaving.

I looked to see and, after I did, I felt sick. It was Gino. Yes, Gino and his ever-hounding musclebound friend. My thoughts were in regress over the agents statements. No, there was nothing said that could finger me as the one who'd taken their stuff.

Arriving at the house, I couldn't eat. The babysitter had gone home, so I went in to play with Tricia. She was real glad to see her daddy. I know she wondered where I had been all day, since I had made an effort to spend as much time with her as I could. You must realize, I didn't know if it would be years before I would see her again.

That night was the worst. Stella woke me up, and I was completely wet with sweat. The next morning, I had a glass of orange juice and that was my breakfast.

As we were driving to court, Stella spoke up. "Trickshot, tell me about those men?"

"What men?" I asked, knowing all the time who she meant.

"That fella we saw at the clinic. What's his name? . . . Gino . . . Yeah, that's it, Gino," she said, without looking at me.

"I'll tell you about it after the case is over," I said, pushing the windshield wipers as it began to rain. Did you bring an umbrella?" I asked.

"I think . . . yeah, here it is," Stella said, reaching in the back seat.

The expressway was crowded and it was now raining buckets.

"I hope we won't be late," Stella said, looking exceptionally worried.

I assured her they would wait on us. Once in the courtroom my lawyer called me to his side.

"I think you were right," he said.

"Right about what?" I asked.

"About the Professor," he answered, pointing.

There, sitting in the courtroom as big as day, was the Professor. I tried to catch his eyes. Not with any motions; I just wanted to see if he would look at me. He never dared to look my way. I knew then, the Professor was the pigeon. The prosecutor obviously figured, if he opened up with his best and final blow, it might knock us out of the contest. He called the Professor to the stand and told him to tell the court in his own words of his dealings with me. I imagined that the man with the Professor was a prison guard or a government marshall.

I looked at this small-eyed black devil as he rattled off. In retrospect, I needed him patting me on the shoulder and telling me how he'd never forget me. Well, he's living up to his word. He remembered every damn thing we said or did. He told the court I gave him fifty thousand dollars worth of heroin. When he said this, there was a shuffling of feet. Someone was leaving. I turned to see and wished I hadn't. It was Gino and company. They had finally heard all they needed to hear!

The lawyers carried the case on, but I was just there. I didn't hear anything else that was said. The whole courtroom seemed to spin around and around and around. I was looking straight ahead but I wasn't seeing anything. As the cobwebs slowly cleared away, I heard my lawyer ask the Professor, "Will you tell the court if any promise of leniency had been offered you."

Before the Professor could answer, he shot another question at him. "Or did you volunteer to come forth with this information because you were an honest, upright citizen?"

The prosecutor objected, however my lawyer had

accomplished his purpose. The jury had heard, and once heard, it was in their mind. I remember a phrase used by a very famous lawyer. He said, "You can't unring a bell!"

I told my lawyer to give Stella a note on which I had scribbled. It instructed her to call the house and tell the babysitter to lock all the doors. I recalled what Gino had said at the clinic. In his closing remarks, my lawyer brought out the blatant fact that here was a convicted felon, serving fifteen years who, with a deal, would say anything against his own mother. On the other hand, here was I, a noted businessman with no previous record. The master stroke was, however, when he recalled the freckle-faced agent to the stand and asked him if it wasn't true that he had tried to get a statement from a Miss Ginger years ago concerning me. The agent had to say yes or perjure himself. My attorney asked him if it was true that at the time of my arrest, he had made a statement, "I've been after you for a long time, Trickshot."

All of these things he might have been able to explain, even if the prosecutor had recalled him to the stand. However, all of those previous things went to influence the jury of a possible frame.

After each lawyer had made his final summation the judge sent the jury to its quarters for the final verdict. Stella returned telling me that she had talked to the babysitter and Tricia was fine. I wondered if, possibly, I could arrange to pay the hoods for their stuff? Nope, I had violated their code. Anyway, the only person who could have arranged it was gone. Dino! Yes, Dino could have done it. But that was water over the dam. It really appeared hopeless.

Finally, my lawyer called me in. The foreman of the jury was a brother, but he didn't look like my type of brother. I had noticed him during the trial. Whenever I could catch his eyes, he'd look away. I just didn't like him. There was one other black on the jury. A lady, who gave the appearance of a housewife. This I knew could go either way. The judge asked if they had reached a verdict. The foreman, my black brother, answered him, "Yes."

"We, the jury, find the defendant *Not Guilty!*"

I looked around towards Stella. She had a Kleenex up to her face. The few business associates who were present, came forth to shake my hand. As we entered the hall, two reporters snapped pictures.

We were about to enter the car, when Gino pulled upside my car and said, "Like I told you, Trickshot, a pimp should stick to his game." With that said, he drove off smiling.

As soon as we entered the car, Stella said, "Trickshot, you must tell me about that man!"

Briefly, I gave her a detailed account, going back to the days when I had first met Dino and Tony. I told her everything leading up to that minute.

"Oh, Trickshot, why didn't you tell me? All this time you've been carrying this thing around by yourself!" she said, grabbing my arm.

"Well, I knew you would worry, not only for me, there is Tricia to consider."

My God! Tricia! I turned on the starter. "I know these people. They don't play around," I said, as I moved out into the traffic.

"Maybe we could pay them and move somewhere else?" Stella suggested.

"Where is that?" I said, without looking at her.

"Yeah, they'd find us, wouldn't they?" she asked, with questioning eyes. "But if we paid them?" She was still looking at me, waiting for an answer.

I don't think so; naw, I don't think so. Oh, why the hell did Dino have to die? Why didn't he take better care of himself?

## Chapter Twenty-three

WHEN WE REACHED THE HOUSE, everything seemed in order. I rang the chimes and unlocked the door at the same time. We waited for Sue, the babysitter, to take the night latch off. Opening the door, she had Tricia in her arms. We went in and closed the door. Stella took Tricia and thanked Sue for being so efficient.

My mind had been turning. I was going to try and live. I had money, but what good was it? If I could live, I could get more money. Yes, I was much older, but I still had knowledge, and I still had Stella.

Realizing my time was limited, I called a friend who owned a kennel. Yes, he had a couple of Dobermans, but the price was rather high. I didn't give a damn about the price, as long as they were good watchdogs. It was two days before I received the well-trained dogs. I had to make arrangements for their quarters and other things. However, when they took over their yard duties, a fly couldn't come near the house without putting himself in danger.

This done, I proceeded with Plan Two. I knew an old Italian buddy who had a store on the west side that was similar to mine. In fact, I had quite secretly bought a truckload of dresses from him a few months previous. Worried, I called him the next day and told him it was urgent! I saw no reason to hold back anything from Sal. He was in the position to find out anyway.

I ran it all down to him the next day in my recreation room. Salvidore was about sixty or seventy years old. He knew something about everything. I told him I wanted to try and square myself with the north side family. I wanted him to see if I could pay off the whole seventy grand, even though Gino had heard the Professor say he had only given me fifty grand for the package. Salvidore looked at me. In his broken English, he said, "That'sa bad. That'sa bad thing you do, Trickshot!"

"I know! I know I did wrong, but I'm trying to square it. Can you help me?" I asked, looking at him with the same pleading eyes I'd shown to Dino in the garage that day.

"I da no, I da no; it'sa bad thing."

"Damnit, will you stop saying that. I know it was a bad thing. But I'm trying to pay them off. Listen, Sal, didn't I give you a nice price for those dresses? We've always gotten along all right. I know you've made some mistakes in your time. Somebody had to give you a break at one time or another."

He looked up at me. My mind instantly flashed back years to Jim, the con man. I remembered again what he'd said about watching the eyes. When Salvidore, who was sitting on the bar stool, looked up, I could see in his eyes that I had brought a memory back to him. I had been standing and now I sat down on the stool facing him.

"How old are you, Sal?" I asked.

"I be, ah, sixty-eight years old soon," he replied.

Walking to the window and looking up, Sal glanced past the dogs that were playing. He didn't seem to notice the branch from the hedges that was tapping against the recreation room window. He began to speak.

"I tol' you, I know this man. Yeah, I know him many, many years ago."

Saying this, he turned and faced me. "I will send you something. When you get this, you will be O.K."

After saying that, Salvidore started to leave. I thanked him for his help, even though I didn't know what kind of help it was. You see, I had known Sal before I opened my store. He was one of the fences I would sell Ginger's hot clothes to. He had become rather wealthy through his fencing business; though he kept his small department store as a front. He had a son who helped him in the store. I had often heard that this son had had a twin. But what had happened to the other son had, to some, remained a mystery.

As he headed for the door, he was mumbling to himself, "Killing, killing; always dis killing." I let him out.

Stella, who had been upstairs with Tricia, entered the room and asked, "Well?"

I looked at her and said, "I don't know. I just don't know."

"He said something, didn't he?" Stella asked, looking questioningly.

"Yeah, he said that he would send me something."

I said this, becoming irritated with her persistence. Sensing this, Stella turned and went back upstairs.

The next evening when the phone rang, it was Sal. He was calling to tell me that he was sending a fella to my place.

That night Nancy had Paul lock the store. She then brought me an envelope. I knew why Sal hadn't sent it directly to my home. The less people who know where you live, the better. Today this fella worked for Sal; tomorrow he might work for who knows? I thanked Nancy, and asked her if anything seemed suspicious around the store. She left after assuring me everything was all right.

It was a large brown envelope. I opened it. There was an old clipping in photostatic copy. It was a clipping from a newspaper. I couldn't make out the writing that showed beneath the two pictures. It was some kind of foreign writing. I called Stella, who had had much more schooling than I.

"What kind of language is this?"

She looked at me and shrugged. "It looks like Italian. I don't know," she answered.

"Ain't this a bitch?"

I took the clipping and headed to the phone. I dialed Sal, and asked him what should I do. He told me he would send his son over tomorrow.

The next morning the dogs woke me up barking. I looked out from the upstairs window, and saw this tall white guy standing at the gate. I called the dogs off and let him in. He told me that Sal had sent him. I could see a likeness to the old man. We sat in the upstairs living room. Ben, whose name I found out later was Benatelli, began to read the photostat. The newspaper clipping had been written in Sicilian. It gave an account of a gang war between two families. The two pictures were about two of the people involved. One of them, a young fella, had been killed. The other man had disappeared. After reading it through, Ben told me where to send it. And before he left, he said, "Don't worry. It's been our life insurance for a long time."

I let Ben out and went back to the living room. I picked up the clipping and reviewed what Ben had read. Then it hit me! The young fella in the picture. That last name, Mariello. It was Sal's other son, Ben's brother. It all fell into place!

I remembered Sal telling me he knew Nick from the old country. There had always been talk of Sal's other son. Everyone knew he had been killed, but no one seemed to know where or why? Sal's name was Salvidore Mariello.

The clipping spoke of the disappearance of this man, Spilini. Evidently Nicky was in the United States illegally. That's it! That's it1 Nicky is here illegally, and he's changed his name. His name was Nicolani Spilini.

"Stella! Stella! We're safe, baby, we're safe!" I said, running up the stairs to Tricia's playroom. Waving the clipping and talking at the same time, I must have looked and sounded like a man who'd just gotten a reprieve from the electric chair.

I followed Ben's instructions and mailed the envelope with my telephone number inside. I thought about Sal. Nick would know who gave me the information. After thinking it over, I knew it made no difference. Nick had built a small empire in this city. He had made millions and was still getting richer. I remembered the day they had me in the garage. Gino had said he was checking the juke boxes. I'd always thought that to be Johnny Boco's territory, but obviously, Nick had gotten a piece of the action.

He wouldn't dream of harming me now! I wasn't worth the risk, plus there was a warrant for him in Sicily. The more I thought about it, I agreed with Ben; the clipping was good life insurance!

It was two days before I received a telephone call. It was Nick. He was surprisingly calm.

"O.K., Trickshot, you got lucky. How long have you know Salvidore?" he asked.

"Salvidore! Who's that?" I asked.

"O.K., O.K. Keep your mouth shut and you've got a friend." Saying that, he hung up.

I called Sal immediately and thanked him for getting me off the hook. I was about to hang up, but not before I listened to Sal, giving me some fatherly advice.

"This ting you do very bad," he said. "This ting I do for you, because I tink of my son. He too, did a bad ting, but he have no one to get him off hook. You have good business. Take care of it, and it take care of you."

Thanking him again, I started to hang up, but before I could, he interrupted me again. "Say, Trickshot, you run into good deal, like mink coats, you call me, huh?"

Smiling, I told him, "O,K." and hung up. The old guy didn't know it, but the next time Stella brought a mink coat home, it was his for nothing. And I mean nothing!

**THE END**

# TO KILL A BLACK MAN
### By Louis E. Lomax

**A compelling dual biography of the two men who changed America's way of thinking—Malcolm X and Martin Luther King, Jr.**

Louis E. Lomax was a close friend to both Malcolm X and Dr. Martin Luther King, Jr. In this dual biography, he includes much that Malcolm X did not tell in his autobiography and dissects Malcolm's famous letters. Lomax writes with the sympathy and understanding of a friend but he is also quick to point out the shortcomings of both Dr. King and Malcolm X—and what he believed was the reasons for their failure to achieve their goals and to obtain the full support of all their people. And he does not hesitate in pointing a finger at those he believes to be responsible for the deaths of his friends. "A valuable addition to the available information on the murders of Martin Luther King, Jr. and Malcolm X," says the *Litterair Passport*. Louis Lomax gained national prominence with such books as *The Black Revolt, When The Word Is Given*, and *To Kill A Black Man*. At the time of his death in an automobile accident he was a professor at Hofstra University.

---

**HOLLOWAY HOUSE PUBLISHING CO.**
8060 MELROSE AVE., LOS ANGELES, CALIF. 90046

Gentlemen: I enclose _____ ☐ cash, ☐ check, ☐ money order, payment in full for books ordered. I understand that if I am not completely satisfied, I may return my order within 10 days for a complete refund. (Add 75c per order to cover postage. California residents add 6½% tax. Please allow three weeks for delivery.)

☐ BH731-4 **TO KILL A BLACK MAN** $3.25

Name _____

Address _____

City _____ State _____ Zip _____